It's the trilogy everybody's lusting after!
BEAUTIFUL AMERICANS

"The kind of glossy social upheavals that belong to a season of your favorite guilty-pleasure TV drama."—*USA Today*

"Part traveling-pants sisterhood, part *Sex and the City* quartet."
—*Kirkus*

"Glamour, histrionics, and mad, groping sex."—*SLJ*

"Silag's debut has four angst-ridden teenagers alternating narratives, providing plenty to keep readers interested."
—*Romantic Times Book Review*

"If you love *Gossip Girl* and the classic teen drama of the characters in *My So-Called Life, Beautiful Americans* is for you."
—*Justine Magazine*

"Ooh la la! Lucy Silag gives a wickedly juicy tour of the city of light."—Lauren Mechling, author of *Dream Girl*

"The writing in this book was really good. It was soft, mysterious."
—Reading Keeps You Sane

"The writing's extraordinary."—The Story Siren

"An engaging and exciting book."—Pop Culture Junkie

"Copious amounts of drama in another country? Sign me up."
—Frenetic Reader

"Pure entertainment."—LitMuse

"Silag has interwoven the lives of four very different teens. Each one is vastly different than the other and yet in only a few months they've forged unshakable bonds."—Chick Lit Teens

"I can't wait until the next book."—Juiciliciousssness Reviews

"Thrilling."—RimasBookJournal

"*Beautiful Americans* is a meaningful guilty pleasure with international flair."—The Book Muncher

"I loved seeing Paris through the eyes of PJ, Alex, Olivia, and Zack."—Mrs. V's Reviews

"Once I started reading this book, it was hard to put down. Setting the story in Paris just added to the intrigue. This is the perfect summer beach read."—Flamingnet

Beautiful AMERICANS

by lucy silag

razOr
bill

An imprint of penguin group (USA) Inc.

Beautiful Americans

RAZORBILL

Published by the Penguin Group
Penguin Young Readers Group
345 Hudson Street, New York, New York 10014, U.S.A.
Penguin Group (USA) Inc., 375 Hudson Street, New York, New York 10014, U.S.A.
Penguin Group (Canada), 90 Eglinton Avenue East, Suite 700, Toronto, Ontario,
Canada M4P 2Y3 (a division of Pearson Penguin Canada Inc.)
Penguin Books Ltd, 80 Strand, London WC2R 0RL, England
Penguin Ireland, 25 St Stephen's Green, Dublin 2, Ireland
(a division of Penguin Books Ltd)
Penguin Group (Australia), 250 Camberwell Road, Camberwell, Victoria 3124,
Australia (a division of Pearson Australia Group Pty Ltd)
Penguin Books India Pvt Ltd, 11 Community Centre, Panchsheel Park, New Delhi—
110 017, India
Penguin Group (NZ), 67 Apollo Drive, Mairangi Bay, Auckland 1311, New Zealand
(a division of Pearson New Zealand Ltd)
Penguin Books (South Africa) (Pty) Ltd, 24 Sturdee Avenue, Rosebank,
Johannesburg 2196, South Africa

Penguin Books Ltd, Registered Offices: 80 Strand, London WC2R 0RL, England

10 9 8 7 6 5 4 3 2 1

Library of Congress has catalogued the hardcover edition as follows:

Silag, Lucy.
  Beautiful Americans / by Lucy Silag.
      p. cm.
  Summary: Four high school students on a study abroad program in Paris hide
secrets, party, and revel in the glamor of the city, until one of them disappears.
  ISBN 978-1-59514-222-1
[1. Foreign study—Fiction. 2. Missing persons—Fiction. 3. Secrets—Fiction.
4. Interpersonal relations—Fiction. 5. Paris (France)—Fiction. 6. France—Fiction.]
I. Title.
  PZ7.S5793Be 2009
  [Fic]--dc22
                                        2008021075

Razorbill paperback edition ISBN: 978-1-59514-227-6

Printed in the United States of America

For Jeanne

SEPTEMBER

1.ALEX

Au Revoir, New York

The New York City skyline glitters outside my open window, the late summer breeze flowing off the East River and into my third-story bedroom. My mom's calling me from the stairwell, but I can't tear myself away from the view of my city right now, all lit up with the nostalgia of summer ending.

A horn honks from the street outside. I shake myself out of my reverie and scan my bedroom, wondering if there's anything else I need to stuff into my Vuitton duffle bags. I drop to my knees, remembering a few last things.

In the back of my bottom desk drawer is my Jeremy collection—letters, demos, even an old red handkerchief that he used to keep in his pocket to wipe off his face after his rock shows. He'd get so sweaty when he played under all the lights.

There's stuff in here that I haven't looked at in ages, but suddenly I don't want to take the risk of being so far away, needing to have it and not being able to. *What Alex Wants*, for example—what if I want to listen to the CD he burned for me, a mix of rough cuts he made on Garage Band with ironic old songs he knew I'd like? Even the title of the mix was a joke between us. I pestered him for weeks to burn me some of his stuff, and on the last day of sophomore year at Brooklyn Prep, he handed me this CD.

"As if that's an easy thing to ascertain," he deadpanned, "what Alex wants."

I glance up at my calendar hanging next to the window. Each month has a print of a vintage photo of a Paris scene. For September, the photo is of a man and a woman hanging their legs over the banks of the Seine, their feet bare and the woman's too-adorable white pumps sitting next to her. Today's date is circled a dozen times with a black Sharpie. Today's the day of my escape, my starting over.

"The car's here, Alex!" My mom bursts into my room. I shove the handkerchief and the CD into my tote bag before she can see them. "Aren't you ready to go?"

My mom stops in her tracks. "Oh, my," she says, her fire-engine red lips spreading into a smile. "I can see that you are most *definitely* ready for Paris. Spin."

At her command, I rise to my feet and twirl in a circle in front of her, showing off my linen high-waisted Thakoon pants paired with a nautical-stripe tank and my favorite red stiletto heels. "You are so gorgeous," Mom says. "Now come! Paris waits for no one, not even you."

We clatter down the stairs and out the front door, breathlessly struggling with my two enormous bags, each of us trying not to fall over in our high heels and laughing hysterically. A black town car idles on our quiet tree-lined Brooklyn Heights street. In the distance, I can hear the chatter of the people strolling the Esplanade as the sun sets, remarking on the view of downtown Manhattan, how beautiful New York is.

Right now, I can't even see the city as anything but a place that *isn't* Paris. Paris is where I am meant to be. All of the ups and downs of the last year were just a rehearsal for all the great things to come in Paris.

"All right, my darling," Mom says. I take a deep breath, knowing I will cry when Mom tells me how much she is going to miss me. "Time to go." She twists one of the large rings on her fingers, a habit she has when she's sad or nervous.

The thought of my poor mom, banging around in this big, drafty townhouse all alone for the next nine months turns my Louboutins to stone. I *absolutely* cannot go to Paris, I think rashly. My mom will never survive it! We're never apart for more than a week, when she goes to report on the fashion shows in Rome, L.A., Milan, and Paris for *Luxe* and can't take me with her.

But then she smiles. "I can't wait for you to get to Paris!" Mom giddily throws her arms around me with wild laughter. I bury my face in her long dark hair, cloudy with the scent of Chanel perfume. "Go make me proud!"

"But Mom," I say, wriggling away for a second. "Are you sure you're okay with this? Really, truly sure?"

"Yes, yes, yes, of course!" Mom smacks my butt and points to the car. "Now go!" With one last hug and kiss, she pushes me toward Paris.

Thrown off balance by the heft of her push, I stumble a little bit. The way she's hustling me to the car, you'd think she was thrilled I was leaving.

"One last thing," she says when I roll down the car window and look up at her, trying to get myself to grasp that this is it, I'm leaving. Paris is finally happening.

Mom hands me a thin, creamy envelope. "For you," she says. "It's not what you think," she winks. "Now seriously! Go. I love you, darling."

She's right. It *isn't* what I expected. Mom usually sends me on a trip with a wad of cash and her American Express Black Card. Since the Amex card is already safely tucked into my camel-colored leather Hogan tote bag, I thought I'd find a few hundred euros slipped in with a note on my mom's heavy monogrammed stationery. Instead I just find the note.

Dearest Alex,

I always knew this day would come, but I really thought I'd have a couple more years, at least till you went to college. Today your life finally becomes your own.

Your escapades this year, while always charming and indicative of great spirit, have been often very foolish. Young people make mistakes—hell, everyone does.

What I hope you've learned, though, is that women like us can't wear their hearts on their sleeves, darling. You come from a long line of passionate women who fall in love much too fast. Whatever you do in Paris, don't get carried away over there the way you did last fall with Jeremy. Seeing you in so much pain made my heart break. I couldn't stand it if you let another loser walk all over you like that. Be careful falling in love in Paris—you'll never come back the same. I should know.

Good luck and all the love in the world! I'm so proud of you.

See you in November for Fashion Week!

All my love

Now I'm crying for sure. I look out the window, but we've already pulled onto the Brooklyn-Queens Expressway, and my mom is long behind me. It's too late to tell her again how much I love her and how much I am going to miss her. It's also too late to ask her for some cash for the trip! I chide myself and get to work fixing the eyeliner I smeared as I was reading her note.

The brightly lit, lofted International Terminal at JFK airport is abuzz with thousands of people heading off to all corners of the globe—Beijing, Budapest, Buenos Aires. I scan the monitor for Paris. My flight is on time. I realize with a start that while I've flown without my mom plenty of times before, this is the first time I've been on my way to *Paris* without her. It's odd. I can't say it feels bad, but I'm too distracted, too anxious to get to Paris to be proud of my independence.

In line at the French Airways counter, we move ahead slowly. I text my cousin Emily, a brand new freshman at Georgetown. GOOD BYE!!!! I brag. SEE YOU AT CHRISTMAS!! KEEP IN TOUCH!!! The thing is, Emily's been miserable since she got to college. What she wouldn't do to be getting on this flight with me. Instead she's desperate to rush a sorority and can't get a single guy to take her on a proper date.

What's taking me so long to get to the front is a tall blonde girl having some sort of argument with the check-in counter personnel. Her face is unsmiling but nonetheless very, very pretty. Thin, sharp hipbones jut out above her loose, faded jeans. The girl turns around to pull a thick stack of papers out of a retro brown camping backpack that looks like it was unearthed from a time capsule buried in 1970. I can see she's wearing no jewelry or makeup. Just a mane of waist-length, disheveled blonde hair accessorizes her dazzling features—the most arresting of which is a wide, strawberry mouth with full lips set in a strange and downtrodden expression.

The girl is waving around a fistful of hundred dollar bills, but the French Airways clerk just shakes her head and frowns.

It's not like me to stare, but I recognize the stately logo of the Lycée de Monceau on the front of what she is trying to show the French Airways clerk. My eyes widen. Could it be that another student from my program is on the same flight as me?

How thrilling!

I whoop with excitement, eliciting a cranky look from an elderly Frenchman standing next to me in line. Is there another New Yorker attending the Lycée with me? The Programme Americain at the Lycée de Monceau is one of the most respected and exclusive high school study-abroad programs in the world. Students from all over the United States sign up to go to Paris for a year--an entire *year*—and live in homestays while they study French at a very competitive private school. I barely got in myself, despite having spoken French since I was just a baby. Your whole transcript is considered when you apply, as is your disciplinary record. In my case, let's just say I was lucky my mom's a contributing editor at *Luxe* and my being there brings a certain cachet to the student body this year.

I can't help it—I push past the old guy and rush forward to the counter. *"Excusez-moi!"* the Frenchman protests, but I just giggle in his general direction in response.

"I'm Alex!" I place my hand on the girl's bony arm, delicate blue veins streaking her translucent skin. "You're going to the Lycée with me!"

"What?" Her plump lips form a startled "O" as she turns to face me. "Who are you?"

"Alex Nguyen," I reiterate. "We're studying abroad together this year! I saw your registration packet from where I was standing in line!"

She looks at the papers in her hand, and then back at me, confused. I notice as I wait for her to react that she needs some concealer in a bad way—the bags under her eyes make her look like she's been popping amphetamines all night.

She *wouldn't*. Would she? And I thought *I'd* be the token wild child at the Lycée de Monceau.

"You haven't been abroad before, have you?" I ask her. She has the that nervous twitch of a newly minted traveler.

"No, I haven't," she says. "But that's not my problem right now. My problem is that I don't have a reservation and French Airways only has first-class tickets left. And I don't have enough cash for first class, just coach."

"There's one first-class seat left," the clerk tells me in French. "Coach has been booked for weeks."

"You haven't bought a plane ticket to Paris yet?" I ask in disbelief. My mom's assistant at *Luxe* booked my trip last June.

"Can you fly tomorrow?" the clerk offers. "There's a middle seat open if you can go on the six pm flight tomorrow night."

"No, no, no," the girl says, kicking her backpack in frustration. "I have to go to Paris *tonight!*"

"*Oui, oui, oui,*" says the clerk. "Do you have a credit card? The only way French Airways can accommodate your request to go to Paris tonight is if you buy the last available first class seat."

"No!" the girl moans.

"Well, then, please step aside so I can help the next *ticketed* passenger."

"Hold on," I stop them, glancing down at the wad of cash in the girl's hand. "I'll buy her ticket. I have my American Express card. Will that be okay?"

"What are you doing?" the girl asks me.

"You give me the cash you have, and take my seat. I can't bear coach, anyway. You're doing me a favor," I tell her.

"Really?"

"Sure!" I hand the black Amex to the clerk. "So, what's your name, anyway?"

"Penelope Jane Fletcher," she says, putting her passport on the counter so that the clerk can type in her name and information. "But you can call me PJ. Why are you doing this for me?"

"Well," I say with my brightest, most charming smile, looking down at the euros in her hands. "I can always use cash. I forgot to get some before my driver dropped me here. You can pay me for the ticket I just bought for you."

PJ pushes the money toward me as if she can't wait to get rid of it. "Here, take it," she says. "I can't believe you are doing this for me."

I'm stoked, but I'm already picking up on the fact that something is not quite right about this girl.

PJ is *precisely* the kind of girl that the program is supposed to weed out, I think as we walk toward Security. The Lycée is for the best of the best young American students, the kind that have summered on the Riviera, the ones that know the Musée d'Orsay like the back of their hand. PJ looks like she's never been off the ranch.

For one thing, PJ is dressed like an absolute fugitive—dirty, ripped jeans from JC Penney's and a thin, shrunken black T-shirt with the silk screened words "Live Free or Die" starting to crumble and fade on her chest. As I give her a once-over, I notice that it is more than just her ragamuffin clothes that are making me uncomfortable. Her hands are trembling as she sets a cloth purse onto the conveyor. She keeps looking at her boarding pass like it might not be real.

Unpacking my laptop and all my cosmetics, not to mention taking off my gold filigree hoops and unloading my BlackBerry and everything for the metal detector, means PJ is waiting for several minutes by the time the TSA is done with me.

"Listen," PJ says. "You really helped me out just now. I'm totally grateful. My dad gave me all that cash. . . . I was sure it would be enough."

"Please," I guffaw. "Tell me about it. My dad is the same way. He assumes that a stack of hundreds can solve any problem."

PJ looks at me peculiarly. "Really? Your dad always pays for everything in cash, too?"

"Totally!" I nod. That's not exactly true, but she seems so embarrassed about not having a credit card that I want to put her at ease. I'm sure my dad has a dozen credit cards, each with an enormous spending limit that I am sure he takes full advantage of. My dad works for the Commonwealth Trust Bank in London, where he oversees all ventures in Southeast Asia. He also comes from old money, since his family was one of the first noble Vietnamese families to get rich off of French trade during the colonial era. Educated at the best schools in France, my dad ended up on Wall Street, then rose the ranks of the City in London, and is now an inspiration for b-school graduates everywhere, with homes, cars, and girlfriends all over the world.

I know my dad's story like I know Jeremy's acoustic ditties, but the truth is I barely know him. If it weren't for the photos of him in the *Wall Street Journal* whenever he makes some massive overseas shipping deal, I wouldn't even know what he looks like. My mom caught him cheating with our *Quebecoise* nanny when I was about five, and he's been the invisible man, so to speak, ever since.

"It's really no problem," I tell PJ breezily. "You want to take a spin through Duty Free with me before we take off?"

PJ hesitates. "I don't think so," she says. "I think I'd rather just go to Starbucks. I need a cup of coffee really badly." There go her hands again, trembling as she pushes her long blond hair off her face.

"Okay," I say. "I'll come with you. I could use a picker-upper, too."

PJ's blue eyes meet mine. "Alex, I could never repay you for how you swooped in today. In Paris, I am going to try. But right now, can I just be by myself?"

I nearly choke. Is my company that terrible? It's just a cup of coffee. I know her type: ungrateful, awkward loners. Her beauty clearly does not match her personality.

"Well, okay," I say, shocked. "I'll go to Duty Free alone then."

Three lip-glosses, four packs of gum, and a new Burberry rain hat later, I emerge from Duty Free.

I spot PJ, shivering from the overly air-conditioned terminal in a seat by the gate. I don't make eye contact, but I'm carefully aware of her, of what she's doing. Even in her brown, unseasonable wool sweater, she looks elegant and somehow poised despite how she fidgets. Her chilly dismissal of me, how she rejected my friendship before we even got to Paris, leaves a bad taste in my mouth. Good thing I bought all that gum.

I'll outshine the blonde spazz sitting in coach with no credit card. I'll bet PJ is not even from New York. No New Yorker *I* know would ever wear *Birkenstocks* to Paris.

French Airways is boarding first class passengers to Paris. I line up to swipe my boarding pass and flash my passport at the gate agent. This is it!

This is the end of Jeremy, of New York, of failure. Paris is my chance to start over. And I can hardly wait.

2. OLIVIA

The Dance of Discovery

I try to get comfortable in my seat at the back of the shuttle as I stare at Madame Cuchon, the director of the Progamme Americain at the Lycée de Monceau. She is *totally* not what I expected from the first actual French person I met. Mme Cuchon is eccentrically dressed in a getup consisting of several layers of Indian-print flowing rayon and pointy, elfish clogs on her large, long feet. She looks more like she belongs in the desert at the Burning Man festival than as the person in charge of one of the most well-respected high school study-abroad programs in the world.

"Do you have kids of your own, Madame Cuchon?" PJ, an ethereal blonde from Vermont, asks her in perfectly accented French. I envy how cool and ungreasy PJ's skin looks, despite the mugginess of the van. I'm roasting and near passing out from exhaustion. Not to mention, I have motion sickness like I'm on a ride at Disneyland. That and my heart is pounding wildly at the realization that I'm in a foreign country, halfway around the world from California.

Don't puke, don't puke. I take a long drink of water from the liter bottle I bought as soon as my plane landed. I can barely focus on the new world outside the van's windows—the beautiful, long-dreamed of streets of Paris! Is this nervousness or is Mme Cuchon just a really, *really* bad driver?

Mme Cuchon talks nearly as fast as she drives.

"Do I have kids, you mean, besides the hundreds of Americans who've passed through my program at the Lycée?" she chuckles. "No, the antics of *les étudiants* turned me off that notion long ago."

How Mme Cuchon manages to expertly field our many questions while also weaving a fifteen-passenger van in and out of Paris traffic I will never know. As far as I can see, that's just Madame Cuchon. She has a voice like a foghorn and must have eyes on the back of her head, hidden by the taut chignon of her bright red hair.

The Lycée van, jerking along the highway from Charles de Gaulle airport, is packed with kids fresh off flights from the U.S. Every time we turn a corner, my stomach lurches.

Sticky with sweat and stale airplane grease, I'm squished between a leggy South Carolinian named Sara-Louise and Mary, who's from L.A. Mary is almost as short and small as I am, so we're sharing a seatbelt.

When Mary leans forward to hear Mme Cuchon better, Sara-Louise widens her eyes at the tattoo in the shape of an anchor on the back of Mary's bare neck, just above the collar of her formfitting black t-shirt. I try not to give away my disgust—the idea of a needle polluting my body with permanent ink is just *too* gross for me to take seriously, even if the design *is* pretty awesome. Sara-Louise, in her pink sundress and blonde Shirley Temple curls, looks absolutely scandalized and *totally* impressed.

"Well, I'll be darned!" a guy named Zack hollers as he spots the Eiffel Tower in the distance. Zack has the tousled, shaggy haircut and hipster outfit of a shoe-gazing emo rocker, but his Southern drawl gives away his Memphis roots before he can tell us where he is from. Zack is already chummy with Alex, who is from New York. Everyone besides Alex (who can't be bothered by it) leans forward to try to catch *La Tour Eiffel* before it disappears again behind the skyline. PJ, in the front seat, has her mouth hanging open at the sight of it.

"Wow," she breathes. It *is* pretty spectacular. Alex looks up at me from the message she is texting on her BlackBerry and gives me a generous smile. When she looks at PJ, though, her smile turns into a look of disdain.

Alex and Zack keep rolling their eyes at PJ. I can see why Alex might feel threatened by her—PJ is a dead ringer for Heidi Klum. But it would be stupid for Alex to feel that way—she herself is a total knockout. Alex, with her creamy skin and almond-shaped, heavy-lidded eyes, her bouncy layered black hair and huge boobs, is easily the envy of every girl in this van and surely will be the envy of everyone in our program that we haven't met yet, too. She also has a killer outfit on. The body-hugging top shows off her great cleavage and small waist to full effect. On her lap is an enormous leather tote bag, which she cradles as lovingly as one might a newborn kitten. On her face are Gucci sunglasses that probably cost more than my entire outfit from American Eagle. I'd been excited about making a good impression when my mom bought me the denim carpenter shorts and the white ruffled sleeveless top, but now I just melt into the crowd. I'm not wearing any makeup, and my hair is pulled back into a simple ponytail to keep it out of my eyes, like always.

Back at the baggage claim at Charles de Gaulle airport, Alex told us as we waited for our bags that she's been to Paris many, many times. Her dad is French-Vietnamese, and her mom lived here for several years after college. Because of her mom's magazine job, Alex gets to tag along on trips to Paris all the time.

"Oh, look you guys," she points out, casually motioning toward some patisserie where she once had a fabulous *coq au vin* with some of the actors from *Amélie* several years ago. "One of the guys told me," Alex says, "that my French was the best he'd ever heard an American speak."

"Really?" I gasp, immediately self-conscious of my own French. Besides my ballet teacher back in San Diego, I've never even tried speaking French with a real French person. Even our French teacher back home isn't really French—she's from Fresno. Alex's self-confident grasp of Paris is enviable. And I can't help liking her more and more.

"Look!" Alex says again. "See the Moulin Rouge? That was one of my favorite movies." She points to the windmill on top of the famous Paris cabaret. Her smile is infectious.

"Me, too!" Zack and I exclaim in unison.

I, for one, have never been to Paris. Once off the freeway, the city is, in a word, *amazing*. I feel like I'm at Universal Studios or something—everything looks like an old movie set. There are women in five-inch heels leisurely walking lanky Great Danes along with a sack of baguettes tucked under one arm. Flower shops on the corners overflow with roses in every shade, along with lilies and tulips and every other beautiful, tasteful flower. Men in trim-cut suits are running down the street, clutching their cell phones and briefcases, and still looking as agile as Baryshnikov as they rush by. Paris, like a grand ballet, seems expertly choreographed, with each dancer and player knowing just their part, how much to shine and how much to contain. It's breathtaking.

And all I can think about is how much I wish my boyfriend, Vince, were here, too, his arm around me, protecting me.

"Paris is *so* cute," the Texan girl behind me coos to her twin sister. "Isn't this just the *best*?"

This elicits more eye rolls from Alex and Zack. I do have to admit, the twins *are* a little grating. Their squeals are disorienting, making it hard to shake off the feeling of dread that descended over me as soon as my flight from San Diego pulled off the runway.

I'd be mortified if anyone knew this, but if someone had asked me five hours ago how I was feeling about coming to Paris, I would have ended up sobbing face-first in their lap. Maybe because I was flying over a strange black ocean I've never seen before, or maybe because I was dehydrated, or cramped from sitting still for so long, but I woke up a few hours after takeoff, shuffled to the bathroom to pee, and ended up bawling my eyes out over the little sink. All I wanted to do was to turn the plane around and go right back to San Diego where I belong.

But back on solid ground, and a little high on the adrenaline of so many new things at once, I'm feeling excited, if unsettled.

Even if you end up hating Alex, Zack, those twins, everyone, I think with a deep, decisive breath, *don't forget that this is a chance of a lifetime. You came here to dance. You came here to land a UCLA scholarship. Don't forget why you're here. Dance is first. Everything else is second.*

For a moment, I get anxious all over again, remembering that, unlike the rest of these kids, I have a dance audition to prepare for.

"This is the Lycée," announces Mme Cuchon from the front seat as she pulls over in front of an impressive stone building. I look up. Several stories high, the Lycée looks more like a fortress than a high school. I recognize it from the Lycée's glossy recruitment brochure. Like the buildings around it and all the buildings we've passed as we got deeper into the crooked streets and alleyways of central Paris, the Lycée is built from brushed stone bricks in the washed out gray-tan color of centuries past. Every time I couldn't sleep over the past few months, I would get up, turn my light on, and look over the orientation materials from the Lycée again. And yet the Lycée itself is more majestic than I ever could have predicted.

"Your host families will meet you here and take you back to your respective homestays to get settled," Mme Cuchon explains as she pulls forcefully on the parking break. "Then we'll meet here tomorrow morning for an orientation session and your first day of classes." With a jerk and a shudder, the van stills, and we pour out into the soupy heat of the street, pulling our suitcases and backpacks through the heavy iron front gates of the Lycée.

In the large foyer, we sort out our luggage and greet the group of French people, our new "parents" and "siblings," waiting and smiling hesitantly at us as we come in. Mme Cuchon directs me to my host mother, a middle-aged woman with a thick gray pageboy haircut and dressed in a silk, salmon-colored suit. She kisses me dutifully on each cheek, and I laugh self-consciously.

I didn't know they really did that! A year from now, will I be kissing everyone like that when I meet them?

"This is Mme Rouille," Mme Cuchon says. "*C'est Olivia*," she says to Mme Rouille.

"Bonjour, Olivia," Mme Rouille says with a tight, formal smile. The way she says my name sounds beautiful and exotic—Oh-LEEV-ee-AH. I can't help giggling.

I can't tell if I am going to always have to address my host mother as *Madame*, which seems very formal for someone whose standing in for my mother, but for the time being she doesn't offer me anything else to call her.

"You'll be living in an apartment not far from Mademoiselle Penelope in the seventeenth arrondissement," says Mme Cuchon. "Though I don't see her host mother yet. *C'est strange, n'est-ce pas?*" She looks around among the quickly scattering students. "Anyway, you two girls might walk together to school in the mornings this year."

"Penelope must be PJ," I think, watching the tall, lonely girl twist a strand of her long blonde hair around her finger as she waits on the front steps. No family has claimed her.

"*Alors*, Olivia, you must be off now," Mme Cuchon prods me toward Mme Rouille's waiting cream-colored Mercedes. "The Opera is expecting you at one o'clock for your placement audition."

"Today?" I say, trying not to show my dismay. Is she crazy?

I've barely slept—my head is swimming from fatigue. I've been prepping for this audition all summer—for the advanced class at *L'Opéra National de Paris*, what everyone in the dance world calls "The Opera" for short. It will most certainly provide me with the training and credentials for the scholarship that I want—no, *need*—to win next year. But I thought

I'd at least get a good night's sleep before it happened!

"*Oui, cherie,*" Mme Cuchon confirms. "Your mother wants you to be able to begin with the advanced class right away. There's not a moment to waste. Good luck this afternoon! *Bon chance!*"

Ah, my mother. Of course. When it comes to me winning the UCLA scholarship, my mother is right—there's not a moment to waste. She must have implored Mme Cuchon to schedule my audition the moment I got off the plane—not realizing that I might have people to meet, or sleep to catch up on.

Mme Rouille and I stop very briefly at her apartment so that I can put on my leotard and tights and throw my toe shoes into my dance bag. The apartment is located inside a gorgeous, stately limestone building with spiraling stairs leading up to a different apartment on each floor. An elderly concierge, complete with a little tasseled cap, greets us and takes my bags from me, disappearing into a back hallway with them.

Mme Rouille lives on the fourth floor, so we take the little wire-cage elevator up. The concierge, like a miracle, has already left the bags by the front door and disappeared again.

A maid, also in uniform, opens the door for us and scurries ahead with my bags while Mme Rouille does a cursory tour of my new home. We're also greeted by three adorable miniature poodles yapping at our feet.

I coo in delight. I've always wanted a dog! When one of the poodles pees on my foot, I don't care in the slightest. These dogs are just the cutest little puppies in the world!

"*Elise!*" Mme Rouille bellows when she sees the little puddle and the drops on my flip-flop. The maid reappears and wipes my foot and the floor aggressively with a hot, soapy towel. I look up at Mme Rouille, laughing. She shrugs. I hope she knows that I don't mind. What's a little dog pee among new friends?

"Seriously," I tell her. "I, like, *looooove* dogs. My mom won't let me have one. I'll walk them, whenever you want. Every morning!"

"*D'accord,*" Mme Rouille accedes, perhaps more to get me to shut up than anything else. The dogs bark their agreement, and it's settled.

Mme Rouille's apartment is not large, but it is very fancy, crowded with furniture and Baroque in its over-decoration. It's almost scarily clean. The polished hardwood floors gleam as though they were still wet from being scrubbed. Every piece of crystal in the gargantuan chandelier in the living room flashes reflections of the light streaming through the spotless, opened window panes.

Mme Rouille quickly explains to me that she's just finished having her apartment repainted. That's why the light green walls of her son's room—the room where I will be staying—are bare. She hasn't hung his posters back up yet.

"Thomas lives in *le dortoir* now," Mme Rouille says, a little sadly. "He is too busy studying to be a *docteur* for to visit his *maman*. He's brilliant, my son." At the French word for *doctor* her voice brightens with pride a bit. "You can make this room your own, if you want." Then she bustles out, clearly not one for long conversations.

I want to flop down on the twin bed and close my eyes for at least the next twelve hours, but my audition awaits. Growing agitated, I choose my favorite leotard, a new black one with halter straps and a sweetheart neckline, to wear for my big moment.

We hop back into the Mercedes and set off for the ballet academy. I steal another glance at my host mother.

Madame Rouille is impossibly put together, unlike the moms I know in Southern California who live in flared jeans and tank tops. She's obviously very rich, with her posh apartment and her live-in maid. Looking at her, wanting her to like me, I resolve to shed all my grotesque American habits as soon as humanly possible. My feet, for example. Sticking out of my flip-flops are dry, callused toes covered in spotty, chipped hot pink polish. No Parisian wears flip-flops, I'm sure. Dance has made my feet as mangled enough as it is—the least I could have done was get a pedicure before I left.

I was too busy saying goodbye to Vince, I guess. I didn't have time to properly prepare for my swanky new lifestyle.

"This neighborhood is called *Ternes*," Mme Rouille states in a nasal, snooty voice as we drive along a wide street called *Boulevard de Courcelles*. "It's a very elite area of Paris. Full of good families." Mme Cuchon had told us that our host families would speak to us in French, but Mme Rouille addresses me in English only. It seems like she has nothing much to say to me, in either language, at all. At this point I'm feeling so weary and overwhelmed that I don't really mind.

Located on the outskirts of Paris, the Paris Opera Ballet School houses the best young dancers in the world. They live and breathe ballet and have to be absolutely committed to a life of dance.

Today I'm trying out for the non-residential program of the Paris Opera Ballet School, the program that allows the students to go to regular school but also get top-notch ballet training. Best of all, classes are at the Opéra Garnier, right in the center of Paris.

"*Pour les danseuses avancées,*" the young teacher's assistant guides me toward a group of ballerinas gathered to one side of the basement studio.

I should be a shoo-in, but when I see the other girls, I'm nervous. They are teeny—the size of twelve-year-olds—and each of them wears a simple, long-sleeved leotard with pink tights and pink toe shoes. Since I abhor pink (I always have) and hate the way bright colors take away from the technique I'm cultivating as I practice, I always go to ballet class in all black. And being from California, long sleeves feel binding and hot. I immediately see, however, that my cute halter leotard, my black leggings, and black pointe shoes make me stand out, even before I've had a chance to show off my dancing.

I smooth my bun and take a place in the front of the group. I relax my face so that I'm smiling—just a little—and cock my head to the right, and to the left, so that my body draws a clean line through space. I keep my fingers soft and never let my face show how tightly I'm hanging on to keep my center.

The ballet matron's face is stern while she watches my dancing. She finally breaks into a grin when I leap into my final grand jeté, my legs doing a full split in the air before I land softly onto the wooden floor of the studio, chalky with ballet resin.

When the music ends, I mop my forehead and wait for the matron's decision. Long ago, in my auditions for everything from *The Nutcracker* to the avant-garde student productions at San Diego State (my mom never lets me miss an opportunity to perform), I learned to keep still while waiting to see if you're in. One tiny movement, the tiniest bit of fidgeting, and the other girls know how badly you want it, how unsure you are that you really deserve it. Let them crack into your insecurity once, and it takes forever to get it back. I wait, frozen, my face impassive.

"*Oui!*" she calls as she points to me and has her assistant check off my name on her master list. Mme Rouille, fanning herself on the sidelines of the hot studio, gives me the first smile I've seen yet from her. Happy to have pleased her, I finally let myself beam back. A huge flood of relief and elation warms my whole body.

I can't wait to tell Vince how I nailed it. Two years from now, I'll be at UCLA right alongside him, just like we've always planned. It's real now. It's happening!

Back at the apartment, the first thing I do (after stretching and cooling down my muscles, of course) is adjust the time on my travel clock. As soon as the numbers change to 5:00 P.M.—8:00 A.M. in California—I want to run out and call Vince from one of the payphones on the Champs Elysées. Driving down the famous boulevard on the way to the Opera earlier, I saw a large block of France Telecom phone booths just across from the Arc de Triomphe, and as far as I can gauge, that's a quick walk from Ternes. I'm not yet comfortable enough with my host mother to ask if I can use her phone, even if I'm using a calling card. Besides, I want to talk to Vince in private.

The second thing I do is hang my Martha Graham Dance Company poster on one of the bare walls in my new room. It's an old black-and-white photo of Martha Graham herself, her skirt swirling around her, her face lit up with exhilaration. Then I hang up all the photos I brought with me, until my little bedroom is covered with images of Vince, my mom, my dad, and my little brother, Brian.

There's only one photo I don't hang up—a close-up of Vince taken on the Fourth of July this year. I put this photo in my purse so I can look at it whenever I want to.

It takes a few tries for Vince to answer his phone. I impatiently stand up on my toes, then down again as it rings, looking through the smudged glass of the phone booth at the bustling, crowded Champs Elysées. The wide avenue, with busy traffic lanes going either direction, is flanked on either side with every major retailer (Gap, Sephora, Prada, and dozens upon dozens of others) and large cafes with tables and crowds spilling onto the sidewalk. It's oddly comforting to be here, despite how hectic it is. I can hear plenty of English being spoken by the tourists ambling across the roundabout toward the Arc de Triomphe and the Tomb of the Unknown Soldier. As the sun starts to go down, the tourists unwrap the wind breakers tied around their waists and slip them on to avoid the chilly September evening breeze. They look out of place, just the way I feel.

"Ugh, baby, what time is it?" Vince groans when he finally picks up. The gravelly sound of his voice makes me feel like I'm curled up in bed next to him and not thousands of miles away.

"I rocked my audition today!" I shout. "I made it into the advanced class!"

"The what?" Vince asks groggily. "You went to dance class? Hold on."

In the background, I hear Vince grunt and then a door closing. "Hey, I'm back," he says. "My roommate looked pissed about me waking him up so early. I'm in the bathroom now."

"Oh, sorry," I say. "I guess I thought you'd be awake by now. Don't you have class today?"

"Yeah," Vince says. "I do. But we were out late at some athletes' meet and greet. Got pretty wild. You know, hazing for the new guys and all that."

"Oh. Sorry."

"It's cool." Vince is starting to sound more awake. "I'm really glad you called. How are you?"

"I'm good." I smile to myself. All I want to do is snuggle into his arms, wrap myself in his morning boy smell, which always makes me instantly calm. "Tired. I can't believe I'm really here."

"I can't either," Vince sighs. "I wish we could rewind to last weekend."

My spine tingles when he says that. Last weekend, I'd gone to visit Vince at UCLA. As a prospective student, I was supposed to stay in the dorm room of a sophomore dance major, but it had been easy to talk her into letting me stay in Vince's room after my mom had called the dorm to say goodnight. While Vince's roommate partied with some of the other guys from their basketball team, Vince and I had stayed up all night making out in his twin bed.

Inevitably, what with Vince being in college now, and me about to leave for a year, we'd discussed having sex for the first time, but in the end I told him I wanted to wait. Now, talking on the phone to him from so far away and him sounding so sad, I kind of wish I hadn't left without doing it with him. Vince might start to think I didn't want to, which I did. I was just scared. And I didn't want to risk his oaf roommate walking in on us! But God, I miss him so badly right now, I feel like I'd risk *anything*. . . .

"Oh, me too," I breathe. "I miss you so much."

I can hear Vince peeing over the phone, the steady stream echoing in his empty dorm bathroom. I'm glad he feels so close to me, but *ew*. He lets out a deep breath. "Much better. So tell me what Paris is like."

I'm about to describe it to him when I see a familiar face in the crowd of passing tourists on the Champs Elysées. It's PJ from the program! That's weird. I hope she doesn't see me. I don't feel like making small talk right now. I feel like gloating with Vince about my victory today.

"It's okay," I say distractedly. "How's school?"

Vince starts telling me how hard one of his classes is while I watch PJ walk into an adjacent café. Mme Cuchon did say she lives near here, too. But shouldn't she be eating dinner with her host family? Besides, the cafés on the Champs Elysées are a total rip-off. Even Alex wouldn't eat in them, I'm sure. The pricey food they are bringing out to the tourist families is dripping with cheap grease.

"Uh-huh," I murmur as Vince continues. PJ walks out of the café with a despairing look on her face. Looks like she realized how much that place cost. It feels like she is looking straight at me with those big, haunted eyes! I turn around and face the other direction so she won't recognize me from the drive over to the Lycée.

"Yeah, totally," I say to Vince as PJ goes into the next phone booth over.

"Well," I say when Vince's story is over, "I think my phone card is almost out. I should let you get to class."

"Okay," Vince says. "I love you. Call me tomorrow if you can."

"Okay, babe, love you too."

I hang up and lean against the glass partition of the phone booth, overcome with weariness and homesickness. It's physical, like a rock in my gut. I didn't want to say goodbye, but talking to Vince like this isn't the same as talking to him from my bedroom at home, being able to flirt with him and tell him how much I miss him and having him say all the right things back to me. It's uncomfortable in here, leaned up against the dirty glass, watching unfriendly-looking strangers, trying to avoid people from my program and feeling guilty about it. Not exactly the best setting for sweet nothings.

"Oh, my God!" I blurt out. Out of the corner of my eye, I see PJ through the partition—she's slumped on the floor of the next phone booth over, passed out. I pop out of my own phone booth and pull the door to hers open with a loud bang. Passersby slow down and stare at us.

"PJ! It's Olivia. I'm in your program. We met today, remember?" I shake her awake. I'm reminded of my brother, Brian, of all the times I can't get through to him.

PJ rubs her eyes exhaustedly and looks up at me. "Oh, hey."

"Are you okay?" I literally thought that my heart was, like, going to fly out of my chest.

"Um, yeah," PJ says, looking around, embarrassed. She pulls her brown cardigan tightly around her thin frame. "I don't really know what just happened. . . . I was so tired. . . . I need to make a phone call. . . ."

"Why aren't you at your host family's house?"

PJ opens her mouth to speak, then clasps her lips shut without saying anything. She shakes her head, her chin trembling.

"What?" I prompt her. "What is it? You can tell me."

She closes her eyes. "They never showed. They never came to the Lycée to get me."

"I don't understand. What did Mme Cuchon say?"

"She doesn't know. There was so much going on with everyone that I just decided to go to the address she had me listed under in the orientation packets she handed out today. But no one was home. When I went back to the Lycée, Mme Cuchon was gone, too." PJ readjusts herself so that she's more upright and combs through her blonde hair with her grubby fingers. Her voice might sound brave and resigned to her fate, but her glassy blue eyes betray deep fear.

"Are you kidding? Mme Cuchon doesn't know that you're homeless?"

PJ nods. "I couldn't find her."

"Give me your orientation packet," I instruct her. "We're calling Madame right now. What were you going to do? Sleep in the phone booth?"

"I was just so tired from the flight," PJ mutters. "And all the hotels around here cost so much money. . . . I tried to get some coffee to stay awake, but that costs too much money, too. . . ." Her blonde head bobs forward as she nods off again. I reach toward her backpack so that I can get out Mme Cuchon's number.

With a start, she yanks her head back up straight. "*Don't* call Madame. I really don't want to cause any trouble. Please don't call her. *Please*." PJ's bright blue eyes start to well up with tears.

I have to say that of all the homeless people I've ever seen trying to sleep in a phone booth, PJ has got to be the most stunningly beautiful.

"Alright, alright," I say, shaking my head and taking my hand off the closure of the backpack. "But you're definitely coming with me back to my homestay. You're crazy if you think you're sleeping here all night. Let's go."

I pull her up—she's shockingly light for being so tall—and hoist her oversize canvas pack onto my back. "You look like you've been dragging this thing around for long enough. Let's just get you to my apartment." I smile around confidently at the onlookers and lead PJ toward Ternes. "Everything's going to be alright, I promise."

"Okay," PJ says, probably too exhausted to protest any longer.

3. PJ

Broken Homes, Broken Hearts

t's too early in the fall to wear my dad's old brown wool cardigan, my favorite of his with the elbow patches, leather-covered buttons, and the dusty smell. I think it belonged to his dad, ages ago. I pull the cardigan out of my shoulder bag and put it on anyway, even if it does look weird, since I can't seem to escape the chill in the classroom where we're all gathered at the Lycée on Monday morning. I wonder if I have a minute to call Dave. If not now, when will I get the chance? I feel like there's no possible way I'm going to get through the rest of the morning if I can't at least duck out for a minute.

"So, how's your homestay?" Olivia asks Alex as she points and flexes her tiny bare feet stretched out in front of her in the aisle between their desks. Point, flex. Point, flex. Alex fixes her gaze at Olivia's weathered feet, then back at her own perfectly buffed and polished ones, the purple nail polish contrasting against her gold Greek sandals. Flushed, Olivia curls her legs under her chair.

It's our very first day of school at the Lycée. I'm sitting with Alex and Olivia in the back of Room 102, the room at the school designated to the Programme Americain, eating the gooey French pastries the school provided as a chance for all the twenty-five students to mingle before our real classes begin later on this morning. Alex and Olivia are the only people I've actually met so far, and neither of them probably has the greatest impression of me. After all, Alex had to loan me money to get here, and Olivia found me asleep in a phone booth last night.

The flaky *chausson aux pommes* is the first food I've had since the reheated breakfast they served on the flight yesterday morning. I should be ravenous, but the buttery pastry tastes like ash in my mouth. When I set it back down after one bite, Alex looks at me curiously.

"You don't want it?" she asks. When I shake my head no, she reaches out and pops a piece into her mouth.

"Hmmm," Alex says, chewing happily. "You're missing out, PJ—this *chausson* is incredible!"

I sip my bitter coffee out of the paper cup, giving her a thin smile.

Olivia reaches into her light blue Jansport backpack and pulls out the two bananas she got on our way from her apartment to school this morning. "They're a little bruised, but they still look okay to me. Would you rather have one of these, PJ?"

I force myself to choke down Olivia's pasty banana, just because she's so nice and I have a feeling she'll pester me to eat something until I do.

"Are you on a diet, Olivia?" Alex asks, wiping her greasy, buttery fingers onto a paper napkin. "Is that why you are so thin?"

I can't help wondering the same thing. When everyone rushed toward the bakery platter a few minutes ago, Olivia held back. She didn't even take any tea or coffee, even though I know she tossed and turned in the bed we slept in together last night. We both did. That's why I keep going up for refills.

That and because I can't seem to sit still. I can't shake the feeling that the other girls can already tell how different from them I am.

Olivia looks embarrassed. "No! No way," she insists. "I just try to keep my diet as pure as possible. No carbs, no refined sugar. I don't really like to eat anything heavy. It makes dance class that much harder." Olivia is petite, about a foot shorter than me, with every inch of her small shape covered in tanned, freckly skin. Her blonde ponytail bounces as she talks to us.

"Not me," Alex pipes in cheerfully. "Butter and salt are my favorite foods. French women never diet. They believe in moderated indulgence." She pops another bite of *chausson* into her mouth.

"So you're a dancer? A ballerina? *Quelle surprise.* No wonder you're always bending all your bones everywhere." Alex raises her eyebrows at Olivia, who is indeed folded into a mini-pretzel in her chair.

"I can't help it!" she says. "I know it's nasty. Everyone tells me that."

Last night I couldn't tear my eyes off Olivia as she stretched in her pajamas before bed—it was like being at the circus. Olivia has got to be the freakiest, most flexible, double-jointed person I have ever seen in my life, let alone shared a room with.

"I'm *so* sore," she laughed, spread out on the floor in an old UCLA

T-shirt and an oversize pair of plaid boxers I assumed belonged to the boy in all the pictures on her walls. Her nose touched the Persian rug as she leaned over her split. "These Parisian ballet teachers are brutal! I better watch it before I get injured."

"How can you keep dancing when it hurts your body so much?" I asked her.

Her response was muffled by the rug. "Oh, I could never stop," she said, then considered for a moment. "Well, I mean, one day, I guess I'll have to." She looked up at her Martha Graham poster. "All I know is that it's the only thing I'm good at, and right now, dancing is key to getting everything else that I want in life."

Olivia twisted her hips around, contortionist-style, so that she was doing the splits in the other direction. I nearly gagged at how excruciating it looked. Olivia seemed used to it, though.

"It seems like you're good at speaking French," I contested, though I hadn't at that point heard her speak any French at all.

Olivia lifted her head and looked at me. "I don't mean to sound conceited," she said. The blood drained from her face. "But I'm *really* good at ballet. Scholarship good. If it weren't for my brother . . ." she trailed off.

"What?" I couldn't help asking.

"I mean, maybe I *am* good at other things. But I wouldn't know— I've never really done other things," Olivia explained. "It's not like I have stage parents—it's just that we're all really counting on me getting this scholarship to UCLA. I'm really close to my family. I can't wait to go home for the three-week break at Christmas." She looks wistfully at a photo of herself with her family at the beach.

"Oh, I didn't mean to pry."

I shifted on the bed so I wasn't directly facing her anymore.

Olivia smoothly took the hint and went back to stretching.

"My homestay?" Alex snorts dismissively as she applies more hot pink lip-gloss. We're still waiting for Mme Cuchon to start orientation, but she and a pretty young history teacher named Mademoiselle Vailland are wrapped into deep conversation in the hallway. Apparently this is just a getting-to-know-each-other session for the Programme Americain students. "My homestay is . . . well, who cares? My host parents are squares—they're the type of family who wants to watch TV together after dinner every night." Alex gags.

"You're funny," Olivia laughs. "That's lucky. I thought I'd have a real family here—you know, siblings, a dad . . . like at home. But it's just me, Mme Rouille and her dogs! And, of course, PJ." She touches my arm with mock sentimentality. "At least we have each other, don't we, PJ?"

"I'm not going to be there forever," I say quickly, shrinking back. I know I must seem like a scared animal.

"What do you mean?" Alex gives Olivia's hand on my arm a puzzled look. "Do you guys share a homestay or something?"

"For the time being we are," I explain, trying not to sound too bitter, considering how nice Olivia and Mme Rouille have been. I crack my knuckles, making Alex wince at the sound. "My host parents never showed on Saturday."

"Ha!" Alex bursts out. "Are you kidding? You really haven't met them yet?"

I shake my head.

"I bet they are just at their house in the country or something," Alex muses. "French people have a very laissez-faire attitude towards dates, deadlines, etcetera. You know how it is."

Actually, I wanted to say, I *don't* know how it is. Why wouldn't they come get me on my first day in Paris? Why wouldn't they call Mme Cuchon if they had other plans? Is it possible they know everything that happened this summer . . . and that is why they don't want anything to do with me?

Alex snickers. "If you'd ever been to the Dordogne, you wouldn't want to come back, either."

Spotting some of the other girls we met at the airport yesterday, Alex stands up and straightens her black shorts and jersey tank top.

"Hi, ladies!" she calls, stepping around the desks to chat with them. Kids gravitate toward Alex as if she has a magnetic switch—she's left alone when she wants to be, but when she's ready to be social, everyone flocks to her. The other girls are admiring Alex's gold sandals, asking if they are real Jimmy Choos (whatever that means), and the guys clustered off to the side all steal appreciative glances of her, surely noticing the way her thin top grazes over her chest with just a hint of sultriness. Alex is not tall, but her shoes and little shorts lengthen her legs. Her shiny blue-black hair, arranged in artful layers with just the right amount of product, is her crowning achievement. She manages to look as put together as if a team of stylists came to her homestay this morning to get her ready for school.

"My BlackBerry is getting wretched service in here," Alex complains to Sara-Louise, the girl I met yesterday from South Carolina, and Zack, another Southerner. "You want to come outside with me and see if I can get it to function from the courtyard?"

"Alex is a lot of fun, huh?" Olivia comments after Alex leaves with Zack and Sara-Louise. "She's so grown-up. And she knows, like, *everything* about Paris!"

"I guess." To me, Alex seems like everything I've always thought I would detest about people from big cities. She's a know-it-all and a name-dropper, a snob who can't resist the opportunity to draw attention to herself. Already this morning, she's told us at least four times how her mom works for *Luxe* in New York. Growing up in the woods of Vermont, I've never met anyone from a town larger than Burlington.

"She didn't mean it the way it sounded," Olivia leans forward to tell me.

"The way what sounded?" I pull at the little pills on my old sweater.

"What Alex said about your host parents. I'm sure they are really excited to come back to Paris and meet you. They probably just got tied up with something, or got confused about when they were supposed to come get you. I'm sure they can't wait to get to know you," Olivia says. "Besides, you can stay with me as long as you need to."

"I just don't get it, though. Why would you sign up to be a host parent if you don't really want to be there for the kid?"

"Maybe there was a family emergency, or they got the flu," Olivia reasons. She offers me a drink from her water bottle. I shake my head. Olivia bends her neck back and takes a drink, wiping her mouth on her small hand when she's done.

"Did you ever follow up with Mme Cuchon about what's going on with them?"

"No," I admit. "I don't want to stir up any drama."

"Well," Olivia smiles, "I really do like having you with me at my apartment. You know so much about Paris, too! I feel like I have a lot to learn from both you and Alex. I'd love to explore some of the museums you were talking about last night while we were eating dinner, like the Picasso Museum. The paintings you were describing sound amazing!" Her freckled face is open and sincere.

I grin in spite of myself. "Even when I go to my rightful homestay," I promise, "we'll definitely have to delve into Paris together."

Alex prances back into the room on the arm of dark-haired, handsome hipster Zack. In the van, I heard Zack tease her about her "Crackberry" addiction, but apparently it doesn't stop him from adoring Alex like I can tell Olivia does, too. I hope Alex's return means that I can finally use the payphone out there without anyone overhearing me.

I'm off to such a great start in Paris, making an enemy of Alex before the plane even took off. Now everyone, probably even saintly little Olivia, will turn against me when she finds out about my past. I know I'm acting totally bizarre, but how can I explain why without revealing everything?

My head is killing me. I need rest. New faces and voices are swimming around me murkily like a bad, weird dream.

Olivia starts to say something about taking a walk along the Seine together later, but just then Mme Cuchon claps her hands and says it's time for orientation to begin.

Oh, no. I missed my chance. I really needed to make that phone call.

After Mme Cuchon does a rundown of our classes—math, chemistry, and history in English, then French class, then art (also taught in French and my very favorite subject), and then PE—she has to spend some time reiterating to Alex and Zack that PE is indeed mandatory.

"Unless, of course, you choose to join one of our many sports teams here at the Lycée. It's an excellent way to get to know the French students here," Mme Cuchon says pleasantly.

I relish the sound of Mme Cuchon's rich accent, the way her mouth moves over our names and explains the things we'll need to know. It's comforting to listen to her because it means that I'm finally here, that much closer to what I've been wanting. Her flowing, whimsical clothes remind me a little of my mom, I notice wistfully.

"I'll join a team over my cold, dead body," Alex tells Zack in a low voice.

"*Entendu,*" Zack laughs. "*Je crois que non.*" He doesn't exactly strike me as the athletic type himself, with his perfectly tailored trendy clothes and accessories, like the leather bands encircling either of his wrists.

"*Eh bien,*" Mme Cuchon goes on. "Shall we introduce ourselves to one another?"

Introductions mean that it's Mme Cuchon's turn to stop talking, and our turn to start. I sit on my hands to keep them from quavering. As everyone takes turns telling us all who they are and where they are from, I can barely pay attention. It's torture trying to keep perfectly still like everything is absolutely normal right now.

I try to listen and remember all their names. The preppy guy from Boston who winks at Alex after he introduces himself. The surfer sitting next to him. A girl in a spiked belt with choppy black hair who unnervingly ends every sentence with "Right?" More and more people, each one happy, well-adjusted, with nothing at all to worry about except getting over their jetlag and being a little bit homesick. I wonder if I will ever experience that luxury again.

"Penelope?" I hear Mme Cuchon calling to me. Olivia pokes me in the side.

"It's PJ!" I say, too loudly. Everyone, especially Alex, laughs. "I mean, I'm PJ. I'm from . . ." *Should I even tell them where I'm from? What if there's someone else from Vermont here? What if they've heard something? They might know that it's me, and then I'll be ruined for sure.*

"*Je suis malade.* I need to get some air," I cry out as I jump up from my chair. "Sorry!" I can't get away fast enough.

I rush into the hallway, needing to get to the phone, needing to talk to Dave right away. Luckily, the front steps are empty and the phone just outside the school's entrance is free. I shakily dial the calling-card number and, finally, after what seems like an eternity, get connected to Dave's cell phone.

"Pick up, pick up," I plead into the phone.

After five rings, Dave answers gruffly. "Who is this?"

"Dave, it's PJ," I tell him.

"PJ!" Dave exclaims. "Man, you really missed a shit show around here. But I guess that's why you left in the first place, so you wouldn't be a part of it."

"I can't talk long," I whisper into the mouthpiece, manically checking behind me to make sure no one is there. "What's happening?"

"Things are not good, my friend. Your parents got busted almost as soon as you got on the bus. Majorly. They're facing time," Dave tells me, reluctance in his voice. "I hate to say it, but you probably shouldn't try and contact them for awhile. Everyone who wants to talk to them will probably have to go through their lawyer. You don't want to get into that mess. It's getting blown wayyyy out of proportion."

This can't be happening. "I can't call them?"

"No, dude!" Dave insists. "Your parents may have been trying to help people, trying to save the world, but they got caught in a freaky web with some shady characters. You and me are lucky we escaped unscathed!"

I feel like I can't breathe.

"So, how's Paris? You been to see the Mona Lisa yet?"

"You know it's not like that, Dave."

"Well, you were always talking about Paris. But this isn't you, not now. Annabel, yeah. She's been a runner her whole life, just waiting for the right moment. I'd do anything to know where that girl went," Dave says. "But you? You oughta help your parents make things right, Penny Lane, instead of heading for the hills like your sister did."

"My parents *want* me to be here," I argue. My knees weaken when he calls me by Annabel's old nickname for me. "That's what my dad told me. Please, Dave, I—" I fight the tears welling behind my closed eyelids.

"PJ?" a shy voice asks softly from behind me.

I whip around, my heart pounding. In front of me is a guy I recognize from the program pastry session back in the classroom. He didn't drive over from the airport with us yesterday; he must have flown in later than the rest of us. He's built, about the same height as me, if not a tiny bit shorter, with olive skin and dark eyes. His dark hair is shorn close to his head in almost a military style. He wears oversize denim shorts and a white collared shirt. On his feet are beat up white Converse sneakers, just like the ones I'm wearing.

"Holy crap!" I nearly scream in surprise. "Dave, I gotta go. I'll call you when I can. Keep your phone on." I slam the receiver back onto the hook.

"Hey, sorry to interrupt. I'm Jay," the guy says. He's got the slightest hint of an accent, but it's not a French accent; it's something else, maybe Spanish, or Italian. "I had to use the bathroom myself. On my way, I saw you over here looking really upset. Is everything okay? Do you need me to get one of the teachers?" Jay looks genuinely concerned.

"I'm fine," I say, trying to catch my breath. What did I reveal before I knew he was standing there? "I just had to make a phone call. Don't worry about me." What is this kid doing, sneaking up on me?

"Were you talking to your boyfriend?" Jay asks. "Are you guys in a fight or something?"

Is this kid *eavesdropping* on me?

"Yeah," I lie quickly. "Yeah, Dave's my boyfriend. We're in an argument. It's complicated."

"Oh, wow, that's tough," Jay grimaces. "Anything I can do? I hate to see such a pretty girl look so sad."

Oh, good, a ladies' man. I snort. "That's okay. I can take care of myself."

"Well, if you ever need anything, just let me know," Jay says, and despite his jokey charm, I can tell he's being sincere.

But I have too much on my mind. My parents have been *arrested?* Can Dave possibly be telling me the truth? My parents went from being questioned at a gas station to possibly serving time? All for trying to do right in a twisted, inhumane system. They never meant for it to take the bad turn that it did. I'm sure of it. It's all I can be sure of.

"Thanks," I say, distracted. What is Jay still doing here?

"Well, I heard you're an amazing French speaker," he says, changing the subject.

"Oh, thanks, not really." Didn't he say he was on his way to the bathroom?

"You want to study together sometime? Maybe get a coffee or something?" Jay offers. "I saw that you like espresso—you were drinking a bunch of them back there."

"Sure, sure," I say. "Listen, is orientation over? I've got to talk to Mme Cuchon."

"Yeah, they were wrapping up when I stepped out."

Dave had probably just gotten home from the bar he tends when I called. After all, it is 4 A.M. in Vermont right now. I can picture what he was likely wearing, an old T-shirt and a pair of Carhartt workpants. I can picture Dave's bed, the way he rolled over to his cell phone on the nightstand when it rang, probably hoping it was Annabel, back from the abyss. Instead, he got me, Annabel's gawky kid sister.

Jay looks at me steadily, nodding his head as if he's just figured something out, something that he's been thinking about for awhile.

"Listen, great to meet you, PJ," he says. "Don't forget about our study date." As he walks down the hall toward the bathroom, he looks behind him and grins when he catches me watching him walk away. Rolling my eyes, I can't help but find him the tiniest bit sweet.

"See you back there," I say, knowing I should hurry back to befriending Alex, Olivia, and the others before it's too late.

Alex reminds me a little of Annabel, in some ways. Like the way Alex surprised me by stuffing herself with buttery pastries rather than eschewing the rich food the way you'd think a girl like her might. Annabel had a huge apetite, too. Me, I've always been different. I'd forget to eat at all if my mom didn't tempt me with her homemade scones or fresh vegetables from her garden.

Annabel was a heartbreaking conundrum, for me and for Dave.

Impossible to live with, impossible to resist. She does everything big. Her steak was always cooked rare. When she helped my mom bake cookies, she drizzled them with rich dark chocolate and ate them for breakfast. She and Dave used to play their guitars together on the back porch, and her voluminous voice would fill up the whole backyard, all the way to my dad's work shed. She really did have a beautiful singing voice.

On the day of Annabel's wedding, we spent all morning curling her hair with my mom's old barrel curling iron, turning her long dark hair into a pile of ringlets woven with fresh wildflowers on top of her head. I dusted her cheeks with sparkly pink powder and dabbed dewy sheer gloss onto her lips. Her face, usually so similar to my own, was transformed from familiar into angelic.

"I can't believe you're leaving me," I told her when she was all ready.

"I know," Annabel grinned. "But you're leaving me, too."

"It isn't the same. I'm coming back from Paris in a year. Aren't you scared?" I asked. She was going to be a real adult now, married, with her own house.

"No, Penny Lane," she laughed. "I never get scared."

She had a point there; she never did. Annabel was the first one to go splashing in the creek behind our house every spring as soon as the ice thawed. She always drove just as fast as she pleased, and gave anyone who cut her off on the road the finger and a big smile. When she stepped on a nail, she pulled it right back out and kept running barefoot through the backyard.

She must have run because of my parents, but why then? What happened between our sweet last moments together and when I heard the shriek of car wheels spin over our gravel driveway, the only goodbye I ever got from my sister? By the time we were gathered in the gazebo that my dad built for Dave and Annabel to get married under, Annabel was nowhere to be found. Her car never pulled back into the driveway. She never showed up to her own wedding.

All I had was an old paperback copy of Annabel's favorite book, *Madame Bovary*, left on my bed in the room we shared, a note inscribed on the title page:

Bon voyage! Love, Annabel.

Annabel always was so excited about my big Parisian adventure. I should be, too. I head into the classroom, determined get through this alone.

I'm going to come clean to Mme Cuchon and straighten out my homestay *tout de suite*.

It's time to make Paris my new life. And turn away from the past for good.

4. ZACK

Maybe Now, Maybe Never

"*Y*ou and I will grab a drink and then meet everyone else at Odéon," Alex suggests on Friday afternoon, twirling a strand of black hair around her finger. We're standing on the steps outside the Lycée, each of us having blown off PE class, Alex to go shopping and me, well, because PE is a massive pain in the butt. Besides, the outfit I have on today, cuffed dark denim jeans, boat shoes, and a white blazer over a navy blue v-neck tee, begs to be taken for a long walk in the Trocadero. I'm headed over to the park after school to people-watch while sitting next to the grand fountain, from which you have the best view of the Eiffel Tower in all of Paris.

"We haven't even *hung out* yet," Alex says. "I've been wanting to get to know you since we met at the airport. I just love your hair." She reaches over and tousles my messy, longish dark hair. It's a new thing I'm doing lately—shaggy chic.

"Thanks! I'll pick you up," I offer, laughing. "You've been in such high demand that I didn't know you had time for us riffraff." I consider asking Alex to join me this afternoon, but I sense that Alex wants to make our time together into an occasion. Rightly so. It's not every day that a girl like Alex asks you out on a date.

"I'd always have time for you, dear," Alex says sweetly. "See you at eight tonight. Don't be late."

I click my heels together as I walk down the Avenue Kléber, following my map carefully so I won't get lost. The fact that Alex is so set on hanging out with me is proof that my quest for love might not be as much of an upward battle as I thought. Even if Alex herself isn't exactly . . . my type.

The fabulous Alex lives in the same arrondissement as me, the 15th, I discover that evening when I go to pick her up. I find her host family's building easily, and in the hazy twilight Alex is leaning over the second floor balcony in a bright pink silk Kimono. She's furiously pounding a text message into her BlackBerry with one hand and smoking a cigarette with the other. A dark, angry expression clouds her pretty face.

"Yoo-hoo!" I call softly up to her. When Alex sees it's me, her face lights up.

She spreads her palm. "Five minutes," she mouths down to me, stubbing out her cigarette and tossing it over the ledge. After a moment, Alex bounds out the front door, wearing a black tube dress and red high heels. Her hair is held back by a wide black headband, and she's carrying her camel-colored tote bag with the thick braided handle.

"*Comment ça va?*" I ask, kissing her gaily on each heavily rouged cheek.

"*Ça va,*" Alex sighs. She lights up another cigarette. "I need a drink *so* badly," she tells me, pulling me down the street. "I'm getting hassled by my mom about the most *ridiculous* things—her texts have me all *tense* this evening. She's giving me *such* a hard time about doing well in school this year—and the school year has barely even started." Alex is wide open tonight—full of energy and spunk.

We grab a table at the first place we see with outdoor seating in the rollicking area near the famous Odéon Theatre on the Left Bank. Alex stares moonily at the cute waiter until he comes over to take our order. I feel the urge to fan Alex's cigarette smoke out of my eyes, but I'm afraid of offending her. I'm just wearing a simple army-green long-sleeved T-shirt and slouchy tapered Wesc jeans, but I starched and ironed each so carefully that I'd hate for all the smoke in this café to soak into them so early into the night.

Of course, in Paris, trying to keep the putrid stench of cigarette smoke out of your clothes and your hair would have been like trying to tell Johnny Cash to stop singing sad old songs all the time, or telling my preacher back in Memphis that I'd rather he quieted down when he was praising the Lord every Sunday morning. In this case, as in many others, you just have to let go and let God. And be sure to wash your clothes with a whole lot of strong detergent when you get home.

"Anyway, let's chat about *toi*," Alex says, flinging her BlackBerry on the table. "Not *moi*. Or my *vache* of a mom, *merci beaucoup*, or my deadbeat ex-*whatever*, Jeremy, back in Brooklyn, or my good-for-nothing dad I haven't seen since I was a baby, nor any of the other reasons why I'm thrilled to be an ocean away from everyone I know. Let's just skip my sob story and get onto the good stuff about *you*." She smiles flirtatiously.

Alex is dramatic. I knew that from the moment we met in the baggage carousel and she swooningly had me carry her suitcases out to Mme Cuchon's van. I am also getting two other feelings from Alex: Number one, that she likes me as more than a friend, and number two, that some of her brazenness is a show to make her look confident. Don't get me wrong—I *love* Alex's shenanigans so far. But her crush has to be put out · of its misery. Before it gets embarrassing.

"Do you think that waiter is cute?" I say slyly, hoping she'll catch on.

"Yeah, I guess," she says thoughtfully. "Though *très petit*. Too short for me."

"I think he's cute," I say evenly. "He has beautiful skin. What if I give him my number?" I ask with way more confidence than I actually have. *As if I ever would! As if he would even want it.*

Alex looks at me for a long moment, figuring out what I am saying. "Sure," she says. "Yeah. Do it."

Alex has a look on her face like she has been duped. It's sweet. She starts to laugh. Just then, things fall into place: Alex realizes that she's got an instant best friend here, a Will to her Grace, a solid rock for her shaky neuroses, and I am happy to note that Alex is smoother than most of the other girls who've ever had crushes on me.

She reaches into that behemoth leather bag and pulls out her hot pink lip-gloss for the tenth time since I picked her up. Watch Alex sometime and you'll see it's just a constant series of cigarette, lip-gloss, cigarette, lip-gloss. That and her obsession with gum.

"Dude, you don't even *have* a number here yet," she says, "but I'd bet my BlackBerry he'd screw you if you went up and asked. Who wouldn't?"

I stick my tongue out at her. She bears her perfectly even teeth at me wolfishly. Our brief, one-sided romance has officially devolved into the snarky friendship I'd been hoping for.

"Well, then, my dear, darling Zack," Alex goes on, "tell me more about your wild youth. I'm counting on you for a year of debauchery, and I need to know your credentials."

"Shhh!" I hiss at her. "Deep down, I'm, well, *you know*," I say. "But let's keep that to ourselves for the time being. Only a few other people on the entire planet know besides you and me."

"You're kidding," Alex says disbelievingly. "You're not out of the closet?"

"Sort of," I tell her. "I came out to my best friend, Pierson, last year."

Alex snorts. "Haha, 'coming out'? Is that what the gays are calling it these days? You and your 'best friend,' huh?" She raises her eyebrows suggestively.

"It's not like that!" I protest with a retch. "Pierson and I have known each other since the dawn of time. We both like guys, but we could never be *together*. It would be like going out with my *brother*. It's too disgusting to think about."

"You didn't even come out to your family?"

"That's how come I applied to the Lycée. I can't be myself in Memphis," I explain. "You can't hardly flick your wrist without hitting some redneck just ready to exorcise all the gay demons right out of your soul in the little suburb where I live. I come into church on Sunday with this hairstyle, and I can just see my preacher itching to bang his Bible right over my head. I'm ready for Paris to just burn itself all over me."

"And *this* is where I come in," Alex galvanizes. "Zack, we were destined to meet, I just know we were. You're obviously never going to get anywhere in Paris without me to help you; I can see that already. Hold on just one second. . . ."

Alex scans the bar inside through the open windows. "Aha! Excellent."

"What?"

"Zack, darling," Alex says, stubbing out her cigarette and lacing her velvety, thin manicured fingers into mine. "You and I are going to make a pact. You want a boyfriend; I want a boyfriend. That's precisely why both of us came to Paris, and that's precisely what we are going to find here."

I can't help but beam giddily at her. In my wildest hopes before coming to Paris, I never dreamed I'd become friends with someone like Alex so quickly. She gets it. She gets me. I reach out and pinch her cheek to make sure she's real. She is. Every glamorous inch of her.

Alex squeezes my hand and removes it from her face. "So right now," she commands, "I want you to finish your drink and follow me over to that table full of total poufs inside."

I look over. She's right. In the corner are three young guys—none of them older than probably nineteen or twenty—each of them emanating a very, um, *inviting* quality.

"What?" I cry out in alarm, trying to keep my voice down unsuccessfully. "Alex, no!"

"*Yes*," Alex insists. "It's now or never."

"But what about you?" I say nervously. "None of them could become your boyfriend. What's in it for you?"

"Oh," Alex waves her hand. "Don't you worry about that. I'm already lining something up at the Lycée, and besides—I don't want a French guy anyways. My mom married a French guy, and look what happened to her."

Of course Alex bails as soon as the setup is in place! Why am I not surprised? After a half hour of the French guys cooing over how cute she is, how much they love her bag and her shoes, she gathers her things, ties a large vintage Hermès scarf around her neck, and air kisses the guys goodbye.

"Zack—call me tomorrow, and I will fill you in on how we're spending *next* weekend. I love you more than anything." Alex leans over, balancing precariously on her red stiletto heels to kiss me on the cheek.

"You can't leave me with them!" I protest quietly into her ear, but she's off, teetering down the Rue Saint Sulpice, already chattering away onto her BlackBerry and waving for a cab. I rub at the lip-gloss, sticky on my face, fuming.

"*Alors, Zack, que penses-tu de Paris?*" one of the guys, a redhead with ruddy skin whose name I think is Martin, asks me. He looks deep into my eyes as he says it, his voice husky.

"Oh, I love Paris," I stammer. "I just love it!"

"You should let me show you around sometime," Martin says, reaching down and putting his hand on my knee. "Tonight we are going dancing at this really great club if you want to come with us." His two friends nod in agreement.

"Oh, maybe," I say. *Is it just me or did they dim the lights in here?*

I look away from Martin for a moment. I *should* go to the club with them. I should go out dancing every night. I should meet guys. I should trust Alex. This is how to get a boyfriend! But somehow—this feels all wrong. It sounds strange to say it in my head, but I realize I've never hung out with openly gay guys before. It's oddly terrifying, I have to confess.

With a sheepish smile, I turn back to Martin to decline his invitation. It's just too soon. Besides, it's getting late, plus . . . I don't even know these guys. Maybe if Alex were here, but not like this. . . .

Suddenly, Martin is leaning in toward me like he is going to kiss me. My first kiss with a guy! In just one second, I'm going to be *kissing a guy*. In public. This is. Absolutely. Unreal.

Martin's two friends have moved away from our table a bit to give us some privacy, and it's obvious that they think he and I are a done deal. How did this all happen so fast?

"Oh, God!" I sputter, feeling a hot, red blush spread from my hairline to the absolute tips of my toes. "I've got to go—curfew—sorry—thanks for the drinks!" I leap out of my seat and hear the crash of our wine glasses as I blindly knock them over. I don't even stop to help clean up the mess. I just bolt for the door.

5. ALEX

Love and Lies in Le Marais

"*T*his joker thinks he knows his way around the Paris metro, but he's *demented*," Drew practically shouts as he and George approach our table, each holding a tacky tallboy of convenience-store beer. "We were all the way to the Porte de Clignancourt before homeboy realized we were going in the completely wrong direction."

A group of us is sitting at the most adorable outdoor garden café, located in the trendy neighborhood of Le Marais on a Saturday night. The café is draped in white Christmas lights and hushed except for a little retro record player warbling Edith Piaf. The patrons, locals dripping with style and class, give us an immediate look of disgust as the boys drag up chairs to join us.

I take a deep breath. Since Zack is clearly out of the question, George is the one I've selected to be my boyfriend this year. Half horrified, half cracking up, I grab the mostly empty cans from the boys and hide them under the table before the waiter turns around and sees.

"Shut up, you idiot! The girls are going to think I don't have any game if you keep that up," George retorts, also way too loud, giving Drew a friendly shove. "Don't listen to him. He's the one that got stuck in the metro turnstile. The dude in the little hut at the station had to come help him out of it. It was priceless."

George and Drew are possibly the most eligible guys in our program, both of them clean-cut sons of New England privilege. They know each other from before the Lycée, since they've gone to boarding school together for the last four years. Though Drew is certainly plenty hot, tall and a little scraggly with shaggy blond hair, George is my favorite of the two. George is preppier and a little stockier than his friend, with a sweeter face and a certain je ne sais quoi. He reminds me of an old-school charmer, like one of the rich kids in an old John Hughes movie. A prepster with a heart of gold. Or something.

"I'm so sorry we're late," George says more quietly, looking right at me with piercing, intent eyes. "I hope we didn't keep you waiting."

He's perfectly captivated by me, his manners honed carefully by his ritzy upbringing. I feel my mom's nod of approval all the way from New York. "That's okay," I tell him, unable to look away.

I noticed him on the first day of school, checking me out as I put on my lip-gloss in French class. It took him a full *three weeks* before finally asking me what I was doing this weekend.

"So, Al," George says, reclining comfortably, still looking just at me. "Now that you took our beers from us, how should we go about getting more?"

I *really* like that he called me Al. Having a nickname for me so soon is surely a good sign. "Um," I say, barely able to think, nonetheless respond like an intelligent person. "Order one from the waiter?"

I usually have an arsenal of flirtatious one-liners to keep me going through the adrenaline high of being with a new crush for the first time, but tonight I'm falling flat. I must like George more than I realized.

Olivia raises her eyebrows at my quavering, nervous response and motions at the waiter to bring everyone a fresh drink.

I'd helped Olivia accessorize the striped baby doll dress I'd loaned her with my red stiletto pumps (I'm already sick of wearing them, anyway) and my wide black belt cinched around her small waist. She looks fantastic, though not quite as good as I do tonight in one of my mom's patterned Diane Von Furstenberg wrap dresses with its plunging neckline. Olivia might have a boyfriend at home, but not for long if I have anything to do with it. Dating is no fun when you can't include your friends.

"What do you care what I wear tonight?" Olivia asked me, disgruntled, when I insisted she changed out of her jeans and Ugg boots and into something of mine. "Besides, it's starting to get chilly out. I'll freeze if I wear this."

"Wear this over it, then," I told her, handing her a black pashmina wrap. "Olivia, it's hardly freezing out. It's not even October. Just wait till January. You'll be begging to get on the first flight back to San Diego."

"Still," Olivia said, fiddling with the belt. "I like to be casual."

"I've noticed," I told her. "You and every other American in our program. How do you guys expect to find boyfriends over here if you're always dressing like you've just rolled out of bed?"

"Alex," Olivia told me for what seemed like the millionth time. "I have a boyfriend. Vince, remember? We've been going out for two years. I'm not about to go out with someone else."

Yeah, yeah, yeah, I get it, I thought. The whole story is tiresome by now. Olivia has known studly basketball star Vince her whole life— their parents are friends or something. They ran around in dirty Huggies together. If you ask me, that's all the more reason she should date someone new!

I made a vomiting noise. "You're in Paris, for Pete's sake! The city of *love.* Life is too short for long distance relationships . . . and anyway, who else am I going to double date with?" Olivia knew I meant I'd picked out Drew for her, but she wasn't taking me seriously.

I wondered, though, when I saw her fluff her highlighted hair (mercifully, she's wearing it down rather than in a boring old ponytail like normal) as the boys approached.

PJ, of all people, is sitting to Olivia's left. I was *so* annoyed when she came over to get ready with us earlier—*of course* Olivia felt like she had to invite her since PJ is *still* living with her. Olivia is far too kindhearted to leave anyone out, even a space cadet like PJ. Since she arrived at the café tonight, PJ has just sat there looking lovely and petulant, drinking nothing but sparkling water and in general making *everything* as *awkward* as possible. She can't seem to stop fidgeting, or saying things out of turn.

Like when she prompts me for the right words to order my drink. Doesn't PJ think I know how to say "*Je voudrais un verre de vin*"? It just takes me a second to think of it. I have other things on my mind. Like George, sitting not even a foot away from me, his smile as beguiling as a heartthrob on the cover of *Luxe.*

The waiter brings over our drinks. White wine for me, beer for George and Drew, a gin and tonic for Zack, and two very demure glasses of Perrier for Olivia and PJ. Olivia, as a dancer, has an excuse for not drinking. PJ, on the other hand, seems to abstain just to be a buzz-kill.

I sneak a look over at George, sipping on his Heineken (which is conveniently pronounced the same way in every language and thus easy to order in French without looking like a fool) and wonder if he thinks PJ is hotter than me. When he meets my eyes with an amatory smile, I have the answer to my question—there is no one in this program better suited to George than myself. Not even the six-foot willowy blonde hippie. I breathe a long sigh of happy relief.

"I can't wait to go to Amsterdam," George says excitedly. "My sister went there this summer; she said it was *sick*. You can take a tour of the Heineken brewery, and then they, like, pour Heineken down your throat at the end, and you get wasted."

"Fascinating," Zack remarks. Before they arrived, Zack had made his impressions of George and Drew well-known: George is a pampered asshat with a sleazy Boston accent, and Drew poses like a chilled-out idiot surfer to hide his suburban Connecticut waspiness. Both of the boys lost marks with Zack for their bad shoes—loafers with no socks for preppy George, and old, dirty Vans slip-ons for Drew.

"And they dress like their moms shop for them at the Nordstrom kids' section back-to-school sale," Zack complained earlier. When Zack is in this mood—judgmental and hyperaware of what people are wearing—I think it's best just to ignore him altogether. He just hasn't seen George's excellent qualities yet—the things that make George absolutely *perfect* boyfriend material.

George's expensive brown leather loafers might be a cliché, but they are also an excellent metaphor for all that separates George out as the man of my dreams. He's *reliable*, unconcerned with trends and what people think of him, and, best of all, he's *rich*. I know that might sound superficial, but I believe it is incredibly important to know what you want. Dating can be such a royal chore when you have to spend the whole time wondering who is going to pay! Believe me, I've been there before, with Jeremy, my Park Slope pauper, art students from the Pratt Institute, cute guys playing Frisbee golf in Prospect Park. I'm ready for a prince.

"That's fabulous!" I say to George more kindly. "Are you planning a trip?"

"Oh, hells yeah. Are we ever!" George shouts, Drew smacking him high-five across the table. "Dude, we are going to get so blazed in Amsterdam, we'll probably never come back!"

"It's gonna be sweet," Drew concurs. "Pot, hookers, whatever we want, whenever we want." He rowdily starts drumming the tabletop with his hands, pounding out a long solo that attracts even more attention to our table. While he does it, he stares me right in the eye. *Weird.*

"Drew!" Olivia scolds with a shriek of righteous, though giggling, protest. She smacks him playfully on the arm. "Prostitutes? That's disgusting!"

"Hey, man," Drew says gamely. "When in Rome . . . or should I say Amsterdam? Whatever. I'm just sayin'." He makes a lewd hand gesture that sends Olivia back into horrified hysterics.

Even Zack, who I can usually trust to act like a gentleman in public, starts making fake-barfing noises. Shooting a look at our disapproving waiter, I flush with embarrassment. PJ, for her part, is at least acting like a grown-up. The rest of our group has devolved into a level of discourse that is just unsuitable for a Parisian café, no matter *how* much we've had to drink. And no matter how much I like George.

"Shhh," I scold them. "You guys are going to get us kicked out! Can't we have a civilized conversation? One that doesn't involve all the criminal activity you two are plotting in my unwitting presence?"

Finally, I think with relief. I'm forming sentences like a coherent person again, rather than being struck dumb and making googly eyes at George. I toss my hair. There we go.

George looks at me with a lopsided, guilty smile. "Of course we can, doll. What do you want to talk about? Jean-Paul Sartre? Sarkozy's foreign policy? The plummeting rates of the dollar against the euro? Any of those civilized enough for you?"

"No," I giggle. "Those things are boring."

George shakes his head. "Alex, I'm quite positive that you've never uttered a single boring phrase in your life, no matter what the topic of conversation is."

"Besides," Drew comments, "don't you worry your pretty little head about our criminal activity. It's 100 percent legal to smoke pot in Amsterdam. Europeans in general are way cooler about that kind of stuff."

"It's true," PJ says quietly. "Things are way easier over here."

We all turn to look at her, since it's practically the first thing she's said all night.

PJ's not even looking at us. She's staring at an older couple, in their fifties at least, dancing slowly in the corner of the outdoor garden next to the old record player. When the man gently dips the lady, the people sitting near them break into pleased applause.

"I love this city, too," Olivia grins. "Zack, come dance with me."

Olivia slips off the red Louboutins and pulls Zack up to his feet. He twirls her over so that they're slow dancing next to the older French couple. A few other pairs join them, too, enjoying what will likely be one of the last warm nights of the year. All around us, groups of people of all ages murmur to one another, smoking and happily clinking glasses. Olivia and Zack are elegant, easy dancers. They don't look a bit out of place.

That's the beauty of Paris. There's always room for an impromptu slow dance. You just have to move some of the tables out of the way.

"Hey," George says quietly, reaching for my cigarette and taking a long drag. "Drew managed to get a joint past airport security for me. Think anyone here will care if we smoke it?"

"Really?" I say, a little scandalized. "Wow." I'm not generally a huge fan of pot, but I will definitely smoke a joint right now if it means I can slip away with George. "Let's go into that little alley over there."

We leave George's Blackberry with Drew so he can call mine if he needs to. As I press my number into his contacts list, my pulse quickens.

Leaned up against the side of the building in the dark, we take a few hits of the joint. The weed hits me all at once. Everything suddenly feels slower, more deliberate.

George puts his hand on my back, rubbing the soft fabric of my dress between his fingers. "This is nice," he says quietly.

"My dress?" I ask, my voice thick.

"Well, that, too," he says. "But I meant . . . I meant this." He gestures around.

I look at the dumpster we are standing next to. It stinks like garbage. And urine.

Past the dumpster, though, is the tiny Rue de Barres, and beyond that, the lustrous butte of the back of the St. Gervais church, one of the oldest churches in Paris. That's what he's referring to—the gorgeousness of Paris, the way romance and mystery creep into every darkened alleyway.

"My mom took me to a concert there once," I tell him. "Like, last year. It was a harpsa . . . harpsichordian . . . *harpsichordist*." Why on earth is that word so fricking hard to remember right now?

George wheezes like this is the funniest thing in the world. Suddenly, it is. It's hysterical, actually. "She . . . she took you to what?"

I can't stop laughing, either. "She really wanted to see it! She talked about it all day. Don't laugh!" I say, busting up.

"You stop laughing!" George says. "You're the one cracking up!" He leans into me a little. "Did you enjoy the concert? Did you like the harpsa . . . harpsa . . . whatever it was called?"

I swat at him. "I *did*. I enjoy high culture very, very much." With that, I take a long, serious puff of the joint. This makes George laugh even harder.

"Whatever," he laughs. "You totally fell asleep."

I double over in hysterics because he's right. "I did!" I snort. "How did you know?" Neither of us can stand up straight after that we're both laughing too hard and too stoned. George pulls me over to him, and just hugs me while we stand there shaking in silent fits of hilarity. I reciprocally put my arms around him, wondering if he'll kiss me if I look up at him at just the right moment.

Suddenly, I feel the insistent buzz of my BlackBerry going off in my bag.

Make it stop, I think in disbelief. *Rewind back to the part where George and I were about to fall in love.*

George throws down the rest of the joint and stomps it out forcefully under his loafer. He pushes me in the opposite direction than we came, toward St. Gervais. "Run, Alex!" he grunts at me. I don't even answer my BlackBerry, I just *go*.

My stomach lurches as I force my legs to move. If I learned one thing from all my escapades last year, it should have been to eat before you party, but I of course skipped dinner so I could spend more time diffusing my hair properly before going out.

We circle the church and find ourselves on the empty, darkened plaza facing the back of the Hotel de Ville, Paris's City Hall.

"Call your BlackBerry," I instruct. "Find out what happened. Should we go back?"

George dials and listens for a second, but Drew doesn't answer.

I'm busy trying not to throw up and still look hot and alluring. Let me tell you, it is no easy task. "Come on, babe," George gestures at me. Despite him holding me for so long before, we don't touch as we walk swiftly down the Rue du Pont and toward the café.

"Shit!" George curses quietly. "What did they do?" There are cops surrounding the table we'd all been sitting at. There are at least four of them, each of them looking sternly at Drew, PJ, Olivia, and Zack, who are staring at the ground. The record player has been turned off, and other patrons are getting up to leave in the commotion. George and I hang back, unsure whether to wait or escape.

"This isn't a playground," I hear one of the cops say to PJ in harsh French. "You kids are causing a lot of trouble here tonight. This is a quiet neighborhood, not your personal *discothèque!*"

"Where did the others go? The ones with the drugs?" another cop demands.

"*Non, monsieurs, vous vous trompez,*" a tinkling, melodic voice says in French. It's PJ!

PJ slips out of her old oversize cardigan and stands up to her full six feet, revealing just a thin white camisole and a wrap skirt. Her hair glows in the candlelight, spilling down her shoulders in messy waves.

She gives the cops surrounding the table an expansive, open smile. I hold my breath. Even I knew Mme Cuchon was serious when she told us drugs were totally off limits in this program. If the cops saw us in the alley, George and I will be booted out of the Lycée for sure!

One of the cops leans in to make his point. "In France, there are serious punishments for troublemaking kids. That's a promise."

"Oh, don't be silly! Drugs?" PJ exclaims, wrinkling her nose like a supermodel bunny rabbit. She's acting like she has known these cops since they all went on family picnics together as young children. "Our friends? They've just been to get some *chewing gum.* See? Here they are now. Alex, *cherie*, show them the gum you just bought." She reaches out to me, pulling me close to her and keeping her slender arm firmly around my shoulders.

As a dedicated smoker who is also dedicated to having fresh breath, I *always* have several packs of gum on me at any given time. Anyone who knows me at all knows that, even PJ. I reach into my tote bag and pull out an unopened pack of Orbit.

"Yup," I say stupidly, hearing my own voice tremble. "I've got the gum. They sent me for gum. And I went and got it. And my friend here"—I cock my thumb at George, who is standing frozen to my right—"he came with me, because he's so nice like that." The cops' unyielding expressions remain unchanged. We're *so* busted. I close my eyes and start rehearsing how I am going to spin this to my mom. After everything that happened last year, she is *not* going to look on this fondly.

PJ takes the gum from me and pops a piece into her luscious mouth. "Hmmm, great flavor, Alex. Want to try some?" she offers the cops. "It's delicious."

They watch her mouth as she chews. Then they look at each other, their shoulders relaxing a bit.

Each cop takes a piece.

I shove a big wad into my own mouth to mask any lingering pot smoke smell. We are all standing there, noisily chomping on the gum. George, Olivia, Drew, and Zack are all staring at PJ and me, knowing all of our fates at the Lycée rest on our ability to charm these cops silly. If we screw this up, Olivia can kiss her scholarship goodbye, Zack will get sent back to the Bible-bangers in Tennessee, and George and Drew will never speak to me again. I pray PJ knows what she's doing.

"Now, is there anything else you'd like to know about me? I mean, my friends and I?" PJ titters attractively. I half expect her to ask one of them to sit in her lap next.

She purses her full lips together. "*Messieurs,* we are *so* sorry to have caused any trouble."

As if transfixed, the cops shrug and shift their weight. They can't seem to figure out what they are doing with us.

"*Non, non,*" one of the cops says with a small smile. One of the other cops takes a long look at me, and then at PJ—quick-witted, beautiful PJ—and shakes his head. Still nestled in the crook of her thin, pale arm, I give the cops my most innocent look.

"Go home now, kids," another cop says with a flick of his wrist. "Don't forget to pay your bill on your way out."

The cops saunter away. I hear one of them say something like, "What a shame the girls were so young!" and all of them laugh. *Blech.*

PJ drops her arm from around me and puts her cardigan back on.

"PJ! You are incredible!" Olivia squeals once the cops are out of earshot. She does a triumphant leap into the air and hugs herself. "Wow!"

"Seriously, great job—those cops didn't know what hit them," Drew agrees. "That was pure witchcraft."

Zack, his brow dripping with nervous sweat, just nods emphatically and pulls at the damp collar of his button-down shirt.

George sighs with dramatic gratitude, staggering comically toward PJ with outstretched arms. "Oh, man, that was close! You really saved our hides there, Miss PJ. I thought I was Boston-bound for sure. How can I ever repay you?"

I feel the vomit creep into my throat when he actually puts his arms around her in a grateful hug. It's a little *too* friendly for my comfort.

"Yeah, thanks," I say quietly. *Now I'm going to have to be eternally grateful to you, you freak!*

PJ just shrugs. "This kind of thing has to stop happening to me," she says.

"What, are you in the business of saving everyone's ass all the time?" George gibes, still standing right next to me.

"With varying success rates," PJ comments. Everyone laughs. Everyone but me.

OCTOBER

6. OLIVIA

Keeping the Faith

"Do your host parents actually talk to you in French, like they're supposed to?" Zack asks us over lunch at Café Dumont, the Ternes café where he and Alex can often be found during lunch and after school.

The French kids all go home for lunch. (Yet another reason that none of us has really gotten the chance to know them . . . that and they avoid us like our lack of worldliness will somehow rub off on them.) Some American guys, like Jay and some of his friends, and George and Drew and their hangers-on, eat at this fast-food kebab place on the main drag, Boulevard de Courcelles. The rest of us split ourselves up between one of a few other dimly-lit cafés near the Parc Monceau.

Most Americans who live in this ritzy neighborhood near our school (like me) go home, too, but today I'm in the mood for a Parisian café. I like this one best because it makes every day feel like a cozy rainy day—

the café is dark and moody, with small candles in red votives, and the air is heavy with steam from hot drinks and the delectable smell of the roast chickens rotating in the rotisserie behind the bar. Today is one of those days when I just want to lounge around and soak up the atmosphere. Paris must be rubbing off on me.

"Mme Rouille barely talks to me at all!" I groan. "And when she does, it is always in English. How am I ever supposed to learn how to speak naturally if we only speak French with our teachers and other Americans?"

The waitress has long since cleared our dishes away, and the three of us sprawl out across the table, lazily looking over our French textbooks. What we *should* be doing is practicing the pluperfect tense, since it's one of those concepts that none of us seem to be able to get a grasp on. What we're really doing is practicing the age-old art of French lethargy.

"I know. It's so frustrating," Zack says. "Finally, I just flat-out asked them to speak to me only in French." Zack, like Alex, lives with a French family who insists on family meals every night. Both Alex and Zack have younger siblings at their homestays that they couldn't care less about, but Zack at least knows their names. Alex calls her little host brother "*le Morceau de Merde*"—the Piece of Shit.

"My family is all trolls," Alex tells Zack and me in a bored voice. "I can't figure out *what* language they're speaking. English? French? Who knows? They all just mindlessly mumble at me." She sips from her frothy café crème.

"Alex, you should try to get to know them better," I urge her. "That's the whole reason you're here. To see how the French live!"

"Honey, I *know* how the French live," Alex says exasperatedly. "I *am* one. My dad was raised here. My mom spent the most important years of her life here and now practices the most Francophile lifestyle possible in New York. Remember?"

Zack giggles. "Pretty soon, Alex, we're *all* going to feel like we're as French as you are. I myself can barely remember what real barbeque tastes like—I don't even know if I can call myself a Tennessean anymore!"

"I can't say I'm sorry to hear that," Alex teases snottily. "I'm really going to miss it when you stop talking about fried okra and Kenney Chesney—it's been so thrilling to hear all about your life back on the farm!" The two of them snicker at each other affectionately, reminding me once again how uncanny it is that they've only known each other a few weeks. Both Alex and Zack seem to have settled into Paris so easily. They hardly ever talk about home except to make fun of something cheesy Americans do for fun.

But me? I never stop thinking about what's going on in California—if Vince is liking school, how my mom is holding up without me, and *especially* about Brian. I still haven't told anyone about my brother, and how horrible it feels to be so far away from him. I want to, but I don't want to bring everyone down, or worse, make people feel sorry for me. Like right now—I could tell Alex and Zack, since they are supposed to be these great new friends of mine, but it would just kill the good mood they are in. They'd never understand how unresponsive Brian is over the phone if I try and get my mom to put him on when I call, and how Brian doesn't actually comprehend what a computer is for just yet. One day, he will, but not while I'm in Paris. And I miss talking to him! I miss the way he lets me in. I miss our special bond.

Even when Zack and Alex do complain about things they miss from the U.S., it's things I can't relate to. Zack misses driving around Memphis in his pickup truck with his friend Pierson, blasting hokey music like *The Best of Dolly Parton*, and Alex misses going to dive bars in the East Village with her cousin's ID that doesn't even look like her. I don't have a car—if I need to go somewhere, I have to arrange it with my mom or ask Vince for a ride. And before the café in Le Marais where Alex almost got us all busted for smoking pot with George in the alley, I'd never been inside a bar in my life.

Over Zack's right shoulder, I see PJ coming into the café, letting in a gentle breeze of cool fall air when she opens the thick velvet curtains that hang in front of the vestibule. I'm not sure where PJ goes for lunch, but she never comes home with me to Mme Rouille. I've always wanted to ask her where she wanders off to, but I sense that she enjoys exploring the neighborhood on her own. When I see her across the café, I'm glad. She'll provide some levity to Alex and Zack's banter. And possibly get them to concentrate more on our studies!

"PJ!" I call out to her. "Hey! Were you looking for us? We're studying; we could use you." Despite his sluggishness today, Zack is as anxious as I am about the end-of-the-semester exam, called the Final Comp, that all the Programme Americain students have to take in order to continue studying at the Lycée. If we fail it, we'll have to go home. At least, that's the rumor—apparently no one has ever failed the test, because everyone always studies their butt off.

Alex brushes it off when we try to remind her how important it is that we stay on top of our French, telling us that she's already fluent and the test will be a breeze.

I've heard Alex in action. Trust me, if she thinks she's fluent, she's going to have a big surprise when she sits down for the final exam! But, people always say that I'm a perfectionist about grades. Maybe I should just leave Alex alone. As she says, she *is* practically French herself.

PJ hurries over, untying a hand knit scarf from around her long, thin neck. She's totally oblivious to the admiring looks that some of the older men at the bar are giving her as she walks by. "Hey!" She pulls out the empty chair next to mine. "Great news. My host parents are back! They called Mme Cuchon just now. I don't have to stay with you anymore, Liv!"

"PJ, that's great!" I lean over and give her a hug. "I know how much you've been wanting to meet them." She feels skinny under her jacket and the baggy wool sweater she always wears. Again this morning, I noticed that she didn't have anything besides coffee for breakfast at Mme Rouille's.

"When you get back from ballet class, I'll be gone," PJ says happily.

"So where does this family of yours live?" Alex asks. "They must be loaded if they have a second home. Properties in France are among the most expensive real estate in the world." She says this as shrewdly as if she's just been perusing the home section of *Le Monde*.

"Just down the street from Olivia in Ternes," PJ tells her without looking at her. "I just went and checked out the building before I came over here. It seems pretty nice." Even though Alex is my friend, and PJ is my friend, the two girls haven't warmed to each other no matter how hard I try.

"I'm sure it will be terrific, PJ," I say. "Don't read too much into the rocky start you guys might have gotten off to. I just know you're going to love your new family."

"I hope they love me, too. Anyways, I better go." She grabs her cloth shoulder bag off the floor, noticeably more sedate than when she walked into the café just a few minutes before. "See you guys," PJ says as she walks out, her voice interrupted by a flurry of activity from the next table.

A group of girls from our program, a few of the others who live too far away to go home for lunch, is getting up to leave for class at the same time. The blonde twins from Texas spot us and stop to chat.

"What are y'all doin' this weekend?" one of them asks us. "Any plans?"

"Get to the point, Tina," Alex says, snapping her red manicured fingers. "Is there something going on that we should know about?"

Zack covers his mouth to hide his amusement.

It drives Alex *bonkers* how the twins literally mosey about every conversation, especially when they've got something important to say. They relish every detail that keeps them in the spotlight.

"I'm Patty," the twin snaps at Alex.

Alex holds up her hands in a mockingly apologetic gesture and smirks. Zack muffles his laughter behind his coffee mug.

"We were just curious to find out if Sara-Louise has invited any of you to her party yet," the real Tina muses.

Zack nearly spits out his café au lait.

"Wait a second," Alex says, her eyes flashing. "Sara-Louise is having a party? At her *apartment*? In *Paris*? This *weekend*? Why didn't anyone tell me?"

"Oh, it's all over school," Patty twitters. "I even heard some of the French kids are going. Saturday night. 8 P.M." Her sister Tina raises her eyebrows at us and pulls Patty towards the door. "See y'all there."

"Well, shit." Alex is truly dumbfounded that she's the last to know.

"Thank God I still have time to figure out what on earth I am going to wear." She immediately pulls out the oversize issue of *W* she's been carrying around today and starts frantically thumbing through it again.

"Well, hot damn and hallelujah!" Zack says with a whoop. "It's about time someone had a good old-fashioned clambake this year! I was wondering when we were all going to get down to the business of getting good and plastered!"

Even I can't help bouncing up and down a few times with excitement. It's not like I'm going to be getting hammered like Alex and Zack, but I don't need to be drunk to have a good time. I just need good music, good conversation, a little distraction from all the pressure. . . .

But back at school, as I quickly check to see if there's anything from Vince in my email before I have to run to class, there's something from my mom.

Hey, long-lost daughter! I'm sorry I've been a slacker about keeping in touch, but I have to say that I really miss you, Livvy, and I'm really starting to appreciate how much you lighten everything up at home. Now that you're gone, all this driving back and forth to Brian's school and all the specialists and therapists is a real drag. I guess you don't appreciate things until you lose them, but I really miss my co-pilot. Sure you don't want to drop out of the Opera and come on home to SD? :) Haha, just kidding (sort of).

Attached to the message is an "inspirational" YouTube link to a recent UCLA dance performance. I don't bother to watch it. Instead I spend the last three minutes of the lunch period scanning Vince's Facebook page for signs that he misses me as much as I miss him.

I message him quickly.

To: Vince Palatella
1:57 P.M.
Subject: French Kiss
  I miss you. That's all.

After I send it, I realize that Vince changed his profile picture. It used to be him in his UCLA sweatshirt, a photo I took of him the day he left for college. Now it's an old one of us, taken the same day as the photo from this summer I carry around in my purse. He does miss me. Sometimes I still can't believe that we are really going out. I remember when I was so shy around Vince that I couldn't even talk to him!

Vince's mom, Liz, has been best friends with my mom since they swam together on the La Jolla High School Varsity Champions team back in the seventies. My mother jokes that Liz is the *real* love of her life, not my dad.

Liz and my mom are best friends like no other best friends I have ever seen. They dress alike. They finish each other's sentences. They go for highlights at the same hairdresser together. And while I take care of my brother for a few hours, they go for a swim in the ocean together, coming back a shade of deeper brown than when Liz picked my mom up. When my mom gets overwhelmed handling Brian's care, Liz steps in for a few days, leaving her own husband and son to take care of themselves. When Vince's parents fight, Liz sleeps over in our living room, and my mom sleeps down on the couch with her. It's always been like that; I'm pretty sure it always will be.

Until my freshman year I always loathed Vince; maybe it was because I really didn't want to live out Liz and Mom's dream of having the cutest-couple-for-children award, but I always hated him before. He was cocky, really good at sports and school, and had a steady stream of different girlfriends at all of Liz's summer barbeques. But something changed when I got to high school. On the first day, I'll never forget it, Vince pulled up into our driveway as my mom was hurriedly trying to get Brian and me ready for school on time. Brian was in the middle of a meltdown, my dad was already at the office, and I was horrified to find that my mom had shrunk my new skirt so that it was a good four inches shorter, leaving my bare thighs horribly exposed.

Vince had called out to my mom that day, I'll never forget it, "Let me take Livvy—you've got enough to deal with right now." And before I could change into something less revealing, my mom pushed me into the front seat of his car.

"You're a lifesaver!" she thanked him.

When he parked I could see the other freshman unloading onto the feeding grounds of the senior lawn, where the seniors lay in wait to torment all the newbies, and Vince casually escorted me in through the side entrance without incident. *You* are *a lifesaver*, I silently told him as he dropped me at the auditorium for freshman orientation.

"Hey, Livvy," Vince called me as I scanned the rows for an empty seat.

"Yeah?" I said shyly.

"Great skirt," he told me, and I blushed so hard I thought I would die. A month later, I was his homecoming date, and two years later, here we are, still the perfect couple.

At least, we *would* be the perfect couple if we were in the same city!

Besides missing Vince—it doesn't matter if it's Paris or San Diego—it all feels alike when you spend all your free time in the same black leotards and tights. Between my insane schedule at school and in dance class, I feel like I never get a moment to myself to even appreciate where I am!

Tonight, exhausted from an *especially* brutal session at the Opera, I decide to skip my usual shower and just go straight to bed to crash. Flinging open the door, I close my eyes, relieved to finally be home after the madness of another day in Paris, so far from everyone and everything I love: Vince, Brian, the beach, Mexican food, *everything*. I don't even turn on the light; I just flop into a heap on my bed.

"Oh my sweet Jesus!" I shriek, bounding right back up as I realize that I'm lying not on the flat surface of my covers but on top of the bulky frame of a real live human being.

A male human being—Good God, some strange *dude* is in my bed!

A young, strange, and actually *incredibly good-looking* dude!

7. PJ

Faded Empire

"PJ!" a voice calls from behind me. "PJ, wait up!"

Oh, God, not now. I turn around reluctantly. I'm in *such* a hurry. I *can't* be late to *finally* meet my host family after all this time.

"Yeah?" I curtly ask Jay, who's jogging toward me down the Boulevard de Courcelles in his mesh Adidas jersey and shorts. He must have ducked out of soccer—excuse me, *football* practice to come talk to me. What on earth does he want?

"PJ, hey," Jay smiles, catching his breath. His cleats are wet with fresh earth from the field.

"Hey," I say. "What's going on?"

"Oh, not much," Jay says casually. His muscular arms and legs are covered in goose bumps from the chilly day. "Just, you know, settling in at the homestay, getting to know my host family."

"Awesome," I say impatiently. "I mean, what did you want to talk to me about?"

"You break up with your boyfriend yet?" Jay asks slyly. "The one you were talking to the other day on the phone."

I blush. "Oh, him!" I stammer. "Yeah. Things weren't working out. So we're not together . . . anymore."

"Oh, good. Then he won't mind if I ask if you have a partner yet for the Louvre project?"

The Louvre project? "Oh, right. No, I don't have a partner yet. Want to work together?" The Louvre project is an interdisciplinary project that Mme Cuchon dreamed up in which the Lycée Americaine students will work together to write a paper in French on the life and times of one of the many artists showcased in the huge Musée du Louvre, the crown jewel of all the art museums in Paris. For extra credit, we can also turn in a painting or artwork that we do in the style of whichever artist we choose. As a massive art history nerd and wannabe painter, I'm really looking forward to working on it. Just not right now!

"Okay, cool," Jay says, invigorated. "Is there an artist you like? How do you feel about doing Ingres? He seems really cool, with all the portraits of all the different people. But if you'd rather do someone else . . ."

"I love Ingres," I interrupt him, turning to go before he's even done talking. It's true, I really do love his work. He's a relatively obscure painter from the 19th century. I'm surprised Jay even knows who he is. From his shaved head and his strong build, I'd take him for more of a jock than an expert on French artists. "Great choice. Look, I've got to be somewhere. Call me over the weekend; we can get started working on the project."

"Definitely," Jay says. When he smiles I see that the corners of his eyes crinkle, like a little kid. "Looking forward to it."

"*Bonjour!*" I call to an older couple coming out of the doorway at the address I have for Monsieur and Madame Marquet just off the Place des Ternes. "*Je suis Penelope! Votre fille!*" The quiet, narrow side street echoes with the sound of my loud voice.

"Our daughter?" asks a tanned, handsome older man in confusion, taking in my loose, wild hair, tangled from running down the wide, windy Boulevard de Courcelles. My cheeks are flushed. I take off my hat and try to smooth out my hair and cool off a bit. I'd hoped to be a tad less bedraggled when I met my new family.

"Oh, yes! *Bonjour!*" the man says, dipping to place a warm, wet kiss on either of my cheeks. He's quite tall, with longish silver hair slicked back with gel. I can't help but be a bit taken with him. My host father looks like an old-fashioned movie star.

"You must be Penelope," says a diminutive woman with high cheekbones and shining white teeth. I tower over her. "I recognize you from your application photo.

"Ah, *oui*," the man jokes. "Your photo was the reason we chose you to come live with us while you study at the Lycée. So much prettier than all the other prospective students!" He bows his head to me. "*Je suis Monsieur Marquet.* Our deepest apologies for not being here to greet your arrival in Paris. We've had so many things keeping us in the Dordogne, new job, blah, blah, blah." He mentions his job as if it's just something he does to fill the time between parties and benefits.

Mme Marquet tenses. "Yes, well. We're here now, aren't we?"

"I'm so glad to finally meet you!" I say enthusiastically, resisting the urge to pull them both into a bear hug of gratitude.

"Penelope, *ma belle*, we're just leaving for a gala for *Médecins sans Frontières*—we've had the tickets for months and we only just remembered that the benefit was tonight of all nights," M. Marquet clucks his tongue in apology. "We'll be there until late." He takes Mme Marquet's elbow and steers her toward the waiting limousine.

"Oh," I say, hoping to hide my bitter disappointment. "I didn't realize . . ."

"*Cherie*, just run upstairs and introduce yourself to our housekeeper, Sonia," M. Marquet says. "We'll all get to know each other over the weekend when you join us at our house in the Dordogne. That is, unless you have other plans."

"Really?" I squeak in disbelief. After just a few minutes of knowing me, they are inviting me to their house in the Dordogne for the whole weekend? Getting them to love me might be easier than I thought. "No, I don't have any plans!"

"*Oui*, darling, of course you don't," Mme Marquet says. Her mouth is set in a hard, unyielding line as they wait for me to go inside. She taps her gold watch.

"See you Friday then," M. Marquet says, wiggling his long fingers at me as Mme Marquet gingerly steps into the limo, careful of her dark red beaded gown. His eyes sparkle as if we've shared a secret. I smile back though I'm still hurt that they've abandoned me so quickly. "*Bon soir* for now!"

I'm pleased to find that their housekeeper, Sonia, is as warm and friendly as the Marquets are rushed and distracted. A plump, heavyset

Caribbean woman, Sonia speaks a clipped, accented French that puts me immediately at ease from the moment I walk through the front door.

Like Olivia's apartment down the street, the Marquets live in a splendor that most people only dream about. The main difference here, of course, is that the Marquets' apartment is nearly three times the size of Mme Rouille's. Mme Rouille only has two bedrooms and a maid's quarters, but as Sonia shows me around, I count at least three bedrooms besides the master suite and my own sprawling room on the opposite end of the apartment. This apartment is also much darker, with the thick brocade curtains drawn, and dingier than where I was staying before. Elise keeps Mme Rouille's apartment sparkling clean, but there is a distinct layer of dust over all the surfaces here. It's obvious the Marquets have not been spending much time in Paris lately.

"That will change with the season," Sonia explains. "Fall is philanthropy season in Paris. But weekends, they still go to the Dordogne. They can't stay away. You'll see. You'll fall in love with it, too."

Friday afternoon, I can't stop squirming as I sit on the TGV high-speed train racing its way to the southern coastal French city of Bordeaux. At the Bordeaux station I'm going to switch to a train to Périgueux, where M. Marquet will meet me and drive me to the Marquets' château in the Dordogne.

Just listening to the French announcements over the train loudspeaker makes me shiver with excitement. I've always loved France, loved the language, the culture, the artistic heritage. Annabel loved France too, but for different reasons—she loved the romance of it, the idea that Paris was where you found yourself. But Dave would always tell her they had all the romance they needed right there in Vermont.

Annabel and I used to have a big, classroom-sized map of the world on the wall in the bedroom that we shared. For fun, we'd close our eyes and spin in place, then poke our finger on a spot on the map, pretending it was where we were destined to end up one day. We'd always try and aim for France, and usually end up somewhere in the Atlantic off the coast of Spain when we opened our eyes. We'd get Africa, England, Russia, Israel . . . but never France.

The night Dave asked Annabel to marry him, she came home giddy. She spun around with her eyes closed while I watched her from where I was tucked up in my twin bed.

"Aha!" she cried as she put her finger down on the map. "I got it!" The memory makes me smile a little bit.

So far, my brief meeting with the Marquets just as they were leaving for the benefit is all that I have seen of them. The day after we met, they left for the Dordogne again while I was at school. Sonia is there during the day, but at night I stay all by myself in their palatial apartment. Sonia doesn't seem too interested in housekeeping. She mostly talks on her cell phone or reads tabloids in the kitchen.

Olivia stopped by briefly to make sure I was okay, but then had to run off to a study session with Sara-Louise and Mary. Olivia is obsessed with the Final Comp, in case anyone hasn't noticed.

"I found out that your host dad is a magistrate," Olivia told me before she left.

"Oh, really?" I'd been wondering what M. Marquet's seemingly negligible job was. Except a *magistrate* doesn't sound so negligible. "What's a magistrate?"

"It's like a judge, but also, like, a political office. Mme Rouille told me that your host dad was just recently elected to the district court in the Dordogne, which explains why they've been so absent. But the rumor is," Olivia whispered in an uncharacteristically gossipy tone, "that he wants to run for national office."

"Ooooh, Olivia, how scandalous!" I teased her.

She laughed. "Well, that was how Mme Rouille said it! I guess it's not that big a deal. Still, sounds like you're living with high society over here."

The last few days living there have been something out of *Eloise in Paris*—velvet Louis XIV chairs, glittering chandeliers, eight-foot mirrors in gilded frames. I didn't know anyone besides maybe Marie Antoinette who had ever lived like this—I certainly never expected myself to be in the lap of luxury.

And certainly not after everything I've done.

Last night, I bought a baguette and some gruyere on my way home from school, and after Sonia left, I made a sandwich and ate it in the middle of their elegant living room floor, facing the ornate doors leading out to the terrace. The sun was going down, and I opened up the drapes so I could watch the dusk settle over the Place des Ternes. Hilly, animated Montmartre, with the Sacre Coeur crowning its top like a white star in the misty evening, rises just beyond the Marquets' safe, placid residential neighborhood. Careful of the crumbs on the carpet, I chewed thoughtfully, contemplating the strange roller coaster of the last few months. When I finished eating, I flossed and brushed my teeth, and lay on my bed for several hours, wide awake.

It was the most alone I've ever felt.

The train is packed with weekenders, but my seatmate disembarked at the Poitiers station. Families and couples are crowded all around me, restless with anticipation for the weekend as the train chugs across the valleys and hills of southern France. The atmosphere is hospitable, but I feel removed from it.

I open my notebook, thinking (as I often have in the last few weeks) of Annabel. I know my older sister will never get this letter, but I write to her anyway.

Dear Annabel,

You'd never believe it if you could see me right now. You'd be so proud of me. The Marquets barely know me, and already they want me to stay with them at their house in the country.

You're the only person who could ever understand how much I want this. How much I need them to feel bonded to me, and ask me not only to come for this weekend, but to stay for winter break so I won't have to go home to Vermont anytime soon. It was the one flaw in my plan, the one thing I didn't think of until I got on the plane. The program specifically says that all students have to leave their French families for the three weeks of winter break unless formally invited for the holidays by their host families. That only gives me three months to secure that invitation. Only three months to secure my fate.

Besides the things I want to tell Annabel about my own new life in France, there are a million questions I want to ask about hers. My sister was always a mystery, but now, after this long separation, she's an enigma. Whenever I picture her, she's running, her hair a dark streak behind her. Her legs even longer than mine, I could never keep up with her.

I love trains. I wish we used them more in the States. It's dreamlike to be sitting on a train, looking out the window. Even loneliness, even gloom, seem comfortable on a train whistling and rolling through the French countryside in the dark.

Where are you out there, Annabel? I ask my dimly lit reflection in the window. *Will I ever get to see you again?*

All of a sudden I'm reminded of Jay, how he noticed my caffeine habit, how he wanted to work with me on the Louvre project. I'm missing our study date! And the party at Sara-Louise's, too!

Oh, no, I despair for a moment. Then I brush off all thoughts of Jay. I'll deal with that later. Nothing could ever be more important than this trip.

I find a very jolly M. Marquet waiting for me in Périgueux. He picks me up and swings me around like a little girl. I laugh, too loud.

"Eh, I would have sent Charles—that's the groundskeeper, the man who tends to the animals and the gardens—but I wanted you to feel welcomed, at home here," M. Marquet tells me as we loop around the windy roads leading up to their estate. "Marie, the housekeeper here, will get you some dinner, and in the morning, Mme Marquet and I will show you the place. It's very special. This land has been in my family for a long time."

The château *is* very special. It's dark, the way I would imagine an old castle to be, and creaks and shudders in the windy night. I fall asleep immediately in the huge feather bed I'm sent to after eating roast quail and *haricots verts* in the big dining room.

Decked out in sturdy rubber boots and stiff, starchy jeans, the Marquets take me for a robust hike around the grounds the next morning. I'm practically jogging to keep up with them, thinking of questions I might ask to get to know them better.

The house itself, built from bricks that are an almost fluffy pink, is flanked by two cone-shaped towers on either of its rear corners. Surrounded by lush green gardens on all sides, the landscape of the grounds becomes gradually more rugged the farther you get from the château. Each doorway to the house is oversize and regal, fit for kings and queens and the banners and flags that would have attended them and their entourage. The gravel paths trace the rolling hills for miles in every direction, leading to barns, fields, and pastures full of the Marquets' sheep and horses.

My own sketchy knowledge of French history is based purely on the old portraits I've seen in the meager collection of art books at the library of my old school in Vermont. This house looks like the houses I've seen in those paintings. At least three hundred years old.

"Five hundred, actually," Mme Marquet sniffs. "Not including the additions our family has put on over the generations."

I give her my most genuinely impressed expression. She doesn't react to it, just carries on admiring her own house.

The front entrance of the château is several stairs off the ground, about as high as a horse's back.

"So that you could just hop onto your horse without ever stepping on the ground," M. Marquet elucidates. "The ancestors so hated to get themselves dirty."

I chuckle. In contrast to their somewhat decrepit, dusty home, the Marquets' boots, jeans, and barn jackets are spotless. Meanwhile, I've managed to get completely sodden with dirt during our exertions.

M. Marquet leads me out to the pasture, a green expanse dotted with black horses. It's starting to feel cooler now, even in the middle of the day when the sun is high in the sky. I'm glad I brought my dad's old baggy sweater with me, even if Mme Marquet did give it a funny look earlier.

"Do you like to ride?" he asks me.

"Sure," I say. "I mean, I've never done it before, but I'd love to try." That's not exactly true. Dave's parents have an old pony, and when I was little I rode it bareback along the creek while my sister and Dave made out behind a tree. Somehow I don't think that's what the Marquets have in mind.

Mme Marquet looks down at my Converse sneakers. "You can't ride in those. The soles are too soft. The horse won't understand your commands."

"*Pas de problème,*" M. Marquet says, motioning for Charles to take the horses to the stable and saddle them. "Go ask Marie for an old pair of boots. There are dozens in the mud room; there's sure to be some in your size."

Mme Marquet sighs. *"Dépêche-toi, Penelope."*

"I'll be really quick," I promise, running down the hill toward the house.

I bang open the back door and look around for Marie. I remember that when she served me breakfast this morning, she'd said something about going to mass down the road. The mud room, just off the kitchen, is easy enough to find without her, as is the closet where all the outdoor wear is stocked. It doesn't look like the stuff in here gets worn very often.

There are cobwebs laced around the half-dozen pairs of boots. I kneel on the floor, picking through them, willing myself to quickly find a pair that fits. I imagine Mme Marquet with one hand on her hip, the other tapping that gold watch.

From far away, I hear a noise like the shutters slamming.

"Marie?" I call, rising to my feet. No one answers.

I haven't been gone that long. Is it Mme Marquet, impatient to get our horseback ride underway? I go back through the kitchen to the hallway that connects these old housework areas—the kitchen, the laundry room, the stairs to the wine cellar, the mud room—to the rest of the château.

The château, even during the day, is dark and musty from lack of sunlight. The darkness makes me unsure, afraid. It's so dark that I wish I had a flashlight.

The hallway is empty, of course. But that tingling at the top of my spine, that horrible feeling, is the same one I got when I was pouring the coffee for my parents up at the gas station near the Canadian border this summer. That night, I didn't have to go outside to know something was off. I could just feel it.

I creep into the sitting room. Like at the Paris apartment, the furnishings at the château are old and slightly decayed. The yellow curtains in the sitting room are browning at the edges, and the ancient pianoforte in the corner is covered in a thick layer of dust, despite the presence of Marie. While the Marquets are most certainly living in absolute splendor, their homes are the tiniest bit decrepit, just about to give way to neglect and disrepair. The chandelier hanging above the little armchairs set in a half-circle has several bulbs out. The majestic fireplace is covered in soot.

Hardly able to breathe for the sensation that I am being watched,

I reach out toward the yellow drapes, pulling the fabric back an inch, then slightly more. When I see a face at the window behind them, I let out a bloodcurdling scream that sends the face bounding away from the window. There are several flashes of light, all in a row, and then a shout to *run* in French.

I realize, after a moment, that I'm squeezing my eyes closed. I open them and look out the window, up the gravel driveway that leads to the main road back to Périgueux. There are two men dashing toward a Peugeot hatchback, cameras and flashbulbs hanging off their bodies and bouncing along with them.

From the pasture, on horseback, comes Charles, the groundskeeper, shouting at the men with the cameras in harsh tones. He has a horsewhip in one hand, raised above his head like he will strike them with it if they return to the château.

"I see you've met our friends," a low, deep voice says from behind me.

"M. Marquet!" I jump away from the window, jostling the curtain so that it leaves me covered in a shower of dust. "You nearly gave me a heart attack!"

"*Bonjour*, Penelope," M. Marquet says tiredly. "Adele! She's in the sitting room!" he calls behind him.

Adele, better known to me as Mme Marquet, comes in, followed by Marie, back from church.

"Did you say anything to them?" Mme Marquet asks me sharply. "Did they ask you any questions?

"No!" I answer her. "I'm so sorry I took so long getting the boots. I suddenly felt like someone was watching me, so I came in here. . . . Who were those men?"

"This is no place for you to be sneaking around," Mme Marquet says, her back rigid. "You have to be more careful! Did they get photos of this room?"

I shrug. "All I know is that they flashed the camera right at my face."

"Photos of you would not be bad," Mme Marquet says, almost to herself. "But this room—with all these old things in it, all this old junk— that would be a disgrace to the Marquet name."

I don't understand. Suddenly, before I can stop myself, I start to cry.

"Ah, Penelope," M. Marquet breaks the tension and gently puts his arms around me. "Off with you. Marie, take Penelope to lunch in town. Penelope, Périgueux is *très, très belle* this time of year. Every time of year! Marie will take you to lunch, and then perhaps we'll ride tomorrow."

"But those men," I say, still confused, still afraid of the way Mme Marquet has her hands on her hips like I've messed something up, big time. "What were they taking pictures of?"

Mme Marquet sighs. "They just want photos of the new magistrate's house. Now that M. Marquet is in the public eye, the tabloids are just a part of our lives. But whatever you do, Penelope, don't ever talk to them. You hear me?"

"They were photographing *me*?"

"Yes," Mme Marquet says, exasperation in her voice. "God knows why."

I nod. I feel like I can't catch my breath. The Marquets are public figures. If they find out who I really am, what my family has done, they will want nothing to do with me.

"Good girl," M. Marquet says, patting the top of my head and pushing me toward Marie. "Now go on with Marie. Don't worry anymore about those silly men."

Marie whisks me down the hall and into an old station wagon parked in the garage. I help her shop in the market in the town square, picking out vegetables for *dîner*. When we return to the château, I'm looking forward to eating with the Marquets, but I find out that they're having dinner at a friend's house. I'm not invited. I can't help but wonder if they're shunning me, if I've offended them. Do they think I was poking around in the sitting room on purpose?

It's true, I can't explain why I was drawn into the room I think as I fall asleep, how I knew there was someone else looking in on it, but it's not like I was trying to sneak around.

Mme Marquet swishes by me in the kitchen the next morning, wearing a fancy dressing gown with sable trim.

"Penelope," she says, much more warmly than she'd addressed me yesterday. "M. Marquet must have left for his ride without you. How odd of him not to wait. He must have thought you weren't interested."

I'm befuddled. "Really? Why would he think that?"

"Hmm, unclear," Mme Marquet says. "Care to join me for some tea upstairs? I've got to get ready for a brunch we've been invited to at the château of *les Lafontants*. Their good favor is important to us."

"I'd love some tea," I tell her, and follow her to her bedroom. As in her apartment in Paris, Mme Marquet has a large boudoir where she gets ready. The vanity is lined with bottles, compacts, brushes, and pencils. I whistle at the sheer number of products she has in her collection.

"Sit," she commands me, pointing toward an empty chair across from the bed. I lift a cup and saucer from the tray on the table and help myself to some hot tea with lemon. It helps calm the shivers I can't seem to get rid of in this big old house.

Mme Marquet is what the French call *jolie-laide*—"pretty-ugly." It means that in her wide features, her pronounced overbite, and her deep-set eyes, there is a kind of beauty that is far more than the sum of its parts. Many members of the French aristocracy have this look, I've noticed from looking through old issues of *Paris Match* around the Marquets' Paris apartment. Both Madame and Monsieur Marquet heavily resemble old paintings printed in French history books with the medieval sensibility of their looks. Despite not being a natural beauty, Mme Marquet obviously takes her regimen quite seriously.

"I don't have it as easy as a natural beauty like you, Penelope," Mme Marquet comments, noticing my looking at all of her makeup and perfumes. "I need all of these." She gestures with the eyeliner in her hand.

I shake my head at the compliment. Mme Marquet has a look a girl like me could never replicate—self-assured, elegant, established. Next to her I feel like a farmhand, like I belong in the pasture picking mud off the horse's hooves.

I watch Mme Marquet get ready in silence for a while, not sure why she's invited me in here.

"So M. Marquet is the magistrate in Périgueux?" I ask, trying to make conversation.

"*Oui,*" Mme Marquet answers. "His position is one of great importance in this region."

"Oh," I say.

"And this region is of great importance in France," Mme Marquet continues.

"Is he really thinking of running for a national political office?" I ask, stirring some sugar into my bitter tea. I wish she'd asked if I wanted some coffee. Tea doesn't quite zap me awake as much I'd like it to.

Mme Marquet sets down her eyeliner and stares at me. "Who told you that?"

I bite my lip. Maybe it was as big a deal as Olivia had thought. "My friend Olivia, from the Lycée. She's living with Mme Rouille, on, um, the Boulevard de Courcelles. . . ."

"Ha!" Mme Marquet practically spits. "Clotilde Rouille! That widowed hag. She doesn't know anything that she doesn't read in the society pages. You tell your friend M. Marquet wants nothing more than to bring justice and peace to the Dordogne. National politics! How tacky. Never!"

Mme Marquet stands up and folds her arms across her chest. "What else have you heard about us? That we've lost our fortune? That we're selling the château? The local papers will tell any old story to sell a few extra copies."

I take that as my cue to excuse myself. "I better let you get ready for that brunch," I say, not understanding how I've, yet again, managed to offend her. She offers me a small, jerky wave in response.

On the train back to Paris, I read over the letter I wrote to Annabel on the way here, not quite feeling as happy about my host family as I was when I wrote it, and more unsure about my future in Paris than ever.

"Where on earth did she go?" Dave asked me after all the wedding guests finally went home, the buffet left untouched. "Did she tell you anything before she left?"

I shook my head. She didn't tell me anything. All I had was a map of the world with a bunch of lousy fingerprints all over it as clues to where she might be.

Dave suggested that we take a trip to Montreal and ask around for her up there. Since I spoke French, he wanted me to come with. My parents, who must have thought it sounded like a great alibi, came with us.

"Stop here," my mom told my dad, who was driving Dave's car. "This place looks good."

We stopped so that I could pee, at a gas station just across from the customs check. My dad had begged me to wait till we got across the border. He was getting nervous about something, but I couldn't hold it. I'd had to go since St. Albans.

I suddenly spotted Highway Patrol cruisers, a long line of them getting off the freeway and heading our way.

They told me to hurry inside to the bathroom. Dave took a deep, audible breath. "Really, you guys?" he asked my parents.

"I thought you said if we took Dave's car . . ." my dad said to my mom.

"Get me some coffee, with plenty of cream and sugar," my mom said to me, not taking her eyes off the cruisers as they got closer. I took my time, careful to make the coffee smooth so they wouldn't have indigestion from drinking it so late at night. When I came out of the shop, cops were surrounding the car.

It still gets to me, remembering it, even now on the train, so many months after it happened. It's still so painful to recall the looks on my parents' faces that night: not of bewilderment, but of surrender.

8. ZACK

Falling Fast

"Oh, Zack, you should have seen your face when I left the café that night. You gave me a look that could have shattered glass," Alex crows as she grabs a bottle of Stella Artois from Sara-Louise's fridge. "I gave you the perfect romantic setup with those guys and yet—here you are, as virginal as when we first met. What are we going to do with you, my dear? Will I have to deflower you myself?"

Believe me—I've been tempted by girls in the past. Sometimes, you just want to do the deed and get it over with. But never *that* badly.

"Give it a rest, Alex," I say, looking around to make sure no one heard her mention my romantic affinity for guys—or heard her make reference to my virginity. "It's not like you've hooked up with George yet, either. We're both still at square one."

"Oh, so it's a competition, is it?" Alex fluffs her wavy, wild black hair

in the reflection of the mirror in the foyer. I look at my own reflection—
my hair tousled just so, the way I always do it. I'm letting it grow a little
longer here in Paris. I wore my glasses tonight, thick black hipster frames
with square lenses. I think they are the perfect accessory for the little
argyle sweater vest I've pulled over one of my button-down shirts and
my favorite jeans.

We're giving ourselves a pre-party tour of Sara-Louise's homestay,
which doesn't take long. Sara-Louise lives in a tiny, two-bedroom
apartment in an uninteresting housing development full of other
apartments just like it. No matter how it lacks charm, it is certainly the
place to be tonight. It's the first party of the year!

Sara-Louise's host parents are on a weekend trip to Bruges, leaving her
alone in the apartment with their eighteen-year-old daughter, another
student at the Lycée. We got here sort of mortifyingly early, when Sara-
Louise and her host-"sister" Anouk were still setting out cheese and
crackers and stocking their fridge with all the booze they bought for the
party. Tried as I might have, I couldn't keep Alex away tonight. She
didn't want to miss a *second* of the soiree.

Perched on the little stools at Sara-Louise's tiny kitchen counter, Alex
is using the down time before the party takes off as an opportunity to
alternately make fun of me for being a prude and preen in front of the
mirror. She's looking uncharacteristically preppy this evening in a white
Polo shirt, a dark denim miniskirt and a green canvas army jacket from
Marc Jacobs. On her feet are bright yellow Jack Purcell sneakers. She
must think the way to George's heart must be by dressing like his New
England boarding-school classmates. Regardless, Alex looks amazing.
She always does.

"You look like a soap commercial," I tell her. "George will be smitten."

"You think?" Alex says, taking a sip of white wine from a glass tumbler. She insisted that Sara-Louise serve her in a real glass, rather than the plastic cups she and Anouk bought for the party. She gives her reflection her most captivating glance. "I'm as ready as I'll ever be. Wish me luck!"

Just then, we hear a big group of French kids come into the party—Anouk's friends. They crank the music and glare at us Americans. Alex beams at them—what she wouldn't *do* to be good friends with just *one* of them, to count just one Frog on her list of cohorts. I'm aching to be friends with them, too. But they're too good for us, and they all know it.

"Tay-*ex*-US!" comes a sudden, almost barbaric cry from the entryway. The twins.

I turn back around, horrified at the sheer unpleasantness of the noise my poor ears have just been subjected to. Framed by the doorway, Patty and Tina are decked out in cropped black tube tops and matching A-line miniskirts, with Mardi Gras style beads laced around their necks. True to form, Tina has her hair up in a high cheerleader-esque ponytail, and Patty's hair is feathered out around her small face like Farrah Fawcett. That's the only way you can tell the twins apart—they wear the same outfits every day but different hairstyles from each other. Champagne bottles in hand, they are both making rock-star poses in the doorway as if there were a group of paparazzi taking their photos. Many more partygoers shout hello to them than they did to us. Triumphant, the twins air kiss and high-five their way to the fridge to cool their champagne.

Right behind the twins are George and Drew. And right behind *them* is Olivia, gaping at the twins.

"You are never going to guess what happened to me!" Olivia moans to us when she makes her way past the crowd surrounding the Texan twins.

"Holy smokes!" I hear one of them squawk at George. "You're lookin' *fine* tonight!"

"What?" Alex demands, keeping one eye on George and the other glued to the twins. "Tell me." Like Mme Rouille's yappy mini-poodles, the twins circle George and Drew, desperate to be petted. The sight of it has Alex breathing fire.

"You guys." Olivia shakes out of her jacket, revealing a typically laid-back California outfit of a white peasant dress with a simple pink cardigan and flip flops. "You have to hear this story—I need your advice! So, I got home the other night, and I literally—I literally cannot explain just how literally—I *literally* jumped onto a strange man who was lying on my bed."

"What?" I laugh. "How did that happen?"

"His name is Thomas," she explains. "He's Mme Rouille's son. He came home from the Sorbonne to grab some books from his room and apparently got so wrapped up in Rilke's *Letters to a Young Poet* that he didn't notice me until I was on top of him, legs sprawled in the air. Oh, my God! I'm officially in a shame spiral."

"Livvy, that's *hot*," I say. "So what happened next? Don't leave out *any* of the sordid details."

"Oh, Zack," Olivia rolls her eyes, laughing. "What do you think I did? I ran to the bathroom! I was all sweaty and stinky from ballet. When

I finally came out, he apologized and left. Mme Rouille was horrified by the whole thing—it was so *improper*."

"So what do you need advice on?" I ask.

"Well, do you think I should tell Vince?" Olivia blushes.

"Ach, you're a prude," Alex says flippantly. "Get a beer and let's go dance."

"I'll pass on the beer," Olivia answers cheerfully, "but let's definitely hit that dance floor."

Olivia waits patiently as Alex and I chug some beers with Sara-Louise and her good friend Mary, the punky girl from L.A. Once everyone is good and buzzed, Alex drags us both out onto the makeshift dance floor in Sara-Louise's miniscule living room. The apartment is already packed with kids. It seems like every single Programme Americain student is here, with a fair amount of Anouk's friends, too. Alex bops her way over to the stereo and turns up the volume even higher.

Olivia is, of course, a phenomenal dancer—we already knew that. But Alex isn't too bad herself. Just watching them shake their hips seductively to the French hip-hop on the stereo makes a bunch of other kids start to move to the music alongside them, swaying and grinding to the beat.

Alex and Olivia dance on either side of me, Alex facing me and grazing the back of my neck with her hands, Olivia shimmying her back against mine. Right now, I'm likely the envy of almost every guy in this room.

I can't deal. Alex's hair keeps getting in my eyes, and Olivia keeps knocking me off balance, bumping me with her little rear end. I extricate Alex's arms from around my neck and leave them to each other.

"*Salut!*" one of Anouk's French friends calls to me, motioning for me to join her on the couch. I perch on the armrest next to her.

"Hi," I greet her, forcing a smile. She's petite, with a cute pixie haircut and dimples in either cheek.

"What's your name?" she says.

"I'm Zack," I say, trying to stay friendly.

"You're American," she notes. "I couldn't tell."

"Really?" I'm flattered.

"You're very handsome," she says, reaching out and stroking my face. She takes a long sip of her beer. "*Voulez-vous danser avec moi?*" She puts her hand on my knee and squeezes it a little bit.

I want to laugh at the irony—a beautiful girl throwing herself at me, when all I want is a beautiful *boy* to throw himself at me.

"No, thanks. I'm not really fixin' to dance right now," I cringe at how my Southern accent just crept right out without me doing anything to stop it. Often happens when I'm nervous.

In the middle of all the action in the living room, Olivia and Alex jump up on the coffee table. In a blissed-out trance, Olivia twirls with her arms over her head. The neck of her dress is hanging off of her tanned shoulders, leaving them bare and sexy. Alex, gyrating like a stripper next to her, could be auditioning for a rap video. Her skirt is hoisted so far up from her outrageous dancing that she might as well be in her underwear.

"Come on, kiss," I hear Drew heckle them. "Just once! We'll give you five euros. Ten!" A group of guys around him dissolve into laughter. Alex and Olivia remain totally oblivious.

The Texan twins, for their part, glower in the corner. Alex and Olivia are the hottest show in town. Despite Patty and Tina's bold entrance (not to mention the fact that they came with the two most desired guys at the

Lycée), no one is paying any attention to them at all.

"I'm Tallis," the pixie girl breathes in my ear. Quickly and gracefully, she hoists herself up onto my lap. With one leg on either side of me, she leans down and kisses me on the lips, softly, but obviously wanting more.

Whoa. I can feel my heartbeat hammering. I'm trapped!

"Sorry—I've got to go—there's someone over there I want to talk to," I squeal.

Tallis is so little I can easily lift her up off my lap and set her right back down to where she was sitting on the couch. She pouts at me, her arms folded angrily across her chest.

"Don't worry, *cherie*," I say as I walk away, though she can't hear me. "There's plenty of other takers here tonight. You'll get over it."

Jay's sipping a beer by himself in the dining room, checking out some book on the shelf in there.

"Hey, man, how's it going?" I say, giving Jay's arm a friendly punch.

"What's going on, man?" Jay says, shaking my hand. "I didn't think I'd see you coming up for air for awhile." He nods behind me, toward Tallis. *He was watching?*

"Oh, well," I say, not knowing how best to deflect the truth of why I couldn't hook up with Tallis. "She was hot, but . . ." *But what?*

"You just couldn't do it?" Jay asks. "I know what you mean." He leans back against the bookshelf.

"You do?" I say, nearly spitting out my beer. Could it be?

"Oh, yeah, man, I've been there," Jay says easily. "Wrong person, wrong time. Someone much better will come along, I guarantee it."

I'd thought Jay was straight, but this was too weird. Could Jay be gay, too? Is that why he said "wrong person" and not "wrong girl"? Because he knew what it felt like to have a girl hit on him and wish it was a guy? Or maybe I've had one too many beers. I search his smooth, angular face for a clue.

All of a sudden, a loud crash comes from the living room. "Oh, shit," I say before I even see the damage. It's got to be Alex—she was drunk even before the party really got going, and just before Tallis kissed me I saw someone passing out some kind of shots on the dance floor. When the shots come out, Alex is done for.

I push through the thick crowd of people. I'm shocked to find Olivia—Olivia who is usually so together—crying in hysterics on the living room floor. Most of the dancers have moved out of the way.

"What happened?" I ask. "Where's Alex?"

Olivia shakes her head, sobbing. "I fell—I fell on my ankle—please help me up, Zack . . ."

I bend down and lift Olivia to her feet, but she crumbles in pain. She can't put any weight on her ankle.

Jay, who's right behind me, helps me get Olivia to the kitchen to make an ice pack. "It looks like you sprained it," he tells her sympathetically.

"It can't be! Noooooooooooooooo," she wails.

"I better get you home," I say, and pray Jay sees me looking hopelessly strong and handsome as I carry Olivia out to the street to hail a cab.

In the cab, Olivia passes out. When I wake her to take her up to her room, she starts to cry again. "Oh, Zack, now I'll never get my scholarship," she frets. "And Brian . . . and my future . . . I didn't tell you this, but Brian is autistic . . . I have to get this scholarship, for nothing else if not for him."

Autistic? Olivia never mentioned that her brother was autistic. And what does that have to do with her scholarship?

"Livvy," I tell her as we hobble into the elevator, "you're going to be fine. Tomorrow morning you'll feel fantastic. I bet you'll be dancing on it by next week."

In truth, I think she's going to have to stay off that ankle for at least a month, and I'd bet my cab fare that she'll be at the doctor for a good portion of tomorrow morning—feeling anything but fantastic.

"Really?" she asks me sleepily, giving me her keys and letting me guide her into her room and put her on the bed.

As I remove her flip-flops and cover her in her bedspread, I look wistfully at all the pictures of Olivia and Vince on the walls. It would suck to have to miss each other so much, but Vince and Olivia don't know how good they have it. To know, to actually *know* in your soul, that someone loves you more than anyone else on the whole planet— what would that even be like? To be absolutely secure that you wanted to be with that person in college and for the rest of your life? I can't even begin to imagine that.

As I run back down to the waiting cab, I wonder if Jay got home okay. I didn't even really get a chance to say goodbye.

9. ALEX

The Best Laid Plans

*Y*ou know, I was relieved when Olivia told me that PJ would have to miss Sara-Louise's party because she'd be in the Dordogne. But as I watch Patty and Tina unpack the supplies for body shots—salt, limes, a handle of tequila—I realize how foolish I've been worrying about PJ's supposed hotness. It's *Patty* sprinkling salt on George's neck right now. Patty's the competition here.

My vision might be hazy from all the shots I've taken tonight, but even I can see that George isn't exactly pushing Patty off of him, either.

I stumble over to them before Patty can get her tongue anywhere near *my* George. Tina may already be getting close to scoring with Drew—the nerve! After Drew is clearly meant to be *Olivia's* boyfriend—but there is nothing I can do about that right now. I have other, much more important matters to attend to. And the more I hang out with Drew, the less I actually believe he's boyfriend material for anyone. He never quits with that annoying drumming thing. He's doing it right now on the countertop. Tina seems to think it's actually really cool and interesting.

"Hey, babe," I say to George, nuzzling his neck in greeting. He smells like Old Spice, one of my all-time favorite smells. "I haven't seen much of you tonight."

Patty hasn't gotten the hint yet. Having taken her shot without the salt, she's now rubbing her ass—oh, excuse me, is that what she calls dancing?—up on George far too suggestively for me to let it go on any longer.

"Al!" George says, taking me in appreciatively. "You're looking awfully hot tonight. What's the occasion?"

"Do I need an occasion to turn you on?" I say, turning him around so that Patty's rear isn't so close to his Abercrombie cargos anymore.

George's eyes register a little surprise at my forwardness—all along, I've been trying to keep my game sweet and simple. You've got to be careful with guys like George—there might be less bullshit with a straightforward guy like him, but I've had to be careful to act like a lady at all times. A common whore might be able to get his attention at a party (see Example A—Texan Twin Patty humping his leg in Sara-Louise's kitchen), but that's not the kind of girl (Example B—me) George wants to spend his time with in Paris. He needs someone *cultured*, with *class*, who wouldn't throw herself on him at a house party.

But desperate times call for desperate measures. The more shots Patty and her slutty sister Tina take, the more likely they'll chuck their virginity promise rings out the window and trap George and Drew into some sort of highly unnecessary hookup scandal that I just can't have right now.

I slip my arms around George's neck. "What are you doing in here with Patty?" I say in a sultry whisper. "It's been so lonely at this party without you. And this apartment is amazing! You want to see the view from the master bedroom?"

Sara-Louise's apartment is hardly amazing—it's so tiny and drab that I can't really fathom how four people manage to cohabitate here without killing each other. But from Sara-Louise's host parents' bedroom, you can see the Eiffel Tower, all lit up.

"It's almost worth it, sharing a room, just to look at that all day and night," George jokes as we sit on the bed and take it in. I recognize the bright blue bedding we are sitting on from Ikea. I'd never been to Ikea until my cousin Emily went to college and I went with her and her mom to the one in Elizabeth, New Jersey to help Emily load up on dorm supplies. I run over the silk-screened fabric with my fingertips, wondering what it would be like to get under the covers with George.

"Imagine looking out this window on Bastille Day," I say. "With all the fireworks going off over the Seine. I bet it's to die for."

"Totally bitchin'," George agrees. He's just inches from my face. I'm drunk, that's for certain, but I also can't take it anymore. His musky smell is drawing me in. I turn and plant my lips on his, kissing him softly and slowly.

George kisses me back, just as softly. I love how confident he is, how good his lips feel on mine. "Hey," he mutters when our lips part for a second. "Are you trying to take advantage of me when I'm drunk? Is that why you brought me in here?"

I giggle at his teasing. "It's not like I had to beg," I say. "You followed me in here of your own volition."

George takes a swig of the whiskey sour he made himself in the kitchen. "That I did," he concurs. "That I did." He kisses me again, this time with more fervor. He obviously wants to take it to the next level.

I don't want to be trashy, I reason to myself as we settle back onto the bed. I stare up at the dimmed light fixture and the fan coming from the ceiling above us, trying to decide how far to go, as George kisses my neck. *But this feels amazing—I'm finally getting what I want. And if I don't do it, he'll find a girl who will.* Patty's overly painted face pops into my head. *Patty will get him if I don't.*

No matter how chaste I am trying to be, I always choose my lingerie carefully—you never know when passion might overtake you, after all. I had worn a light yellow, very girly bra under my polo shirt. George is pawing at the front clasp clumsily. He gives up and peels off my skirt to reveal the matching yellow thong instead. I pull his shirt off, running my hands up and down the smooth skin on his back, slipping my hands around his waist and undoing his belt and his cargo pants.

"Man, Alex, you are *sexy*," George breathes as he starts to struggle out of his boxers.

"Wait," I say, hating to interrupt him. "We need a condom." I jump up to get my bag, tingling with excitement.

I can feel George's eyes on me. I stretch out the task of finding a condom in the side pocket so that he has to wait, just those few aching moments of wanting me so badly that *he* can't take it anymore.

I'm shaky with nervous expectation. *Be brave,* I tell myself as I crawl back onto the bed. I kiss him again to quell my nerves.

"Al," George says, holding my waist. "Let's wait. Let's not do this right now."

The fan spins above us, whirring and ticking. Beyond the door, I can hear shouts and music from the party. It sounds like the twins are trying to organize a game of beer pong, and the French kids—those of them still left at this lame, too-crowded party—are not understanding the rules.

"Why?" I fret. "Do you want to wait because you like me . . . or because you're too drunk right now?"

George, his eyes already closed, smiles. "Both. Now, come here." He spoons me, circling me into his arms.

"Oh," I whisper back. Within seconds, he's snoring right into my ear.

When I wake up, George is gone. There's just a bunch of wrinkles in the bed next to me. I stare at the blue sheets for a minute. Then, gathering the blanket around me, I hobble around collecting my polo shirt, my jean skirt, and the little yellow shoes worn in an effort to appear down-to-earth and unaffected.

At least a walk of shame is better in Paris than in New York. The sun is just starting to rise, and with the bakeries all opening their doors, letting out the delicious smell of fresh bread and croissants, I could *almost* convince myself everything with George is just as it should be.

Back at my homestay in the Cambronne, I try to call my mom's cell phone. In her last email, she told me she'd be on a trip to San Francisco researching a story for *Luxe* all week. It's still early evening in San Francisco—she shouldn't be sleeping—but she must be out already because she doesn't answer.

After the disaster of last night—George fell asleep, and he *snores*, for God's sake—all I want is some affection, my mom's careless laughter in my ear. I want some fabulous piece of advice, like, *You will have many lovers, Alex darling. Some of them are bound to be disappointing.*

After listening to my mom's voicemail greeting for the fourth time, I dial Zack's cell phone.

"What are you doing?" I ask him when he yawns a greeting. "I found a place that does American brunch on Sunday, just like you've been wanting. I'll text you the address—meet me there?"

We meet at the restaurant, comically called Thanksgiving and kitschy the way American diners are. Zack is chirping happily about funny things at the party—Tallis, the pixie girl; how Tina's polyester miniskirt had unsightly static cling all night; how wild Olivia had gotten dancing with me on the table, even though she was stone cold sober.

Zack howls with laughter. "I had no idea how bad Patty was jocking George before last night but now—now she might as well broadcast herself on France 2's evening news! So what happened with George once you got him away from her?"

"Hmm," I say blithely. "We hooked up."

"Girl!" Zack says. "It is a *scandal* that I've been sitting here all this time, just waiting for my pancakes and watching you smoke those God-awful Gauloises, without knowing that you and George did the *deed*! How could you keep me in the dark for such a very long time about it? Are you in *heaven*?" He looks at me, his dark brown eyes gleaming and expectant.

"Oh, Zack," I say heavily. "I think I put too much on the table last night."

"I'll say!" Zack guffaws. "Sounds like you put *everything* on the table."

"Shut it," I say grumpily, even though he's right. "We didn't even have sex. We want . . . we want to wait."

"Wait for what? " Zack says, getting confused. "Wait a second . . . is George into you or what? Why on earth didn't y'all go all the way?"

I can't tell him the truth. "George likes me a lot. I can tell. We're going to do it, but that isn't the important thing going on here. He might even—he might even love me too much to go all the way yet." I don't know why I'm saying all this. It just sounds really perfect as it comes out. I pick up my mimosa and take a sip.

"Right," Zack says skeptically. "You know . . ."

"What?" I demand. I stub out my cigarette and immediately light another.

"Watch yourself. I mean, all you really have is some drunken fumbling in the dark. You've got a breakable heart, *ma poupette*. Be careful with it. Just sayin'."

Our waiter sets down our plates of pancakes and eggs in front of us with an abrupt clatter.

I glare at Zack. He's wrong. And jealous, most likely.

I'm not letting George get away just because I'm embarrassed he passed out on me, not when we're so close to being boyfriend and girlfriend. The old me, the Brooklyn me, would have been too embarrassed after that episode, but the Parisian me knows it's not over. This is going to happen, whatever it takes.

10. PJ

Promises, Parties, and Problems

"I wouldn't have missed Sara-Louise's party for all the châteaux in France," Alex says superciliously Monday morning, leaning against the locker next to mine just before M. Paton's Algebra 2 class (thankfully for all of us, taught in English) starts off our day at the Lycée. She's still wearing her sunglasses, but I can see her arched, disapproving eyebrows.

Zack nods his agreement as he digs out his Algebra 2 textbook from his leather book bag. "It was out of this world. I mean, *Olivia* was dancing on a *table*. How can you *ever* forgive yourself for missing it?"

"And we met French kids," Alex boasts. "We did shots with them. It was *amazing*."

I grab my own math book, as well as some books on Ingres that I wanted to show to Jay for our project. We should probably do some more research on our painter before we actually go on the Louvre field trip in a few weeks. Plus, I really want to try and do a painting for extra credit. It's been so long since I had an art project to work on, not since before the aborted wedding and the trip up to Canada.

I slam my locker door shut. "Sounds like it. So, where is Olivia this morning, anyhow? Too exhausted from her table dancing escapades this weekend to come to school?"

Zack purses his lips. "Wouldn't you like to know?" Is it just me or does Zack get the teeniest bit femme when he and Alex are together? "Olivia—get this—*fell off* the table and tore up some ligaments in her ankle during her little show on Saturday night. She's going to be out for a few days."

"Oh, no!" I stop and stare at them. "You're kidding!"

Zack nods and puts his hand on the chest of his light blue sweater. "I swear. Honest to God."

"Poor Liv," I say, filling with sadness. Of all the nasty things to happen to someone so kind and good! You'd think, the way Alex likes to party, that it would have been *her* falling off a table. "How long does she have to stay off her ankle?"

"At least six weeks," Alex informs me casually, finally pushing up her Gucci shades. "She gets to miss school this week, too, lucky bitch. She's all doped up on painkillers. Anyway, you really should have been there. Was the Dordogne worth it?"

My heart skips a beat at the mention of pharmaceuticals. It always does.

How could Alex and Zack treat this like just some other piece of gossip? Olivia must be heartbroken—not to mention scared out of her wits. What if she screwed up her ankle permanently and won't be able to apply for her UCLA scholarship?

And not to sound selfish or anything, but the thought of a whole week without Olivia at school is dizzying. She's my only ally here. Moreover, I'd been wanting to see if she might like to go to an African folk dance and drumming performance I'd heard about. Of all the kids at the Lycée, I thought she might actually be interested in seeing a band not in heavy rotation on MTV Europe.

"The Dordogne was fine," I answer Alex carefully. She doesn't respond. She's reapplying her lip-gloss.

I'd tossed and turned all night on Saturday, wondering if I'd greet Sunday morning with an exposé on the mysterious American foster child living with the magistrate of Périgueux. I'd thought for sure a reporter would want to cash in with a big story on me, about my parents, and how the Marquets' good name would be forever tainted. At the Périgueux train station Sunday afternoon, I'd scanned all the Sunday papers, making sure there weren't any photos of me taken by the paparazzi from the day before. There was nothing, of course. I laughed at myself. I'm getting paranoid on top of everything else.

"It was great, actually," I tell Alex, reminding myself to act normal above everything else. "The château is incredible."

I take my seat and start unpacking my homework to turn it in to M. Paton. I'd had trouble concentrating on it last night; I know it isn't my best work. I'd been anxious to speak with Dave again. I still am. He hasn't been answering his cell phone the past few times I've tried to call him.

"Olivia told us that your apartment blew her mind when she came over," Alex says, grabbing a chair in our first class right next to mine. She never does that. "She said it was positively *massive*."

Zack takes a seat on the other side of me. "I can't wait to see it!" he gushes. "Olivia told us it's a mini-Versailles. Living there must be to die for. Who decorated it? Has it been featured in any magazines?" He crosses his leg and clasps his knee, all ears for more descriptions of the apartment.

Okay, *definitely* getting a gay vibe from him today.

"A mini-Versailles?" I say doubtfully. "No. It's more like . . ."

"A faded empire?" Zack says, almost panting.

"Well, yes," I say. That's exactly right. The apartment feels like a museum, a relic.

The château is like that too, though to a greater degree. Its many rooms are in various stages of upkeep. Certain wings of the house seem to be off limits. When Mme Marquet had given me a tour Friday night, we'd skipped over the rooms she was in the process of remodeling, which was many of them.

"I know just what you mean," Zack says. "I bet it's all just divine. I can't wait to see it for myself."

"Are you going out of town again this weekend?" Alex asks pointedly "It'd be such bad form to isolate yourself again so soon. I mean, our program hasn't even bonded together yet. People are going to start thinking you don't *want* to be friends with them."

"That's not true," I protest. "I just really wanted to get to know my host family. But no, I'm not going away again this weekend. Even if they invite me I don't think I am going to go back at all until after our trip to the Louvre. I really feel like I need to catch up on my studying. I'm behind in almost everything."

"Well, that's good," Alex says. "I mean, everyone is so busy getting to know each other that after awhile they might forget about you entirely. And you don't want to risk that."

Zack shakes his head. "No, you wouldn't, girl. Our program is just starting to gel. I bet you don't even know everyone's names yet."

I look around the classroom. He's right. I don't know everyone's names yet.

"Like that there is Katie Dinkus," he says in a low voice, pointing to a curly-haired girl in jeans and a lavender crewneck sweater. "Katie's from Ohio. Last year, she started a nonprofit at her school that benefits teen mothers. She's a major feminist."

"So?" I say. Sounds like Katie's a nice person, and I would like to get to know her better. I don't understand why Zack's tone is so accusing.

"Well, at the party, I found out, while we were shot gunning beers with Sara-Louise," Zack continues, "that Katie Dinkus has been getting freaky with that Justin Timberlake look-alike from Orlando over there." He cocks his head at a baby-faced guy who's in my French section named Robbie.

"That's Robbie," I say, to prove that I'm not totally out of the loop. "I've worked with him in our conversational French exercises." Because of this, I know that Robbie dreams of being in a band one day and used to perform in musicals at his old school. I also know that he thinks women shouldn't work but should stay home and raise their families. He told me this during an ill-advised exercise our French teacher created in which we all expounded on our political beliefs in French so that we could eventually understand how to argue with the French kids who will likely attack us for our beliefs if they ever deign to talk to us. This exercise, of course, broke out into general hostility.

"Well, him and Katie are like, nymphos. They do it every night, because Katie's host mom is a nurse who works until almost midnight. Bet you didn't know that about them," he tells me.

Alex looks at me. "It's true," she says solemnly. "They do it every day. But they never talk at school. They pretend like they don't even know each other!"

I burst out laughing. I glance from Katie to Robbie and back to Katie. There is no way they are a couple. "You guys are full of it. Tell me another one," I say.

"PJ!" Alex scolds me. She reapplies her lip-gloss and smacks her lips together. "Zack would never repeat a rumor unless it was true. Would you, Zack?"

"On the grave of my daddy's daddy," Zack says with a goofy twang, "I cannot tell a lie."

I can't stop laughing at them. "What do Robbie and Katie have to do with me having a party?"

"PJ," Alex says, tucking her makeup case back into her leather tote bag and slinging the strap over the back of her chair. "We tell you these things because we want to be your friend."

I stare at her. Alex has been icy to me since day one. What changed?

"We do, Miss Penelope Jane," Zack backs her up. "We want you to know that we don't want you to be left out. And the easiest way to fit in is to have an awesome welcoming bash at your apartment and everyone will get drunk and throw up and bond and then we can all call it a day. Don't you want to?"

"Well, thanks," I say, meaning it. "I mean, for not wanting me to be left out. But there's so much I need to catch up on before the Louvre trip."

"You sound like Olivia, always *catching up* on everything," Alex scoffs. "What's there to catch up on in Paris? Paris is about living. It's about loving. Laughing. Having fun. It's not about some stupid trip to the Louvre."

"Louvre, schmouvre," Zack chimes in. "I'm so sick of museums."

I can't help laughing. "We haven't even been to one as a class yet. Have you guys been going to a lot of them on your own?"

"Well, no," Zack divulges. "But Alex has been to them all already, and besides, I prefer the *real* Paris. The Paris that can't be contained by *institutions*." Even though his tenor is pretentious, I can tell that Zack is mocking himself. It's times like these when I really want to get to know him—and even Alex, really—better than I do. Both of them are really witty, and I'm envious of how they are taking Paris by storm, going out, eating in great restaurants, getting up and dancing when they feel like it.

They were actually the kind of people I'd been hoping to meet here, carefree, as in love with Paris as I am, but so far, I've been too torn up about my parents, and Annabel, to really put my best foot forward.

"The day of the Louvre trip would be perfect!" Alex says, the bangles on her thin wrists jangling as she claps her hands together with pleasure. "We can all celebrate getting through the dreadful field trip alive."

"No!" I gasp in horror. "Alex, I *can't*." It's only now that I'm getting how serious they are. It was funny to joke about it with them, but the idea of our entire class coming over and potentially wreaking havoc on the Marquets' apartment makes me nauseated.

"Now, why on earth not? It's just a few people, and Zack and I will help you clean up afterward," Alex coaxes.

Just then, Jay walks into class and takes the seat in front of mine. He swivels around to face me.

"Hey, Jay," I say before he can remind me again of our study date. "So sorry about this weekend—I had to go out of town. "

I look over at Zack and Alex, who hover, still waiting for my answer.

In a nervous flash, I decide to go for it. "I'm going to have a couple people over the night of the Louvre fieldtrip if you'd like to come. You know, like to celebrate getting through that part of the project." I sound like I'm parroting Alex. I can't believe this.

"Jay! You should totally come," Zack says, overhearing us as he sits back down holding a steaming Styrofoam cup of espresso in his hands. "PJ—great idea. Jay, it should be a great little shindig. Alex and I are helping PJ organize it."

Jay beams. Maybe I'm finally starting to do things right. Maybe I have a chance again at a normal life.

Alex passes me a note while M. Paton explains some theorem or another. *You're doing the right thing*, it says. *Imagine what stories Zack might have to make up about you if you weren't there to defend yourself, like Robbie and Katie.*

I look at her and roll my eyes. I *knew* Robbie and Katie weren't a couple. I just knew it.

Besides, if someone wanted to spread rumors about me, Zack wouldn't have to make any up. He'd just have to know where to look for them.

Before I run home for lunch, I swing by the computer lab to check my e-mail.

News from Vermont! I click it open as soon as I check to make sure no one's behind me. It's from Dave!

PJ—

Majorly bad news. This is awkward, but I thought you should hear it from a friend. I'll be blunt—it's about your house. It's been repossessed by the bank. I guess your parents got pretty late on the mortgage. I saw them, like, carting stuff out of there yesterday morning—the rocking chair your dad built for your mom, things like that. Harsh, I know. If you ever hear from Annabel in this wacked-out mess, tell her I saved our prom photo from the dresser in your room.

If I talk to your parents, I'll tell them I told you.

Sorry for the bad news.

Peace,

Dave

I stare at the screen. I almost think it's a joke—he just got high with some friends and thought he'd prank me or something. My dad built our house from logs with his own bare hands. He and my mom have lived in the cabin since they first got married, adding on a room for Annabel and me when we got too big for our cribs on the sun porch. Set in a clearing not far from a little stream, my mom and dad always talked about growing old there together, eventually putting on another addition, helping me raise a family of my own there one day.

My parents owned that house fair and square . . . no matter what. And yet—it looks like they didn't. They must have taken out a mortgage at some point. When they knew shit was about to hit the fan . . .

How could they have made such a terrible mistake?

I used to feel proud of my parents. But now, they are shameful and pathetic, locked up, shunned by one daughter, abandoned by the other.

Careful to log out of my email, I get up and go to the payphone on the steps of the Lycée with a heavy heart. Dave answers on the first ring.

"Have you heard from Annabel?" he asks at the same time I tell him, "I got your email."

"No," I say. "I haven't heard from Annabel."

"Oh," he says. "Well, I wrote you everything I know in the email. I got nothing else to tell you, no silver lining. I was hoping *you'd* have a silver lining."

"I'll let you go back to sleep," I say, and hang up.

As I walk back to Ternes, I wonder what Annabel did with her engagement ring, the little diamond in it's gold setting. It wasn't worth enough to sell. Does she still wear it?

I bet Dave thinks about that question all the time.

I unlock the doors of the apartment and call out for Sonia. She's not here. Not hungry, I go straight to the living room and lie down on the glorious Persian rug that covers the whole of the living room floor, staring up at the molded ceiling. *This is your home now*, I tell myself. That house, regardless of all the memories we made there, doesn't matter. *That house is full of lies.*

I roll over onto my stomach, my arm brushing over a ridge in the carpet near one of the end tables. *Did my notebook somehow slide under the carpet?* I worry. I'd hate for Sonia to pick something like that up and show it to the Marquets, not knowing what kinds of things I've written about them in my fake letters to Annabel. Also, the other things I've written to Annabel wouldn't be good for the Marquets to see, either.

I reach over to the edge of the rug and pull the slender object out. When I realize what it is, I drop it back down to the floor in fright.

It's a porn magazine called *18*. Across the bottom of the magazine is a promise that all the girls photographed within the magazine *are* legal, but just barely. One of these girls smiles out at me from the front cover, her breasts large and exposed above a short schoolgirl's kilt.

I jump up, not quite sure what to do. Finally I just kick the magazine back under the rug and sit on the couch like a normal person. Why am I always lying on the floor in here? If Mme Marquet saw me, she'd think I was a bigger freak than she does already.

I look up at the portrait of one of M. Marquet's great-great-great-grandfathers hanging over the mantel. My stomach turning, I imagine Alex defacing it with a marker, drawing something lewd coming from the old patriarch's sternly set mouth.

I realize I don't know the Marquets at all. I have no idea what kind of people they are. But, who knows where the trashy magazine could have come from? It probably isn't that weird. Isn't that what people are always saying about Americans? That we're priggish, shameful about the human body? And it *was* hidden.

Still, I'm not super comfortable with the idea of M. Marquet having that magazine. I'm seventeen, turning eighteen later this year. That's almost the age of the girls in the magazine. I gag a little. Am I really going to risk it all—the only house, family, protection that I have left in this world—to have a stupid party? So that I won't feel so guilty bailing on some half-assed plans with Jay? To get on Alex's good side?

What would my older sister do?

Of course, Annabel would have the party. And it would be the best party anyone had ever seen. And the next day, Annabel would bag up all the trash, scrub the house till it was sparkling clean, and no one would be the wiser.

Because if there was anything my sister was good at, hiding the evidence was it.

11. OLIVIA

Raison d'Etre

"*Bonjour!*" a friendly voice greets me as I hobble out of the wire-cage elevator. "Olivia!"

Perfect, I think grimly. *Just what I need right now.* I'm tired from the walk home, tired from the week I've had, back at school, avoiding the humored comments about how I hurt myself. I've forced myself to take the jokes kindly, but inside I'm simmering with humiliation and resentment.

It's the boy from my bed—that is, Mme Rouille's son from the Sorbonne, a beat-up notebook tucked under one arm. Carrying his bike up the spiral staircase, he clucks his tongue in sympathy at my crutches.

The accident at Sara-Louise's party left the ligaments in my ankle shredded, but even worse than the throbbing pain is the forced rest.

I've been dancing for at least four hours every day after school since I was ten. When they figured out that Brian was autistic, my parents warned me that they might not be able to send me to ballet class anymore. Then one day, as my mom and Brian waited for me to finish a recital rehearsal, the dance teacher noticed that Brian was keeping time to the music by tapping on the floor in the studio. His development coaches thought that not only the music but also the social aspect of watching my classes really helped Brian. So my mom let me take as many classes as I wanted, and by the time I could go on pointe, I was done for.

There is nothing more soothing than counting out your *degagés* at the *barre*, no greater release for your soul than that split-second in a *tour jeté* when you are actually flying. It is a joy that I cannot live without.

And for the past few weeks, I've had to.

"*Maman* told me you have hurt yourself," he says with concern, wheeling his bike over to me. His English is just the slightest bit off, sort of like his mother. "I think I did not properly introduce myself—*je m'appelle Thomas Rouille.*"

"*Bonjour*, Thomas," I say, leaning forward for him to kiss my cheeks. "*Enchantée.*"

Of course, there are many pictures of Thomas around the apartment, but what looked like shy dorkiness in school photos actually seems to be part of Thomas's charm in person. In a grey toggle coat and charcoal corduroy pants, he's a picture of what a scholar should be—rumpled, academic, sweet. His face is so smooth and sweet it's almost pretty. His curly hair makes him seem a little younger than someone in college, closer to my age. He takes my books from me with the hand not holding his bike.

"Now. Let's have some tea, yes?" he offers, and gallantly holds open the door to my—well, *our*—apartment for me.

• • •

I find out that Thomas would rather study here at home than at school. "I can't concentrate in the dormitory," he confides. "We debate the philosophy all night and never write the papers. I come here so that I can finally learn in peace!"

I smile politely. In truth, I've never been much for school beyond just getting the 3.6 GPA I need to land my scholarship. The idea of losing precious sleep just to discuss the meaning of life seems like overkill to me.

"*Maman* says you are a beautiful dancer. She told me about watching your audition," he says as he boils water for some peppermint tea. "*Elle m' a dit que tu es très douées.*"

I blush at the compliment. I wonder why it seems to mean so much, coming from someone I barely know. I feel so awkward, like I can't stop staring at his mouth. But he's the first person besides a teacher who'll really speak some French to me!

That night, Thomas teases me a little when I emerge from my—his—room to use the restroom.

"The apartment was so quiet I was sure you had fallen asleep!" he teases me from his nest on the couch. "Your Friday nights are so very exciting, Olivia."

"I was studying," I inform him. "We have a big test at the end of the term that I am just so nervous about, so I've been going over all my irregular verbs and all the tenses and everything—"

"You've been studying French by yourself, all alone in your room, when France awaits you just beyond your front door? You've been speaking French with yourself instead of speaking French with all the citizens of France that you could meet if you only shut your books and experienced it?" Thomas's French lilts with good-natured ribbing.

"You think I need to go out on a Friday night to do well on the test?" I ask him, trying my very best to keep my French up to par. "As if! You're delusional," I add in English.

"I'm telling you that you could use more *experience*," he says.

I go back into my bedroom, not sure of how to answer him.

Mme Rouille, with her harsh, tough-love French attitude toward me, hasn't indulged me too much since I hurt myself. I told her I did it by falling down some stairs at a movie theatre while out with Zack, but I can tell she doesn't buy it. Besides relieving me of my miniature-poodle-walking duties, she certainly hasn't been waiting on me hand and foot the way I notice that she dotes on Thomas. She puts Elise to work right away, baking *sablés au citron*, Thomas's favorite cookies, and making rich, nourishing *pot-au-feu* every night before he goes back across the Seine to the Sorbonne on the Left Bank.

During Thomas's midterm break, which lasts a week, he comes back to the apartment every day. I don't ask why he doesn't just go to the Sorbonne library. Maybe it's closed for the holiday. But the way Mme Rouille fusses over him, it's not a shock that he prefers hitting the books at his mom's kitchen table. She's thrilled to have Thomas home again, even for just a few hours at a time. Instead of going to lunch and shopping with her high society friends, she invites people over for tea and cocktail parties to admire her brilliant son. Besides a few awkward questions about what I did to my ankle, Mme Rouille's elegant friends can't be bothered with me.

Wednesday afternoon, we sit in comfortable silence in the airy, old-fashioned kitchen, him reading a medical text book at the heavy wooden table as I drink up one of my carrot-juice smoothies on a breakfast nook barstool, my left leg—the healthy one—twitching with restlessness. Even though it's over a month away, I'm horrified at how ill-prepared I am for the Final Comp. The Final Comp will have questions on all of our subjects, and according to the program alumni who interviewed me for my Lycée application, it will be the hardest thing I've ever attempted in all of my sixteen years.

"I love to write," Thomas tells me suddenly.

I turn to him quizzically. "*C'est bon*," I say lamely. "That's wonderful."

"I always have my notebook with me," he says, lifting the notebook in question up so that I can see it. "And everywhere I go, all day long, I always have something I want to write down. The expression on the face of the cashier at the fish market—the choir I can hear practicing in the basement of the Saint-Germain-des-Prés—the way it feels to walk along the Seine in the dead of winter. To not be able to write—I would be in hell. So you—you must be feeling like that, without dancing, *non?*"

I stare at Thomas.

Never once in the last two years of going out with Vince, has he ever been able to sum up how I feel about dance so succinctly as I think Thomas just did.

"Olivia!" Mme Rouille's maid, Elise, calls me from the foyer. "Alex is here to see you!"

Still thinking about what Thomas said, I call out to Alex that we're in the kitchen.

"Hey," she says, kissing me on either cheek. "I dig Elise's outfit, man."

Elise always wears a typical black and white French maid's costume. I couldn't get over it when I first met her, either.

"Well, helloooooooooooooo," Alex drawls when she sees Thomas. "You must be the mysterious boy Olivia pounced on unawares all those weeks ago. Nice to meet you in the flesh, finally. Your reputation for a wild night precedes you."

"Oh, Alex," I say with impatience. "Sit. You want some tea?" I reach up to the dark mahogany shelves above the sink for a clean cup and saucer.

"If that's all you have on tap at the moment," Alex jokes. She leans over the granite countertop, chomping her gum and openly gawking at Thomas. "Though I'm more in the mood for a dirty martini." Alex unwraps the oversize silk scarf from around her neck. "Listen, I came to tell you that PJ is having a party this weekend."

"*PJ* is having a party?" I ask in disbelief. "You've got to be kidding."

"I swear on my Hermès," Alex says, briefly touching her scarf in mock reverence. It's a nod to her hero, the one and only Carrie Bradshaw. She turns to Thomas. "Well, well. And you would be. . .?"

"*Je m'appelle Thomas,*" Thomas answers with a bemused grin.

"Well, then, *Thomas*," Alex says with an irresistible smirk, "I hope I see you on Saturday night. Listen, forget the tea—I can't stay. I'm meeting Zack at the Galeries Lafayette in ten minutes to pick out something new for the party. *Au revoir*, darlings!"

The miniature poodles nip at Alex's heels as she crosses the foyer toward the front door.

"Toodles, poodles!" The dogs bark in response.

I hear Elise let her out. Too impatient to wait for the elevator, Alex's banging high-heeled Chloé boots—her new ones—echo down the spiral marble stairs to the lobby of the building.

"Olivia, do you mind if I accompany you girls to the party? I'd love to meet your friends," Thomas beseeches me. I gaze out the kitchen window, then back at him, touched by his concern at intruding. I'm also wondering what Vince would think about Thomas coming to the party. It's not like I invited him, after all.

"Oh, sure," I reply, not wanting to offend him. "Of course. I mean, it'll just be high school kids. Tons of Americans. Are you sure you want to come?"

"*Bien sûr!*" Thomas affirms. "It sounds like a fun time."

It does sound like a fun time, one that I wish Vince could be there for. It's easy enough to get through the school day and ballet class without Vince, but social events make me miss him so much. Vince is so funny at parties, always right in the center of things. When I became his girlfriend in the ninth grade, I remember feeling so lucky that my boyfriend was so popular and well-liked. He never ignores me when we go out, either, or pressures me to drink. He always used to get me home right at eleven, and come in and say hi to my parents. Remembering him, the way he used to come around to the passenger side door of his car and let me out, and reach down and help me out of the car and hold my hand up the front walkway of our house, how safe I always felt when I was with him, fills me with yearning and sorrow.

After dinner, I walk with Thomas to the Villiers metro station, planning to go call Vince before bed.

We pass the Lycée, where Thomas tells me he used to be a student. "Don't let them fool you," he says of the French kids who I complain ignore us all the time and make us feel like idiots. "We were always fascinated by *les Américains*. They will come around."

Past the Parc Monceau, this part of the seventeenth, Clichy, gets a little sketchy. More bustling than Ternes, the boulevard is full of people even at all hours. As we part ways, I jump a little when a bar erupts with cheers, the crowd enraptured by a soccer match playing on the TV in the corner.

"Olivia," Thomas calls before he climbs down the stairway to the metro. "*Ça va bien?*"

"*Oui, bien,*" I assure him. With a flash of his impish smile, he disappears into the station. I take a moment, then maneuver around on my crutches to turn around and head back down the street, looking for a payphone. I still feel weird calling Vince from Mme Rouille's house phone.

I find one near the bar with the soccer fans.

When Vince answers, I have to struggle to hear him over the noise.

"What?" I say, turning away from the bar toward the busy street. "Say that again?"

"I said, how are you?" Vince repeats.

"Good. I found out that *PJ* is having people over this weekend. Can you believe it?"

"Who's PJ?" Vince asks. "Is that a dude?"

"No, Vince," I say. I'm irritated that he forgot. "PJ is my friend, remember? The one I told you about because she had to stay with me for awhile?"

"Oh, the hippie chick?" Vince says. "That's cool. You gonna drink?"

"No, Vince," I snap. "I can't exactly get wasted right now. My body needs to heal from my accident at the movie theatre."

Like with Mme Rouille, I told Vince that I'd tripped at a movie theatre with Zack. For some reason I didn't think he'd be pleased to hear I was dancing on tables. And then I'd told him how Zack was gay, so that he wouldn't worry about what I was doing at the movies with another guy. Zack's never actually *told* me he's gay, but I just assume so. Hang out with enough male ballet dancers as I do and you'll get a pretty good gaydar going.

Repeating the lie makes me feel even worse than snapping at Vince. I continue, keeping my voice light. "It's just so surprising! PJ is not the party type."

"The party sounds cool," Vince says, missing my point. I hear noise in the background and wonder what is going on.

"Yeah, well," I respond. "My calling card's almost out. I better go. Love you."

I hang up and hobble home, shivering all the way. The fall air, now that the sun has set, is biting and uncongenial.

I wish I had my mom to talk to about everything. We always did everything together—from getting our highlights touched up to going grocery shopping. Whenever I used to need advice, my mom and I could just talk it out. She was always just right there.

Friday morning I feel the best I've felt since Sara-Louise's party—no, the best I've felt since I got to Paris. I swing my legs out of bed far before my alarm starts going off, and when I step onto my right foot, my ankle doesn't buckle. It barely even hurts at all.

I stay on my crutches all day, but I test my ankle again without them at the end of the school day. *I could dance on it*, I think. *I should at least try.*

I slip into class late, wearing a black scooped-back leotard and a high, tight bun. As I run through the *barre* exercises with the rest of the ballerinas, my muscles cry out in delirious happiness. To be moving again!

Despite my three-week absence from ballet class at the Opera, my arms feel light and graceful, my legs strong and sturdy.

"*Bon, bon*, Olivia!" the teacher cries as I attempt a simple series of jumps while holding the *barre* with both hands. When we form a line to *piqué* turns in quick succession across the polished wooden floor, I surprise myself at how smooth and steady it feels after so long with no practice. My spot is right on; I don't feel dizzy at all.

By the end of class, I see my ankle swelling when I look at it in the studio mirror, but I'm too euphoric to notice if it hurts or not. The music sweeps over me, pulling me along the movements, over and over again. The final combination would have been hard even in flawless health—it's dangerous how hard I'm going after it.

An American teacher would never let me do this so soon after an injury, I think as I whip around gleefully like I've been longing to do. And for the first time since I got to Paris, I'm dancing with all the joy that ballet is meant to be danced with. There's no Brian here, no Vince, no scholarship. Just me and the gorgeousness of Paris—the faces of strangers, the songs coming from open windows, the wind off the Seine—just like Thomas was saying. Spreading myself into the air, executing all my leaps and turns flawlessly, I'm so moved by the experience that a few tears streak down my cheeks.

All at once, the pianist stops playing and I'm frozen into the final position. Gulping for air, I realize Thomas is behind me, his hand held up to his face like he's seen a ghost, or maybe an angel.

"Thomas!" I say, astounded. "What are you doing here?"

"*Maman* told me to come find you," he replies. "She says you are not supposed to be dancing." His face is stern. I can tell he left the house in a hurry. Despite the windy, rainy day outside, he's wearing just a windbreaker over his wrinkled T-shirt and slacks. Thomas is wet from his dash into the dance studio, and I feel terrible for sneaking into dance class and Mme Rouille sending him after me. Like me, he's breathing heavily from the exertion.

"I had to," I say simply.

"I can see you did," Thomas responds. His face is a mixture of alarm, wonder, and pride. "*Tu es ravissante.* Wow." Finally he breaks into a smile that shows off his endearingly crooked teeth. "As a medical student, I shouldn't tell you that, should I?"

I shake my head and lean into him. "I'm so glad you're here," I say. It's the first time I've ever touched Thomas. For some reason, it seems like the appropriate reaction. And my ankle is really starting to throb.

"*Allons-y,*" Thomas leads me to the door. "I think you've done enough trauma to your ankle for one day." Seizing hold of his shoulder for balance, I let him help me up the stairs and out to the waiting Mercedes.

NOVEMBER

12. ZACK

Wishing and Hoping

TO: Chandler, Zachariah

FROM: Randall, Pierson

Hey, guy! Isn't it so crazy being here in Europe, finally? I feel like I'm about a million miles from M-town. Don't you?

Sorry I haven't had a chance to respond to your emails until now. I've been so busy with everything here in Amsterdam . . . especially my new boyfriend!

Oh, Zack, I hadn't told you what was going on until now because I was too superstitious it wasn't going to work out. I mean, me? With a real live, honest-to-God boyfriend? And yet, I met Hannes a few weeks ago at a club . . . and he's amazing . . . he's 23 . . . totally down-to-earth, gorgeous, AND he doesn't mind going slow.

I'm in a constant state of happiness, Zack. You can't even imagine. Unless . . . you've met someone, too? If you haven't yet, all I can say is get to it. This is our last chance till college, bro.

Get a Euro boyfriend while you can!

I read over Pierson's email a second time to make sure I've absorbed it correctly. Have I stepped into a parallel universe? Has Pierson Randall—short, chubby Pierson, whom I've known since we met in the toddler class of the Christ's Message Baptist Church Preschool—actually gone off and found himself a boyfriend, and love, and sex, all before I've even managed to meet anyone datable?

What gets to me is that Pierson and I have always done everything together. We went to school and Bible-study together. We got baptized at church together, twice. (That was when we both thought we could run from this whole gay thing. Ha!) We're both on the JV swim team. We got our drivers' licenses on the same day and even came out to each other when we couldn't come out to our own families. We're like brothers, which, of course, means things that might be particularly convenient to first do together—like, *ahem*, losing our virginity—are simply out of the question. At least, not *literally* together. But that doesn't mean that he can just run off to Amsterdam and lose his virginity to some twenty-three-year-old sex god without me doing the same thing here in Paris! That's just not the natural order of things.

Especially when *I've* always been the more confident one, the one the girls are always calling (to no avail, of course), the one the swim team moms are always cooing over. Pierson is sweetly pudgy, with thick glasses and a slight lisp. His clothes are too big for him, he's a hopeless dancer, and he wouldn't have even made the swim team if I hadn't busted my ass in the tryout relay to make up for his slow time. He wouldn't even be in Amsterdam, for that matter, if it weren't for me. As soon as I signed up for the Lycée, Pierson went out and found some second-rate program in Amsterdam that didn't even have a language requirement!

Don't get me wrong. I'd walk through fire for this kid. He's my oldest friend and the one person who's never let me down. It must be clear, however, that if Pierson or I were ever to take a step without the other one, it should be me that goes first.

I read over Pierson's email a third time, gagging with jealousy, and finally log out of my Gmail in disgust. Alex, sprawled on the dusty old couch in the corner of the computer lab, looks up from filing her nails when I stomp over to her.

"What?" Alex says, hopping to her feet. "Did you get a letterbomb?" she gasps in horror.

A *letterbomb* is what students in the Programme Americain call an email with bad news, made all the worse by the fact that you're a million miles from home. A letterbomb is how Katie from Cleveland found out that her cat was hit by a car and died. It was how Drew's mom told him she'd found his glass bong in the back of his closet and shattered it before she'd thrown it away in the garbage. Other kids have been dumped by their girlfriends and boyfriends, heard their grandparents have cancer, and in general just logged into some major buzzkill by innocently checking their email. Alex lives in a state of terror of the letterbomb. For her, the one drawback of living in Paris is that it increases your chances of being blindsided by (rather than simply made aware of) bad news from home. And if there is one thing I've learned about Alex, it's that she might actually rather die than be the last to know.

"No," I sigh. "No letterbomb. Not really, anyways. It's just Pierson . . . and his new Dutch boyfriend, Hannes." I spit out the ugly, hard sounds of the name as I picture Pierson saying it with his forced Dutch accent.

"Oh, honey," Alex, says, wrapping her arms around me. "Sounds like we need a little trip to the Galeries Lafayette to cheer us up." I shrug unenthusiastically. "Come on," Alex twists my arm, tilting her head coyly at me. "I'll buy you a latte at Maxim's." Maxim's is Alex's go-to destination for all refreshments at the Galeries Lafayette.

I grudgingly agree, despite what I know will be huge crowds and lines at the most famous department store in Paris. But sugar and heavy cream are maybe the only things that could make me feel better right now.

Alex's hyper anxious prattling about George does little to distract me, though it does bolster my ego a bit to think that if the fabulous Alex Nguyen doesn't have a boyfriend after two months in Paris, how can anyone expect me to either?

"I mean, he offered the rest of his *pain au chocolat* to Patty yesterday morning!" Alex moans. "And I was *right* there. And don't even get me started on La Cinémathèque Française . . ."

One afternoon last week, Mme Cuchon took us all to the famous French film center to see a remastered screening of Jean-Luc Godard's *Breathless*. The trip had been a rare school outing that Alex and I had enjoyed more than anyone else. Unlike Notre Dame, which was too crowded and full of docent douche-bags who kept shushing us every time we said *anything*, or the *Tour Eiffel*, where Madame forced us to walk all the way to the top and I had to practically carry Alex in her stilettos. No, seeing *Breathless* in the cool, austere theatres of La Cinémathèque Française's glamorous new building designed by Frank Gehry was a welcome, sophisticated change. Alex and I, giddy with excitement, sat in the first row. George, in preparation for a long nap, took a seat in the back of the auditorium. Alex was furious, at least until she became temporarily distracted by Jean Seberg and she forgot.

I consider for a moment. "George probably assumed someone as thin as you would scorn his highly caloric castoffs," I reason aloud. "And Alex—isn't the whole point of George that he doesn't go ape shit over Godard and the like? Wouldn't you like him less if he was rabid for French New Wave?"

We dart around fancy French ladies, vendors selling crappy souvenirs to tourists, and the very beginnings of holiday shoppers picking through gaudy, glittery merchandise. I guess if your country doesn't celebrate Thanksgiving, it would be hard to know that Christmas decorations the first week of November are tacky.

"You're right," Alex calls to me brightly as we hurry along. "So totally right!" She shivers in her lightweight Marc Jacobs army jacket and skinny jeans. "Okay," she says determinedly when we enter the store, facing the crowds like a bullfighter entering the ring. "Let's be sure and stop off at outerwear before we go up to Maxim's. I've got to find something for winter before I freeze to death."

The Galeries Lafayette is an enormous department store bigger and much fancier than anything in Memphis. Alex will even admit that it is better than any of the stores in New York. From the outside, the Galeries Lafayette looks like a palace or a museum but for the scores of blazing lights and advertisements hanging from its carved façade. Inside, tiers of boutiques—Chanel, Gucci, Louis Vuitton—reach up on all sides to a high ceiling arching into a grand, cathedral-like glass dome. Alex jokes that she could live here, with the restaurants, the beauty salon and spa, the travel agency, and all the other services that the store offers its customers. I joke back that she does practically live here—she trolls the aisles enough that she might as well.

"The only place to beat it is Harrods," Alex told me decisively on our first trip. I didn't tell her I had to Google "Harrods" to find out that store is in London.

"Honestly," Alex says, eyeing a purple Longchamp overnight bag and matching makeup case. "I haven't even been worrying about George. He and I are doing great. We're taking things slow, getting to know each other. What with the birthday party I'm planning at L'Atelier, I've hardly had time to even think about George. Do you want that?" she asks abruptly, pointing to the sleek black leather passport cover I'm fondling on the counter.

"Of course I do! It's gorgeous," I say with a laugh. "But it costs eighty euros."

"Eh, what's eighty euros? You've had a rough day," Alex shrugs dismissively, grabbing it from me. "Hey, do you like this?"

Alex holds up a long cardigan with a rolled collar and covered leather buttons. It looks like the perfect thing to wear with jeans and boots, Gisele-style, for a walk around the city when you are running errands and still need to be fashion-forward. She flips it so that we can see the back. On either elbow is a grandfatherly suede patch.

"Oh, my God!" Alex shrieks. "It's just like PJ's. Get it away from me!" She tosses it back onto the rack as if it were crawling with lice.

"Oh, shush," I say. "That sweater is cute. You're just mad because PJ started the trend and you didn't." All the girls at the Lycée are wearing long, oversize grandpa cardigans lately, just like the one PJ's always wrapped up in. If you have elbow patches, you're at the height of sophistication these days.

We've barely made it off the first floor before Alex has bought me the Longchamp passport cover, a flashy new camo belt, and some very expensive hair-molding crème to keep my hair artfully disheveled. And that's just the stuff for me! Alex has the set of Longchamp bags (which she said she just resolutely needed to have for the class trip to Lyon later in the term); a black cashmere scarf, hat and mitten set; and an at-home facial kit from the Clinique counter.

"But Alex," I protest as the salesgirl rings the last item up. "You go for facials at the salon every month. What are you going to do with the at-home kit?"

Alex rolls her eyes impatiently. "For in between!" she explains.

Once up the escalators, Alex throws all of her bags into my arms and dives into the task of finding a new winter coat.

"Did I tell you that I found out Jay is here on a scholarship?" I ask Alex, wondering if she had known that all along.

"Oh, really?" Alex says without really listening.

"Yeah," I tell her as I wander closer to the men's section, lured by the soft wool gabardine of the winter suits on the mannequins. What is it about a suit that makes every man just that much more appealing? "He can't come back after the winter break if he doesn't score 90 or higher on the Final Comp."

A sales guy wanders over to me, but I give a short jerk of my head to indicate I'm just a lowly window shopper not in need of real assistance. I imagine myself in one of the suits—a Hugo Boss one with bold chalky grey strips, cut skinny all over, would look, if I do say so myself, *marvelous* on me.

"Jay never seems to hit on any of the girls on our program," I call over to Alex, still buried in the coat racks. "Have you noticed?" She doesn't answer.

I start back over to where Alex is trying on a stack of possible purchases in front of a mirror. Alex eschews dressing rooms—even when she is not shopping for a coat. I've even seen her try on a bra right out in the middle of the sales floor! "It's the French way," she always tells me, but the French saleswomen always seem pretty annoyed about it.

I exhale loudly. "What's a boy to do? Single in Paris, alone in the world . . ." I try to sound blithe, but there is a harsh undertone—the reality of the situation—that makes me come off sounding bitter and morose. Alex turns around, piling the rejected winter coats into the arms of a waiting salesgirl.

"Zack," she says, with a mischievous glint in her brown eyes. "L'Atelier is a terribly glamorous place. You're going to need a new suit for the party I'm having there." Alex's birthday party is coming up in a couple of weeks.

"I have a suit, Alex," I say, feeling awkward, on the spot all of a sudden.

"I've seen that suit, Zack, and we both know it was a hand-me-down from your dad that should have been given to a Halfway House or a work-release program. The fabric alone gives me hives—let's not even get into the cut," Alex frowns. She pulls me back over to the mannequin in the Hugo Boss suit and snaps her fingers towards the sales guy I'd brushed off before.

"*Je voudrais que vous lui fassiez un costume Hugo Boss,*" Alex commands. I'm shocked to hear her French sounding so good. Must have to do with the luxury goods we are surrounded by. "The pants should have a slim fit." The sales guy, a young, effeminate dandy, leads me over to the fitting rooms and prods me onto the tailor's platform.

"A *very* slim fit," Alex intones suggestively with a wink as the sales guy starts taking my inseam.

"*Je m'appelle Matthieu*," the guy says, his voice high and shrill. "This suit will flatter you very well."

Prancing around like a recently birthed foal, Matthieu gets my measurements and writes them down. "*Très, très, très beau*," he coos at me, tiny droplets splattering from his lisp. "Hehe," he snickers as he gets closer and closer to my crotch. "*Vous etes nerveux?* Don't be!"

A lump rises in my throat.

"Alex?" I call out toward the sales floor. "Alex, can you hear me?"

Matthieu finds this absolutely hysterical. "*Alex?*" he mimicks me. "*Où est Alex?*"

Just as Alex reappears in the doorway to the men's fitting rooms, Matthieu deftly slides his hand between my legs and gives my nuts a quick tweak.

"Alex, help!" I shriek, buckling over. Matthieu has never seen anything so funny in his life. He slaps his knee and holds his stomach, shrieking in that horrible, high-pitch girlish laugh.

I grab our bags and hightail it back to outerwear.

"What was that?" she hisses in amused confusion. "You could've gotten to at least second base with that guy—right here, right now. He's been watching you the whole time we've been here! I thought you wanted some action in Paris—I thought you wanted to catch up to your friend in Amsterdam."

"Alex," I say, trying to keep the frustration out of my voice. "I am not interested in meeting people that way. Thank you for your . . . *concern*, but that's not what I had in mind when we decided to get Parisian boyfriends!"

As usual, she's not listening. She leaps forward toward a rack she hasn't seen yet, letting the coats hanging from it engulf her. "Zack . . . oh my

God . . . I think I found it," she moans from within the pile of fabric.

Alex has *definitely* found the perfect winter coat. It's a divine Dior berry-red wool coat with big, round black buttons. Almost retro-looking, the top is fitted, with a round collar, and a tied belt around the waist. The bottom opens into several pleats, emphasizing her curves and making her look like a bright red hourglass. The effect is a mix of quirky, trendy, and good taste—in other words, it is pure Alex.

"How much is it?" I demand to know, truly curious. Alex routinely spends more at the Galeries Lafayette than I did on the down payment for my truck last fall when I turned sixteen.

I stare at the coat, waiting for Alex to answer. I'm also suddenly overcome by thoughts having nothing to do with the Dior coat. Something about Matthieu, the way my gut heaved when he touched me, made me think of what it would be like if Jay had seen that. My mind ran to Jay instinctively, to his shorn hair and sheepish smile. I could see him making a face like, "Matthieu was crazy. What can you do about it? *C'est la vie.*" That's just what Jay's like—so easygoing and sure of himself.

I open my mouth, slowly feeling myself about to say what I've just realized. "Alex . . ."

She mistakes me for trying to talk her out of the coat. "I can't tell you how much this coat costs. But I have to have it." A saleswoman comes over and asks Alex if she'd like to take the coat.

"*Oui,*" Alex says, cradling the red wool crepe in her arms lovingly. "*Je le voudrais. C'est parfait.*"

The saleswoman leads Alex to the cash register. Alex aimlessly slips on a Swarovski crystal bangle bracelet, admiring it for a moment as she waits to sign her credit card slip.

Suddenly Alex looks over at me, still wandering around in the coats. There is panic and also anger in her eyes.

"Get over here," she says loudly. "I need you. This woman is babbling too fast for me."

The saleswoman addresses me calmly. "*Parlez-vous français?*" she asks me.

"*Oui,*" I say. "What's wrong?"

"Her card was denied," the woman says in French. "Does she have another card?"

"Do you have another card?" I ask Alex. "That one isn't working for some reason."

Alex is enraged. "No, I don't have another card!" she yells at me. She folds her arms over her chest and blows her side-swept black bangs out of her eyes. "That one does work, you idiot! We just used it all over the store, remember?"

"Hmm," I say, recognizing the signs that Alex is on the verge of a meltdown. This is something that must be avoided no matter what. For the good of everyone, everywhere. "Sometimes the bank will put a hold on a card if you spend too much in one day—they might think someone stole it and went on a shopping spree. You should put the coat on hold and come back after you clear it up with your bank. Sound good?"

Alex shoves her hands in her pockets. "Fine," she says shortly. "Let's just go." Apparently she's no longer interested in a hot chocolate.

The salesgirl gives us a forced, polite smile and wraps the coat in tissue paper to put it in the on-hold shelf. "*Au revoir,*" she calls after us, ever mindful of her manners. The French always are.

Back on the Boulevard Hausmann, under the twinkling lights of the storefront window displays, Alex dangles her wrist in front of me with a sharp peal of laughter. "Look!"

"Alex!" I burst out. "Are you kidding? Did you *steal* that?" The bracelet doesn't even look like something Alex would normally wear. It's shiny and cheap-looking, like something a freshman cheerleader would wear with her Macy's ball gown to the Winter Formal.

"From right under the salesgirl's nose!" Alex giggles. "Serves her right. I mean, what an embarrassing inconvenience she caused just now! She's too much of a ditz to figure out how the credit card machine works—when I can barely wait another *minute* to get my new coat. When I go back for it, I seriously hope her supervisor is there so I can get her fired." Alex stares ahead, her pretty face drawn hotly into a fierce scowl.

This was the same way she was talking about George earlier this afternoon—intensely, a little crazily.

"Hey," I say, pointing. "Your coat's in the Christmas display." We hadn't seen it on our way in, but the mannequin in the window is wearing the red Dior coat with a pair of sparkly silver ice skates. The back of the display is wallpapered in old-timey black- and-white photos of couples—shadowy silhouettes of men and women kissing, holding hands, dancing in the Paris streets.

There's not a single photo of two men or two women. All the romance, all the luxurious happiness, is saved for hetero couples.

Alex clasps her hands in front of her, like a little girl in fervent prayer. "I want that so much," she whispers.

"Me, too," I whisper back, though I can't say for sure what is it that we each want, nor do I have any idea how long it might take to get it.

As the first snowflakes of winter fall onto the darkening Paris streets,

Alex whimpers and pulls her thin jacket around her. It's just a tiny flurry, but I pull her toward me, as if she was my girlfriend like in all those old photos in the display, and hold her protectively close as we walk to the metro station near the Opera, with all its lights blazing in the hazy night.

13. ALEX

Chasing Fate Through the Champs de Mars

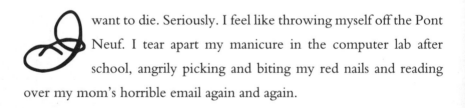 want to die. Seriously. I feel like throwing myself off the Pont Neuf. I tear apart my manicure in the computer lab after school, angrily picking and biting my red nails and reading over my mom's horrible email again and again.

TO: Nguyen, Alexandra
FROM: Braun, Caroline

Dear Alex,

Imagine my shock when American Express called me to report that the card had been stolen. Imagine my humiliation when I told them that no, the charges were not accrued by some petty thief on a retail binge but rather my teenage daughter, let loose on the Boulevard Hausmann, the Rue de Rivoli, and of, course, the avenue Montaigne. Are the other 16-year-olds on your program doing as much damage at Colette as you are? I have a feeling they aren't. How could they be? There's probably nothing left to buy after you are through picking the racks.

I've closed the account until you can prove yourself to be a more responsible spender. As for your meager checking account, which to my surprise has been almost drained since you arrived in Paris, I won't cut off your access to that. Really Alex! How dare you run through your money for the entire year so quickly?

I'm extremely disappointed in you. I had really expected better.

CAB

Is she deranged? I don't understand. My mom has *been* to Paris. She has *lived* here. How can she be so obtuse as to not comprehend the basic bottom line for a life in Paris?

I only went to Colette once! And that was because *she* told me about it. And I didn't even get all the things I wanted. Just the most necessary stuff, the two-tone Repetto ballet flats and this little necklace in the shape of a skull that I wanted for *Toussaint*, the French holiday the day after Halloween. Zack and I had spent the day roaming the *Cemetière Père-Lachaise* and spooking each other from behind the graves. It was important that I be nicely accessorized for the occasion.

Really, Alex! I mimic her in my head as I recall her email for the hundredth time since I read it. Since when does she of all people care about overspending? That's how it works—my absent father sends a ridiculously large child support check to my mom, which my mom hands over to her accountant to pay my bills. That is how it has always been. I get no father and no home life to speak of; instead I get a huge wardrobe and all the cosmetic treatments I want. I was always perfectly happy with this arrangement, and now suddenly my mom wants to reassert some authority into my life this late in the game?

And the way she signs her emails with her initials, "CAB," as if I'm a distant acquaintance as opposed to her only daughter! It used to make me laugh when I was little, that my mom was a cab, a yellow taxi we took home from Bloomingdale's after a long day of shopping. Caroline Anne Braun, who never changed her name to Nguyen when she got married, so she never had to change it back when her husband left her.

Zack always refers to my mom in hyper-deferential tones—he calls her *the Countess, the Queen, your lady mother,* always while using his most effeminate fake British accent. I wonder what he'd think of the grand dame cutting off my livelihood. I imagine him taking my face in his hands in mock sympathy.

"Darling!" he'd cry, and everyone would hear. "Whatever will we do? How can we possibly keep up with the Joneses without the black Amex?"

I roll my eyes at this possible state of affairs. That's never going to happen because I'm going to keep the whole thing on the down low until it works itself out.

This is *so* my mom. Volatile personality, extreme changes in temperament. All the reasons my dad left her, probably. I just need to wait it out and hold my tongue.

Swallowing my pride, I punch a reply into my BlackBerry.

SO SRY 4 INCONVENIENCE W/ AMEX. LET'S DISCUSS WHEN U COME 2 FRANCE 4 FASHION WEEK. ILU, AGN

. . .

It makes my blood boil to think that if the American Express fascists had waited just *ten* minutes for me to find the Dior coat before freezing my account . . . then right now, I'd be wearing it as I dash down the Rue du Faubourg-St. Honoré toward the Chloé store. I'd be *warm*. Instead I'm wearing a sweatshirt that belongs to my host-brother, who's eight, layered under my Marc Jacobs jacket. I pray to God I don't run into anyone.

I'm not exactly shopping right now. I'm capitalizing on previous gains.

This afternoon, I left Zack in the computer lab and went straight home to mope on my bed while listening to the mix Jeremy made for me. On it is my favorite moping song, "Just Like Jesse James," by Cher. Jeremy put it on there to be funny, but Cher's bombastics suit my mood more often than you might realize.

With my oversize Bose headphones on, I didn't hear my BlackBerry go off—it was only when I got up to hunt through the piles of crap strewn all over my room for my cigarettes that I saw the red light flashing that I had a new text message.

I could have done a back flip when I saw that the text was from my George!

Let's hang out, the text read—simple enough. Locating my cigarettes on top of my bookshelf, I lit one with one hand while simultaneously texting George back with the other.

Sure, I thumbed into my BlackBerry. Champs de Mars, 5pm?

SWEET, was the response five minutes later as I frantically tore apart my closet in search of something cute enough—and warm enough—to wear outdoors now that I've suggested Champs de Mars. The park is just a few minutes from my apartment—a perfect meeting point that should give me plenty of time to get ready.

Regarding my closet, I realize there's obviously nothing in here at all suitable for my first real date with George.

In the back of my closet is a pair of black stacked heeled Chloé boots with adorable snap detailing on the back of the ankle. Trouble is, they only had my size in black—and now whenever I put them on, all that flashes through my head is *Aldo's*. Don't ask me how my eight-hundred-dollar boots somehow remind me of the dreaded mall chain store, beloved by suburbanites and Texan twins everywhere, but there you go.

I sucked on my cigarette and thought quickly. *If I can get to Chloé by four, return the boots for store credit, select a new dress to wear by 4:30, change into it in their dressing rooms, and grab one of those sidewalk vendor pashminas to wear over the dress and my jacket, I can be sexily perched onto a carousel horse in the middle of the Champs de Mars by 5:05, when George will surely wander up late, as all boys tend to do.*

Digging under my bed (where I always put my receipts in a box for emergencies like this—my mom taught me to never, *never* throw your receipts away), I found little eight-year-old Sebastièn's brown sweatshirt. How did *that* get here? Stained, but possibly cute in a boho-chic layering way that might come in handy in this suddenly frigid late fall weather. I grabbed it, shout a flustered goodbye to my host mother, and run toward the Cambronne metro stop. *Please please please let Chloé take these stupid made-in-China boots back!*

To save time at the register, I select the dress I want in exchange for the boots before I attempt to return them. It's a black wool shift, cut loose around the body, with a tie around the neck and a very short skirt. I grab a pair of cream-colored, lacy wool tights to go with it, then make a beeline for the cash desk so I can get the hell out of here—I wasted too much time trying to decide between the black dress or the brown one . . .

With a hard smack against my right cheek, I find myself running face first into Sara-Louise, standing there in the middle of Chloé like she shops there every day. She's with Mary, the tattooed, punky girl from L.A. with the short, choppy black hair, and Sara-Louise's host-sister, Anouk, whom I met at their party.

"Well, hi there, Alex!" Sara-Louise greets me cheerfully, her South Carolina drawl filling up the otherwise hushed boutique. Mary smiles at me politely, and the host-sister looks me up and down, somewhat suspiciously.

"What are you guys doing here?" I demand, taken entirely off guard. "You don't shop here!"

Mary snorts. I didn't *mean* to sound so snotty.

Sara-Louise looks toward her host-sister. "Anouk is applying to fashion schools for college next year. We came here to get some inspiration for her portfolio. What are you getting?" Sara-Louise delves into the big bag I'm carrying with the boots in it. "Aren't those the boots you wore to school last week?" she asks. "Are you returning them? For this dress?" She holds out the dress to get a better look. "Oh, but Alex, these would be so cute together. Don't return the boots—just get the dress and wear them as an outfit!"

Mary and Anouk nod their agreement.

"Shhhh!" I look anxiously toward the salesgirl, who's starting to have a line form in front of her. "No!" I say, pulling away from them suddenly. "I have to return these boots. I don't need any more pairs of boots." I stick out my leg to show them the French Connection riding boots I'm wearing. "See?"

Luckily the salesgirl is too busy to put up a fight about the already-worn boots. She throws me for a loop when she says something in French I don't catch. Too afraid to find out what it was by asking her to repeat herself, and definitely not about to admit that I didn't understand, I just smile and nod. Whatever it was, she does the transaction quickly and ushers me into a fitting room, as I am already wriggling out of my jeans to get the dress over the sheer grey C+C California long sleeve tee and into the tights and pull my boots back on. Sebastièn's sweatshirt, worn unzipped over the dress, makes me look delightfully disheveled, like an Abercrombie model. My mom would call this "high-low," the fashionista term for the way French women wear couture with clothes from the discount rack. It's such a hard thing to master.

At exactly 5:03 P.M., I pop out of the cab I've hired to buy me some time (thus spending the twenty euros I needed to fund my cigarette and coffee habit for the rest of the week) and race into the Champs de Mars, the Eiffel Tower looming overhead.

The carousel is deeper into the gardens that run between the *Tour Eiffel* and the *Ecole Militaire* than I remember. As I run along the sandy paths that outline the eighteenth-century style grounds, I swallow hard, recalling times I had come here as a small child, small enough that I even think I was once here with my dad, whom I always pretend that I have no memory of at all. The Carousel of all places . . . *why* did I choose the Carousel for a rendezvous with George? I haven't been here since I was a pigtailed, bilingual toddler in a pink Sunday dress surrounded by admiring French grandparents, aunts, uncles. The Carousel makes me feel the opposite of flirtatious, the opposite of outgoing. It makes me feel like a shy little girl again.

"Alex," I hear George's deep, measured voice from a shadowy bench near the Carousel. "You're late."

I flip around.

"Hey," I say, biting my lip. I had wanted him to see me in a different way—less frazzled, less harried.

George pats the bench next to him. In the fading evening light, I can see he's wrapped up in a navy-blue hooded wool toggle coat and a grey beanie with a brim over his dark eyes. His expertly tied ribbed scarf makes him look almost French.

He's hopelessly handsome. I almost can't sit down next to him for fear of ruining this perfect moment of him wanting me. I gingerly take a step forward, examining him examining me.

"I'm not gonna bite you," George pledges. "Well, I won't bite *hard*."

I stand in front of him, still tense.

"You promise?" I ask. "I'm not coming any closer till you promise."

"Get over here," George cajoles me.

"Do it," I say. "Promise you're not going to hurt me." I'm teasing him, but it comes out weird. What I said, the way I said it, lingers between us.

All of a sudden, George jumps up and tackles me, throwing me over his shoulder. I yelp joyfully and pummel his back upside down with my fists. "Put me down!" I howl.

He twirls me around. "Tell me you're sorry for being late!" he taunts me. "You kept me waiting for so very long." He lets me slowly slide down off his shoulder so that we're standing upright face to face, still wrapped in each other's arms. "I missed you," he says when our eyes are finally at the same level.

His arms still around me, we sit back down on the bench. I nestle my head into the crook of his shoulder. "However did you pass the time while you were waiting for me?"

"I did some deep thinking," George deadpans. "Thought about the meaning of life."

"What'd you come up with?" I can't resist that clean, soapy smell of the back of his neck.

"Sex," George murmurs into my hair. "It's the only thing that makes sense in this messed-up world." George slips his icy bare hand up my skirt and lingers on my upper thigh.

I'd just been closing my eyes, letting the events of this afternoon slip away, feeling my body melt into George's, loving just sitting next to him. But George must have had other things in mind. I gaze up at him. His brown eyes meet mine, twinkling with warmth and good humor and sex appeal.

God, he *kills* me!

Looking around us for onlookers and finding no one at all interested in us, I slide up onto George's lap, his two hands firmly placed on my hips. I kiss him with the full force of my passion for him. I'm trying to tell him so many things without words—to be nice to me, that I know he likes me best of everyone, that I want to make love to him over and over again, but never while drunk in some stranger's bedroom.

The Champs de Mars starts closing down around us—the Carousel turns off its creepy circus music, the darkness sweeps over the park toward the glittering *Tour Eiffel*.

Nibbling my lips, George gets it. Doesn't he? He's promising to be everything I want him to be. Lightly rubbing his finger over my tights and underwear, he's moaning a little bit, wanting me as much as I want him. I feel like we are in our own little world.

A bright flashlight in my eyes stuns me into remembering that it is *not* just him and me right now—a park official stands over us, shouting at us suddenly to scram.

"*Soyez prudents!*" he says, spraying us with a shower of his disgusted saliva.

I scream out in fear, then explode into giggles when George starts laughing beneath me. Lifting me off his lap, we run together toward the gates of the park, propelled faster by our breathless laughter.

14. PJ

Everybody Needs Somebody

"We trust you, Penelope," Mme Marquet says as she hands me the house keys Friday morning before I leave for the Lycée. It's almost as if she *knows* I'm about to have a party this weekend. After these past few weeks of not being able to figure out a way to get out of it with Zack and Alex—not to mention all the people they've invited. *A small get-together,* I correct myself, hoping the distinction will matter to her if I ever get caught—*though I will never, ever get caught. Fate could never be that cruel to me.*

All day on Friday, I obsess about all the ways the Marquets could find out about the party. During PE, I'm so wound up, I run around the track again and again, trying to clear my head and calm myself down.

Olivia calls me before she goes to bed Friday night, checking on me like she often does. "You'll never guess what I did this afternoon."

"What?"

"I went to dance class!" she whispers. "Mme Rouille was pissed."

"Olivia!" I scold her. "You shouldn't be dancing on your ankle."

"I know," she says, sounding guilty. "It's actually killing me right now. My mom would freak if she found out. She doesn't even know I hurt myself. I made Vince promise not to tell her."

I laugh. "I can't believe I'm having a party tomorrow night. Can I cancel it?"

"No!" Olivia protests. "You cannot. It's impossible. Everyone would just show up regardless."

I hardly sleep. I'm stuck. This party is going to happen, no matter what I do.

"It's after ten, Penelope," Mme Cuchon scolds me in front of the glass pyramid entrance to the Louvre the next morning. "You were told to be here at 9:30."

"Yeah, so sorry," I tell her, out of breath from running all the way from Les Halles metro station. I look over at Olivia, perfectly punctual as always.

"RER," I mouth to her. In an attempt to cut my trip to a reasonable amount of travel time this morning, I'd paid extra for the RER regional train from Etoile station, right near the Arc de Triomphe. What I hadn't realized is some of those trains come only once or twice an hour on weekends. I'd waited in the drafty train shaft, kicking myself for nearly forty minutes. I'm a stressed-out, sleep-deprived wreck.

"*Alors*," Mme Cuchon continues. "Now that Penelope has joined us, let's begin our tour of the famous Musée du Louvre."

Mme Cuchon's second in command at the Lycée is Mlle Vailland, who does double-duty as our extremely enthusiastic teacher of French and European history. Mlle Vailland raises a red flag bearing the Lycée's logo into the air above her head.

"Follow me!" she cries.

We trudge along behind her. Jay catches up with me.

"Hey, partner. Before you got here," he tells me, "Mlle Vailland said that she'd take us to see the famous stuff before we work on our projects."

"Oh," I say. "Cool."

"You excited about the party tonight?" he asks.

I undo the elastic holding back my ponytail and shake out my hair. "Not sure," I say. "That's weird, right?"

Jay chuckles. "No way. Parties are high stress situations for the host. But I'm sure it will be great. I, for one, plan on having an excellent time. Just don't let me miss the last metro home—I don't live in your neighborhood."

The Paris metro stops running at midnight. Does Jay really think people are still going to be at my apartment that late?

"Look," Jay says. He nods at the crowd gathered in front of a painting. It's the *Mona Lisa*. Velvet rope barricades keep the tourists at bay. The room is already full of people snapping photos of probably the most famous painting on the planet.

"Oh, my God!" I exclaim. "She's miniscule!" I stare at her stealthy little smile, wondering what her secret was, anyway.

"Come on," Jay says, heading for the front of the crowd. "Let's take photos of all these crazy people."

Jay has a beat-up old digital camera. He snaps some close-ups of the tourists gawking at the *Mona Lisa*, their mouths agape, their kids looking bored and sleepy next to them. He does a slide show for me as Mlle Vailland lectures us about da Vinci. The pictures are hilarious. He even caught some kid picking his nose and wiping it on his little sister's jacket. I can't stop cracking up. It gets so bad that all Jay has to do is make a funny face and I know exactly which picture he's impersonating.

Mme Cuchon glares at us, which just makes us laugh harder.

Finally, after standing on my tiptoes to try and get a good look at the famous works Mlle Vailland is telling us about, the *Venus di Milo* and the *Winged Victory of Samothrace* sculptures, Mme Cuchon lets us disperse to work on our projects.

The info desk in the lobby directs us to the third floor to see the bulk of the Ingres paintings on view. Through the maze of the galleries, Jay takes me by the hand. I raise my eyebrows, but don't let go.

There's a whole room of Ingres. The walls of this gallery are painted pastel green. Skylights illuminate the portraits with natural light, making the colors appear almost iridescent. I don't know if it's the bright light of the room, but suddenly I feel faint, like I need to put my head between my knees.

"PJ!" Jay says, steadying me and helping me to a wooden viewing bench in the middle of the gallery. "Are you okay?"

I'm quiet for a long time. "This is the Louvre, huh?"

"Um," Jay says, his brow furrowed in alarm. "I better go find Mme Cuchon."

"No, don't," I say. "Just . . . let's sit here for a minute. Look at the paintings."

"Okay." Jay reaches over and unwraps the scarf from around my neck. "Aren't you hot? No wonder you were about to pass out."

"We're really here," I say, folding my scarf and placing it in my lap. "This is the Louvre. I can't believe I'm really here in Paris. For real. I'm surrounded by paintings that Ingres painted, that da Vinci painted. There are Rembrandts in the same building as me right now. I sort of never thought I would actually get here."

Jay nods. "I know what you mean. It feels fake, right?"

"Yes," I say. Standing up again, I'm less wobbly on my feet. I walk over to one of Ingres's nudes, *Le Grande Odalisque*. The peachy expanse of the model's back curves just so, bending enough to reveal the side of her breast without making the portrait feel voyeuristic. "She's exquisite. Portraits are my favorite. I love studying the expressions on the faces of the subjects, the way the models hold themselves."

"You ready to get to work?" Jay says. I pull my composition book out of my backpack.

"Definitely," I say. Side by side, we sit for hours on the bench, writing down everything we can think of to say about Ingres. I fill half my composition book.

As a safeguard against any unforeseen disasters, I try to party-proof the apartment when I get home from the Louvre. This turns out to be no easy task, what with the Marquets' collection of hugely expensive housewares and *objets d'arts*. I should cancel the whole thing. But I can't back out and risk everyone's suspicion. Alex and Zack will be so mad at me. I don't want to lose our budding friendship.

As I'm debating whether to lock the china cabinets or just empty them and put all the dishes under my bed for safekeeping, the doorbell rings.

"Zack! You're early." I usher him into the apartment. "Where's your better half?"

"Oh, you mean Alex?" Zack says as he gapes at the Marquets' opulent apartment. "Alex is still at her house getting ready. I needed a little breather from her so I thought I would see if you needed help setting up." He whistles. "This place is sensational. I had no idea. Though . . ." Zack marches into the living room and spins around.

"Can I make some changes?" he finally asks. "I mean, can we move some things around? Editorially, I'm just not loving the use of space here."

Editorially? "Sure," I agree.

Zack opens a beer and chugs it. "Beer really gets my creative juices flowing."

"Whatever works."

As Zack and I move the purple velvet French Empire sofa against the window, he also tells me that Jay might be a little late to the party.

"But he's definitely coming," Zack reassures me, though I wasn't worried to begin with. Honestly, one less guest would actually be a comfort to me right now.

"Oh, PJ," Zack says as he takes notice of the portrait over the fireplace. "I know the French aristocracy love their ancestors and all, but that man is just plain repugnant. Can we cover him for the party? Or better yet, move him to an undisclosed location?"

"Don't you dare touch that portrait, Zack," I say warningly. Mme Marquet treats that portrait like a lost relic from Noah's Ark, regarding it with almost religious reverence. She even cleans it herself for fear of Sonia damaging it. "Whatever you do, stay away from the portrait."

"Fine, fine, the old geezer can stay," Zack says, backing away from the fireplace. I notice he's already on his second beer. "So what do you think of Jay? I'm just wondering."

"Jay?" I say. "We're partners for the Louvre project, but otherwise I don't really know him. Seems nice though." I turn away from the framed photos I'm storing in the bureau to look at him. "Why do you ask?"

Zack blushes, looking guilty. "No reason," he says quickly, but he can't hide a small smile. "I'm going to check over the kitchen really quickly."

Did Zack see Jay take my hand at the Louvre today? Could he and Alex have been in the gallery when I almost fainted and Jay took off my scarf for me?

Aside from having moved all the furniture in the living room around "to create a better flow" (Zack's words, not mine), Zack's presence here is a little odd. Since when does he need a "breather" from the magnificent Alex anyways? Likely story.

Is it possible that Zack's trying to set me up with Jay? I think as I hear the doorbell ring. The chimes sound ominous to me. Here we go.

"PJ! You have more guests!" Zack shouts from the foyer, pushing Olivia toward me, surrounded by a group of older kids I've never seen before.

"Livvy!" It's not like Olivia to bring guests without asking me, especially when I just talked to her on the phone about the party last night. She leans in to hug me hello with an apologetic grimace.

"Thomas is my host brother," she explains, gesturing toward a tall, thin guy in a corduroy blazer. "These are his friends, fellow students at the Sorbonne. Sorry I didn't tell you about them before! I hope you don't mind."

Each of the friends grabs me for a *bise*—the familiar French kisses on the cheek—without really registering my name. Olivia giggles. "We had a few drinks before we came over."

"You did?" I ask, a little surprised. Olivia's such a health nut she usually steers clear of booze. Tonight, however, she opens a beer before even taking off her jacket.

"Well, just one. I've been so antsy sitting at my house, waiting for my ankle to heal," she complains. "Right, Thomas?"

"*Oui, oui,* mademoiselle," Thomas jokes. "The doctor prescribed *kir royales.* So that is what the mademoiselle shall have!"

Olivia finds Thomas's wit truly exceptional. "Thomas is a medical student. Get it?"

"Uh-huh," I say.

"Hey," Olivia leans over to me and whispers. "Before I forget. My host mom was talking about your host parents today! With some friends that she had over for tea."

"Oh, really?" I say, going a little pallid at the mention of the Marquets.

"All the ladies think M. Marquet is just the most handsome," she laughs. "You should have heard them all going on about him today."

I wrinkle my nose. M. Marquet is an old man, over fifty. "Anyway," she goes on, "he was this legendary bachelor until Mme Marquet snagged him a few years back. There's a rumor that by the time she married him, he'd practically gambled away the entire family fortune in Monte Carlo! But now that he's the magistrate of the Dordogne, she keeps him on the straight and narrow."

This is odd, talking to Olivia about the Marquets like this. I feel paranoid that they might be listening somehow. "That's just chitchat," I say. "The Marquets are loaded. Can't you tell?" I gesture to the affluence surrounding us.

Olivia looks embarrassed, like she didn't mean to gossip but couldn't help herself. "I'm sure," she says. "They're being nice to you, right?"

I nod. "Of course. I'm gonna go check on the other people who just came in." I leave her with her older friends, not sure how to process what she just told me. Are the Marquets really hurting for money? It makes the train ticket they bought for me that much sweeter.

Zack's already ushering in more guests, acting as the de facto host, offering drinks and showing people how to get to the balcony to smoke.

Placing a beer into my hand, Zack drunkenly gives me a *bise* himself. "PJ! Lighten up, my dear," he slobbers into my ear. "I think Jay will be here soon."

I swig my beer without answering him, registering with discomfort that the party has grown in mere minutes from a small get-together to a raucous house party complete with a game of beer pong being set up on the antique cherry wood refectory table in the dining room. "No!" I dash over to stop them, imagining long, crusty beer stains eating through the three-hundred-year-old varnish, but I'm intercepted by Alex, who's decked out in a brown satin jumpsuit with her red stilettos. The collared halter top stretches low to reveal ample cleavage and the barest hint of a brown lace bra.

"Great party, doll," she compliments me. "It's like Bungalow 8 in here. I'm so proud of you. Our little girl is growing up so fast!" She pinches my cheeks. "Is George here yet?"

"Haven't seen him."

"Oh, too bad. I wonder where he is?" Alex ducks as Zack tosses her a beer from where he's standing near the fridge, talking to Sara-Louise. Luckily, she catches it before it crashes to the floor. "Anyway—I told you the party would be fine. What were you so worried about? This from the girl who got the cops off our tail in Le Marais that night. You're a pro, PJ. I'd think this would be baby stuff for you," Alex tells me as she attempts to pop off the top of the beer with a lighter.

"Give me that," I say, opening the beer with a bottle opener I have on my keychain in my pocket. The bottle opener says Harvard on it— Dave gave it to Annabel as a joke. Neither of them would ever get into Harvard if they tried. They are both high school dropouts. Along with *Madame Bovary*, I took the keychain with me in my backpack to Paris.

I think about what Alex said while we stand there, drinking beer and surveying the crowd. At the time, Alex looked so pissed about what I said to get the cops to go away. She'd never thanked me for saving her ass. I guess I'm a little bit pleased that she really does realize she'd have been toast if not for me.

"Did you not have time to change?" Alex asks me, looking down at my jeans and cardigan, the same thing I wore to the Louvre today.

Never mind. Alex has not changed a bit since her first bitchy days at the Lycée. She wanders off to find Zack again.

Pretty soon, the Marquets' apartment is packed with people, most of whom I've never seen before. George and Drew are here, tucked into a game of Kings with Patty and Tina in the dining room. I guess Alex will stumble upon them soon enough.

I go to the guest bathroom off the foyer to collect my thoughts. I splash cold water on my face, soaking the front of my white T-shirt. I never wear makeup. Tonight, I wish I had some. My eyes are sunken and hollow. I realize I didn't have anything to eat all day. You can see it in my face.

My mom always told me to inhale for three counts, then exhale for six counts, ten times. No matter what, you'll feel better, she always told me. I wonder if that tactic is making her feel any better right now. It's not really working all that well for me.

I step out of the bathroom, running into a long line of waiting partygoers. The girls glare at me for taking so long.

"It's *my* party," I bark at them. "It's *my* house. I can take as long as I want."

"Doctor's orders!" I hear Olivia's host-brother yell over the energetic pop-punk record one of his friends has spinning in the Marquet's ancient turntable. "I have to carry you everywhere you want to go!"

I go back into the living room and see Thomas, whose tweed jacket has been tossed aside, carrying Olivia on his back around the living room, piggyback style. The portrait above the mantle stares down at the party in extreme disapproval.

"Let's get more beer!" she cries with glee. "Take me to the fridge!"

"No, Olivia!" I shout as I see what's about to happen.

Olivia's outstretched, pointed foot whacks firmly into the oversized antique vase on the end table Zack and I just moved across the room for safety's sake, pushing it off its stand and shattering it all over the marble floor.

"Oh, no she didn't. That wasn't a *Ming* vase, was it?" Alex says in horror, for once her face registering a stricken look appropriate to the situation. "Oh, God, PJ."

Thomas and Olivia tumble to the floor, wasted and barely coherent. "Olivia!" I yell. "Look what you did!"

"Oh, Peej," Olivia mumbles sloppily. "I'm so sorry . . . I made Thomas carry me because my ankle was hurting so bad . . . . Didn't you carry me, Thomas?" She giggles, pulling herself onto her knees and crawling over to Thomas in hysterics. He reaches out for her and pulls her on top of him.

What happened to Vince? I wonder briefly as I gather the pieces of the vase into a paper bag and take them into the kitchen.

Jay must have arrived sometime in all the madness. He follows me into the kitchen, obviously concerned.

"I can't talk right now," I say, without meeting his eyes. "Olivia and some college guy just broke this vase. Alex thinks it was super expensive."

"No, I know," he says. "I just thought that I could help you clean up. . . ."

"I'm so stupid," I say bitterly, spreading out the larger pieces of the broken vase onto the kitchen table. "I thought I might be able to put the vase back together, but this is hopeless. I've always hated putting puzzles together."

"I like puzzles okay," Jay comments, surveying the pieces. "Some puzzles are more satisfying to figure out than others, though."

Jay takes the dustpan out of my hand and holds it for me so that I can sweep the smaller shards into the waste basket in the kitchen.

"Listen, PJ," Jay says kindly. "Just because you broke the vase doesn't mean you had a party. You could even—you could blame it on your maid. An apartment like this surely must have a housekeeper, am I right?"

"What?" I choke out. "Are you kidding? What kind of person do you think I am?"

Jay chuckles. Not for the first time, I notice what a nice smile he has. "My mom cleans houses. You should see the stuff she has to take the flack for. It sucks, but it's kind of part of the job description. Don't sweat this. I'm sure your host parents could afford another. No one would blame you if you were forced to tell a little white lie to save yourself."

Jay's right. The vase—Ming vase or not—was an accident. I would never blame it on Sonia, but the Marquets don't necessarily have to find out about the party. It's not like the Marquets ever have to know that Olivia was overcome by a sudden and out-of-character wild streak and knocked it over as she was being seduced by some older dude who's not her boyfriend. I could pretend I knocked it over trying to get a better look at it during a quiet weekend night at home.

No one would blame you if you were forced to tell a little white lie . . .

Tears pricking my eyes, I look at Jay. He's so sweet, so chill. I wonder if he does like me; if what Zack was hinting at was true. Will there ever be a point this year where I could get beyond all the things on my mind and explore whether or not I like him back?

I imagine him taking me on a date, maybe coming over here to work on the Louvre project instead of meeting at the library at the Lycée. In my mind we're walking down the Boulevard de Courcelles with the leaves on the trees turning orange and red and yellow; we're passing the Parc Monceau as the schoolkids in plaid uniforms climb all over the statues. I'd have my periwinkle hat on, the one that my mom knitted for me last winter from wool she'd shorn and spun herself. Jay would be wearing his North Face beanie, and we'd both be wearing our Converse sneakers. About the same height, with his dark coloring and my pale skin and hair, we'd make a cute couple. In my fantasy of us, I'd ask him questions about growing up in Guatemala before he moved to the U.S. in kindergarten, and I could tell him all about my parents, and Annabel, and how everything got so messed up. And he wouldn't scorn me, or want nothing to do with me.

I open my mouth and close it again. I can't do it.

"I have to go," I say, grabbing the paper bag holding the larger chunks of expensive pottery and opening the door to the terrace so that I can empty it into the larger dumpster out there, where I've been putting the beer bottles so they won't stink up the apartment.

"PJ, wait! What were you going to say?" Jay follows me out onto the terrace. "Whatever's going on under there, whatever made you so weak at the Louvre, you can tell me about it! I promise you, I will never judge you!"

The temptation to unload on someone is too great for me to ignore. I exhale slowly, searching his eyes for a sign that this is the right thing to do.

"Jay," I begin. "It's so hard for me to say this . . ."

"Wait, don't. Not yet," Jay says. "I think we have some company out here."

"Oh, God." I can't believe what I'm seeing.

15. OLIVIA

Some People Cheat, Some People Steal

*A*fter we fall onto the ground, I crawl over to Thomas. The short cap-sleeved black dress I got with Alex at H&M is riding dangerously short. I'm wearing opaque black ballet tights underneath it, which I suppose was a good act of foresight, considering Thomas has been picking me up and carrying me around like an invalid all night, making sure I don't hurt my ankle again. The other kids at the party seem surprised to meet Thomas, but I explain over and over again that he's *not* my boyfriend—he's my host mother's son. We *have* to spend time together—it's practically mandatory according to Mme Cuchon!

"*Viens ici,*" he grunts at me. "May we go onto the balcony for some time?"

I snort. I know I must be drunk because normally I would never laugh at someone's language abilities. It is just too comical listening to Thomas, the intellectual, the prized med student and the apple of my host mother's eye, bumble around his English.

"*Quoi?*" Thomas says, trying to look put out. "Are you making fun?"

"Thomas!" I affect astonishment. "I would never!"

"So can I take you to the balcony or no?" He pulls me up off the thick Persian carpet and hoists me onto his back for another piggyback ride.

"*Mais oui,*" I say. Thomas pushes open the French doors leading to the terrace. He adjusts a curled iron patio chair so that it faces the view of the Place de Ternes below, sets me carefully into it, then crouches on the stone floor in front of me.

I look down over the railing and spot a group of revelers, probably in their mid-twenties, raising glasses of champagne right there in the traffic circle. They had to celebrate so badly they couldn't even wait to get to a bar.

"That's what I love about Paris," I say. Cars honk as they drive past the group. "Everyone lives right here in the present. Not all stuck in the future."

Thomas listens quietly.

"I love how everyone just wants to party all the time!" I watch one of the men do a cartwheel for his friends, and the women he's with cheer and beg for an encore.

At least, that's how Paris feels to me. I've never felt like I had so much to celebrate before I got to Paris, even though I'm thousands of miles away from my family and my boyfriend, ballet is kicking my ass, I screwed up my ankle not once, but twice, and I live with a woman whose only compliments toward me have been behind my back. Yet Paris makes me feel light. It sweeps me off my feet. For no reason at all.

"Why did you come to Paris, Olivia?"

"You know," I say, hanging on to the railing and leaning backward. "To dance at the Opera!"

"There are ballet schools all over the world," Thomas says. "Why Paris? Why not Moscow? New York? Even Los Angeles?"

"Well," I say. "Do you really want to know?"

"I would not have asked if I did not want to know."

"I came to Paris because of Madame Brigitte," I say. "Mme Brigitte runs the ballet school I go to in the hills above San Diego. She's amazing— she's this teeny tiny woman who used to dance with the American Ballet Theatre in New York. She grew up in Paris, in a nightclub that her dad owned in the sixties. Everyone thought that she was too wild to be a professional ballet dancer, but she lit up the stage every time she danced. After she'd been dancing with the ABT for a long time, she scandalized everyone by running away to California with a movie soundtrack composer they'd hired to score a performance. They were so in love, and one day, during a rainstorm, his car was the first in an eighteen-car pileup on the 405 right near Long Beach. Mme Brigitte went to live in San Diego with the composer's father, who's like Stevie Wonder. He's blind but he plays the piano so beautifully you would never know. Mme Brigitte and her father-in-law used the money they inherited from the composer to set up a dance school."

I stop to take a breath, embarrassed by how much I've been talking.

"Is the academy prestigious?" Thomas asks me, sipping his red wine. The way he's leaning in toward me makes me all of a sudden feel like he really does find this the most fascinating thing he has ever heard.

"Oh, no," I laugh. "That's why I came here. My mom wanted me to switch to a more institutionalized program. She thought it would help me get a scholarship. I thought I wouldn't be able to bear it, leaving my family, learning ballet from someone new. But my mom really did think it would be the best thing for my future. I thought, *Well, if I can't be with Mme Brigitte, then I at least want to be in her city.*"

It dawns on me how much Paris has captivated me. Now, even though I sometimes ache to be with my family and Vince, I haven't for a long time doubted my decision to come here. My mom was right. This was the very best thing for my future, no matter how much it hurts to be away from California. I'm learning so much.

"Olivia," Thomas breathes. "*Tu es si belle ce soir.*" He rests his head in my lap like a little boy. His curly hair looks golden in the lantern light on the terrace. Once again, I'm struck by how young and innocent Thomas seems, while also so wise. For being so smart, so driven, so infatuated with school, Thomas is playful and joyous. He closes his eyes. His eyelashes are long and dark.

"You think?" I ask nervously.

"*Tu es toujours si belle,*" Thomas says softly. "You're ravishing."

His eyes still closed, I lean down toward his smooth face. Something pulls my lips toward the soft skin of his cheek, his forehead, the tip of his nose. With each soft, tiny kiss, Thomas makes a low, hungry noise in the back of his throat.

I'm almost to his mouth, stained purple from the cabernet he was sipping as he carried me around the living room. I open my lips the tiniest bit and exhale. Thomas shifts, lifts his head, straightens up, and suddenly I know he wants to kiss me. The moment of expectancy is so flawless I don't want it to end.

Finally. We kiss. He's on his knees, at the same height as me sitting in the patio chair, and we kiss and kiss and kiss. My fear of what's happening keeps the rest of my body stiff, removed from him, until I can't take that anymore either. Soon I can't keep my hands off him, clinging to his thin frame, running my fingertips through his silky hair and down the back of his neck.

We're not just goofing around any more.

"I shouldn't be here," I murmur, though I can't remember why not. Then I do. *Oh, Jesus, what I have I done?*

I pull away from Thomas.

I remember Vince and me lying side by side in his single bed in the UCLA dorms, promising to save ourselves for each other, for when I get back from Paris. We didn't just mean save ourselves for sex—we meant *everything.*

I recoil from Thomas. I can't look at him. Thomas takes my face in his hands.

"What's the matter? *Qu'est ce qui s'est passé?*" Tears of shame roll down my cheeks.

"Olivia!" I hear the creak of the sliding glass door to the Marquets' kitchen opening. PJ stands frozen in front of us. Jay is behind her, but when he sees me in Thomas's arms, his eyes widen and he goes back inside.

"Olivia," PJ repeats. "I—I'm sorry . . . What happened to Vince?"

"PJ!" I struggle for breath.

"Who's Vince?" Thomas asks, letting go of me. "*Qu'est ce que tu racontes?*"

I rush to PJ's side, shivering in my sleeveless dress. "Please don't tell anyone what you saw. Can you promise?"

PJ nods at me. "Yeah, sure." She can't look at Thomas.

"Who is Vince?" Thomas asks again, still confused, though growing more perturbed.

"*Vince est mon petit ami,*" I tell Thomas plainly, so ashamed of myself I could break down and sob. "In California. We've been dating for two years."

"Oh," Thomas says. "I better get my friends and go then. Thanks for telling me."

He rushes by me. I reach out to stop him, to explain better, but he shrugs me off.

It doesn't matter. I don't know how to explain it anyway. I've never lost myself like that before.

PJ puts down the dishpan. "Let's stay out here for a minute. Get our bearings."

We stand next to each other, looking over the balcony at the clear night.

"I can't believe I thought this party was going to fix everything," PJ says sadly. "What a disaster."

I nod in gloomy agreement. Down the street, we can see some of the partygoers headed home. From here I can make out the Texan twins, dressed in jeans and matching checkered pea coats and black berets. Following them closely behind are George and Drew, their loud snickers audible in the stark, moneyed calm of the seventeenth arrondissement.

"Rot in hell, you filthy beast! You animal! You prick!"

A vicious, bloody scream erupts from the balcony next to us—the balcony that leads to the Marquets' master bedroom. The kind of scream that can only come from a woman scorned, her anger lubricated by hard liquor.

Alex has burst forth from the empty bedroom, yelling ferocious, ugly epithets at George as he heads down the street, away from the party. You can barely understand her for her slurred, frenzied speech and the hoarse sobs bubbling in her throat. In one hand is a large, almost empty bottle of Maker's Mark whiskey, and in the other is, of course, a lit cigarette, which Alex is waving around like she's possessed.

The last time I saw Alex, she was sporting a slinky brown jumpsuit, but she's changed into something else. Her feet are bare, and hanging off her slight, curvy body is a silver sequined tank dress with a full chiffon skirt splayed out around her, the armholes of the bodice large enough that we can see her strapless lace bra beneath it. A long rope of pearls is wrapped around her neck, bouncing off her torso as she contorts with fury. "You preppy asshole! You loser! You monster!"

With a fresh venomous shriek, Alex hurls the Maker's bottle over the balcony, and it shatters cleanly onto the Place des Ternes below.

"Alex! There are people down there!" I screech. Sure enough, the group of friends I'd been watching are now all watching Alex and laughing their tails off.

When she grabs the crystal tumbler and hurls that over, too, PJ and I gather our wits all at once and scream for her to stop.

We race through the throngs of people still left in the Marquets' living room, who are starting to float out onto the terrace and the master bedroom to watch Alex's antics in glee.

"Leave her alone!" I yell as people heckle her. Alex is too out of it to understand she has an audience, and that George can't even hear her anymore. He's long gone by now.

PJ wrestles Alex back into the bedroom and onto the Marquets' king-size bed, pinning her down with her elbows and straddling over her convulsing body. I slam the doors to the balcony.

"He left with that bitch! With that slut!" Alex screeches. "With that nasty Texan dumpster . . . that trashy hose beast . . ."

Mascara runs rivets down Alex's splotchy face. I grab some tissues and wipe her runny nose, dab at her heavily lined eyes. It's useless. She's a mess.

"Tell Zack to clear the party," PJ orders. "We've got to get her out of here before she pukes. Let's call a cab and get her home."

"I'm not going home without him!" Alex screams.

"Oh, yes, you are, Alex, you are going home right now," PJ says, unpinning her off the bed shoving her into my arms. Pushing her through the last of the partygoers and out of the double front doors, we get her down the stairs, watching her heaves for signs of actual puke. One thing about Alex—she usually can hold her liquor down, for what it's worth.

PJ and I push Alex into a cab. I have to sit on her to get her to be still. PJ fingers the tufts of fabric coming out from beneath me.

"This belongs to Mme Marquet!" PJ wheezes unbelievingly. "Alex, how *could* you? Are you *trying* to get me in trouble? Do you really hate me that much?"

At her wit's end, PJ bursts into tears. "I can't believe you, Alex! You are so selfish . . . you're totally out of control. . . ." Her whole body shaking with fury, she can't go on.

"It's Alexander McQueen," Alex mumbles from behind me. "It's *mine* now."

I can see PJ resisting the urge to pull me off of Alex and slap Alex across her pretty, streaky face.

"I knew you were a bitch under all that fakery, Alex, I knew it!" PJ hisses. "Look at you, stealing a dress—"

"PJ," I beg her quietly, terrified this is going to break out in a catfight. The cab driver is obviously scared of the same outcome—he keeps looking back at me in the rearview mirror with a mix of terror and unbridled curiosity. "Just let her keep it for the night. She'll bring it back to you in the morning—she'll pay for express dry cleaning if she has to. Just let her be. Okay? Please, PJ?"

"Fine." PJ closes the cab door.

I move off of Alex's lap and hoist her up into a semi-upright position. "That's it, Alex, just go to sleep," I say soothingly, letting her rest her head against my shoulder.

"I just can't believe George cheated on me, ruined everything we had together," Alex hiccups, and starts to weep quietly. "Cheating is just so *wrong*. It ruins *lives*. It's ruined my life *twice*. . . ." I put my arms around her, stroking her tangled hair.

Alex is belligerent, but she's right. Thomas is a mistake. Cheating *is* so wrong.

I imagine Vince at an UCLA football game this afternoon, hanging out with his new friends, and then leaving the game plenty early to call me before I go to sleep. I think of Vince's face, his eyes I've stared into so many times.

I want to crawl out of my skin I'm so disgusted with myself.

16. ZACK

Enough is Enough

"**W**hat are you doing?" Alex growls into the phone far too early the morning after PJ's party. "Want to go to brunch? I need a drink."

"You sure about that?" I ask. "I distinctly remember you shutting down a certain Miss Penelope Jane's party after you had a few too many last night. People are going to be talking about last night until they have varicose veins and grey hair. I've got to hand it to you."

"Oh, be quiet. Hey guess what? I just found out that my mom isn't coming for fashion week. I just got a text from her."

"Oh, Alex," I say, my heart going out to her. I know she's been looking forward to CAB's impending descent on Paris the way teenage girls used to wait for the Beatles, frothing at the mouth. "Are you okay about it?"

"Of course I am! She's coming for Christmas now instead. She's going to spoil me out of my mind. So, Le Pain Quotidien?"

"You got it," I say, despite my hangover. I pop some Advil and take a long drink from the Nalgene tossed on the floor next to my pants from the night before. "I'll see you in a few."

My room used to be a maid's room when the apartment my host family lives in was built. I like it. The decoration is spare, with lightly striped wallpaper and a simple white quilt spread over the bed. The room is right off the kitchen, and this means that I can sneak from my room through the kitchen, the front hallway and out the door without ever having to go past the living room or the bedrooms—thus majorly cutting down on run-ins with the fam.

It's not that I don't like my host family. They're very sweet and all. But there isn't much to tell about them. It's just Romy and Jacques and their two children, Mireille, age ten, and Paul, age twelve, who seems to have an unhealthy codependent relationship with the family's elderly cat that's oddly named Kevin.

(After wondering about this for several weeks, I finally asked them where the hell they came up with the name. I found out that Romy was quite the *Home Alone* fan when she adopted the cat right after graduating University. See, I told you. My host family is so uninteresting I can barely bring myself to engage in routine conversations with them.)

I've worked out an arrangement with my host family where they allow me to avoid them as much as possible and in return, I clean their kitchen till it sparkles every night after dinner. Once in awhile I even wax the floor.

I meet Alex at Le Pain Quotidien in Le Marais. When I spot her across the crowded restaurant, I see that in spite of the escapades of the night before, Alex is as put together as ever. Considering how drunk she was the last time I saw her, I half expect her to still be swathed in the Alexander McQueen number she'd filched from Mme Marquet's boudoir, but she's dressed up hangover-chic in her *own* clothes, ensconced in her dark sunglasses while big gold hoops dangle glamorously from her ears. Her wavy hair is clipped back loosely into a tortoiseshell clip. The outfit, I see when she stands to kiss me hello, is a bell-sleeved black jersey tunic over black stirrup leggings. On her feet are the red stiletto pumps she loves so much. Basically, Alex looks like she stepped out of a movie about people far too dramatic and dishy to still be in high school.

Alex is impatient, neurotic and can be cruel, but she's absolute royalty and she knows it. Just look at her, scowling contemplatively across the restaurant. How could anyone resist her?

I giddily prepare for the best part of a really wild night out—the post-mortem. A good hangover always makes me feel like my youth is being well-spent. Even if I *am* a virgin with one foot still firmly stuck in the closet.

I lift the café au lait she has ordered for me, as if in a toast to last night's debauchery.

"Those pieces of Texan white trash," Alex launches in. "They are *the worst*. So unsophisticated."

"Those matching berets! I declare!" I crow.

"All of it—their outfits, their hair, their voices . . . it's all so middle-America," Alex rants. "No offense."

"None taken," I shrug. I might be from Memphis, but I know I don't look like it. At least I hope not. Guys from M-town don't wear cashmere scarves or skinny jeans like I do. They don't wear pointy-toed, distressed-calfskin topsiders they found at the Puces de St. Ouen flea market in Paris. They wear muscle tees, and cowboy hats, and other Godforsaken things.

"Give me a break," Alex says. "If George wants *that*, then God knows we were never meant to be."

"You said it, girl," I agree.

We order quiche Lorraine and a fruit and cheese plate. Alex gulps down her sour Bloody Mary between long, thoughtful drags on her cigarette. I'm famished, but Alex leaves her food untouched.

"Except," Alex says with a pained sigh, "I know that's not what he really wants."

"Don't worry," I console her. "We have the Lyon field trip coming up. You'll have a whole weekend to win George back. You can do it."

"I can, can't I?" Alex says, brightening.

If anyone can, it's Alex Nguyen.

Friday afternoon, I look up and down the aisle of the train nervously, then back at my watch. 1:59 and Jay is still not here. Our train to Lyon leaves promptly at 2:00pm. Where is he?

"Wait!" I hear someone shout, the voice echoing off the vaulted ceiling of the Gare de Lyon. The brakes underneath us shudder and lift, and ever so slightly, we're moving forward out of the station. "Hold the train!" the voice yells.

"Look, it's Jay!" Olivia squeals, pointing out the window next to her. Delighted, she waves as Jay sprints alongside us, a duffel bag bouncing from his shoulder.

The Lycée kids all jump out of their seats and gather around our window, watching to see if Jay will catch up and be able to jump on board. I unlatch the top of the window and push it down as far as it will go.

"You can do it, dude!" Drew yells out the opened crack, jostling Alex as he leans over her. Her face implanted in his armpit, she makes a retching noise.

"Drew, get off of me!" she says with loathing. "You smell like curry."

"It's true," George says, not to anyone in particular. "We did have Indian for lunch."

"He smells like he bathed in it," Alex sniffs. "Or like he just didn't bathe at all."

Drew ignores them both. "Hurry up, dude!"

The train is speeding up. The conductor, hardly pleased, stands in the opened doorway to the train. He realizes Jay isn't going to give up and moves aside so that Jay can jump up. Mme Cuchon looks like she might have a heart attack. The entire Programme Americain collectively holds its breath as we wait to see if he made it.

All of a sudden, the door to the train compartment swings violently open, and Jay's standing in front of us, dripping sweat and wearing a huge, triumphant smile.

We Americans erupt into wild applause. The Texan twins, cheerleaders since elementary school, actually do a chant that involves a lot of clapping and indecipherable lyrics.

Jay punches the air several times. "Go big or go home!" he shouts. "What *what*!"

"O. M. G." Alex sputters. "Did you see that?"

"That's going on my list of top ten Paris moments, for sure," Olivia says, reaching into her bag and pulling out the little notebook she's been carrying around lately, writing down all the things about Paris she loves.

Paris moments? That's going in my top ten *life* moments. I've never seen anyone do anything that cool, ever. Jay just went from class nobody to class hero.

Mme Cuchon recovers, but Jay's antics seem to have aged her about ten years. Their faces hard, she and Mlle Vailland stand up and scowl at us till we shut up.

When Jay makes his way down the aisle, accepting high-fives and congratulations for his killer entrance, Mme Cuchon tells him the seat next to me is the last one available in the block she reserved for the trip. I sit straight up in my chair, thanking my lucky stars.

Jay tosses his knapsack onto the baggage rack above my head. "Hey, man," he says, flopping down beside me. The sides of his face, right where his sideburns end, are still sweaty. So is his upper lip. Jay wipes his face with the sleeve of his Minnesota Vikings sweatshirt.

"Wow. Hey, man. That was pretty sweet. How's it going? Excited for the trip to Lyon? Should be fun, huh?" I ask Jay in a flurry.

Alex looks at me quizzically across the sticky table between us. On most school field trips she and I have adopted a strict no-enthusiasm policy unless, of course, they involve Jean-Luc Godard. Lyon is the second-largest city in France, and according to Mlle Vailland, just full of sublime treasures and apparently tragically underrated. It's about two hours southeast of Paris by high-speed train. But according to Alex, who's been there several times to visit some old friend of her mom's, this weekend field trip is not worth going gaga over.

And yet, the idea of sitting next to Jay all the way to Lyon? That's something I think is utterly worth getting excited about.

"Definitely," Jay says with a big smile. "I'm just glad I made it. Looked pretty dicey for a minute there."

"You're a really fast runner," I comment, and then cringe. Who am I, superfan???

"Ha! You should see me at soccer practice in our sprinting drills. You run, man?"

I make a face. "Only when I'm being chased."

Jay guffaws. "That's a good one. No, man, I'm amped to be getting out of Paris for the weekend. I've been looking forward to Lyon for a while now."

"You don't like Paris?"

"No, no," Jay laughs. "I do. Haven't I told you about my homestay?"

I shake my head.

"Oh, well, let's just say I live on the literal and figurative opposite end of the spectrum from most of the kids at the Lycée. Ever heard of Montreuil?"

I shake my head again.

Jay leans forward and pulls a Paris metro map out of his back pocket. He points to a stop called Porte de Montreuil, on the far eastern edge of the spidery web of Paris metro lines. With one finger he traces the lines he takes to get to the Lycée every day: three stops on the lime-green #9 line to Nation station, then switch to the cobalt blue #2 line, which makes a half ring around the northern side of the city, through Belleville and along the bottom edge of Montmartre, and over to Ternes and the Parc Monceau, home to the Lycée, as well as the ritzy homestays of PJ,

Olivia, George, Drew, and the Texan twins, among others.

"And Alex and I thought we had it rough!" I remark, tracing the lines of our route to show him. It seems long to take the #6 from Cambronne, then to switch to the #2 for a few stops, but in truth I cherish the commute Alex and I take every morning, sipping takeaway coffee from a little shop under the metro tracks, always exchanging a smile as we pass the Eiffel Tower on our right.

Jay's fingers brush mine as he folds the subway map back up. I inhale sharply, shifting in my seat. It's almost unbearable, sitting so close to him for so long. Could he have touched me like that on purpose?

"It's not as rough as I'm making it sound," Jay says with good humor. "Sammy lives out there too." Jay nods towards a kid I've never even talked to before, a guy I always assumed was too big of a nerd for me to associate myself with. "We've had some good times out there, playing video games in the arcade with some of the local kids."

"Oh, really?" Jay has French friends? Could he *be* any cooler? Alex and I are stuck in our little trifecta with Olivia, and that's only when she has time to hang out with us. Most of the time it's just Alex and me, bumming it and gabbing with each other in English about how much we want a boyfriend. No French kids ever talk to us. Why would they?

"Yeah, we've met some cool kids," Jay tells me. "The hood here ain't that different from the hood back in the States."

I have to hide how impressed I am. Jay's so self-assured. If I'd been given his homestay I'd have cried and called my mom to change it. I don't want to come off as unworldly and sheltered if I let on that I've never really known anyone like him—he probably had it a lot harder growing up than I ever did in Germantown, Tennessee. And if Jay is gay, too . . . imagine how hard it might be for him growing up bouncing from town to town with his parents as they search for work. Jay told us in a French oral report that his parents are from Guatemala, and they've lived all over—Texas, Chicago, Arizona, and now Minneapolis. He's had to start over a bunch of times in his life. Maybe that's why he's not out yet—he's never had anyone he could trust to be the first person he told.

"Sucks about PJ, huh?" Jay remarks.

"What about PJ?" I say blankly. I'm too distracted by Jay's handsome face to recall what he means.

"Oh! You mean how she got kicked off the trip?"

"Well, yeah," Jay says. "This is like the last hurrah before the Final Comp."

Jay's right. As soon as we get back, we'll just have two weeks to study for the test, finish the Louvre Project, and then go our separate ways for the holiday break.

"Totally sucks that she is going to miss out," I agree. I feel a tiny stab of remorse when I think about how Alex and I had pressured her into the party. But it wasn't like she didn't *want* to. If anything, she should thank us. After that party, she has way more friends than before.

It's so refreshing to be with someone like Jay after spending all term with Alex's unpredictable mood swings and Olivia's obsessive anxieties and hang-ups. "You should come and hang out sometime," he offers suddenly, looking at me with an open, friendly expression that's impossible to be anything but genuine interest in seeing me, being with me.

I look over to Alex, who's fallen asleep with her gigantic headphones on. Her discarded copy of *Paris Match* lies forgotten on the table between her and me—her French isn't good enough to get her through a whole issue. I pick it up, trying to look casual when I'm actually dizzy with pleasure at Jay's invitation.

"Sure," I answer as coolly as I can. "That sounds like a lot of fun."

Saturday morning, Mlle Vailland wakes us up early and marches us out to the chartered tour bus to see the sights of Lyon today.

The other guys—i.e. the hetero ones, i.e. all of them besides me and maybe, *maybe* Jay—constantly bemoan the paradox that is Mlle Vailland: She's blonde, stacked, and dresses like she's working a Pigalle nightclub—and yet is made totally unattractive and even, some say, *repulsive* by the shrill, nasal whine in which she delivers her lectures.

"My dick shrivels as soon as she opens her squawk box," George remarks to Drew, loud enough for the back half of our tour bus to hear. Alex makes a face.

Mlle Vailland continues her speech unaware of George's disparaging comments. "The Cathédrale St. Jean-Baptiste-de-Lyon is the seat of the Archbishop of Lyon," she tells her sleepy, unappreciative audience. "It's a great example of the French Gothic style . . ."

We climb off the bus, and take the requisite pictures of the church. I think of PJ again. She'd probably study every inch of it, and sketch a frighteningly accurate likeness in her sketchbook instead of taking a photo. PJ is the best artist at the Programme Americain. My conversation with Jay yesterday really made me feel bad for her and how left out she must feel.

Once Mlle Vailland completes her tour of the cathedral, she lets us wander around by ourselves for a while. Olivia, still a little shaky on her ankle after attempting to dance on it too soon after her sprain, drops to her knees in a pew, saying Hail Marys like she has something *major* to atone for.

Alex and I roll our eyes. Olivia *would* be a Catholic—I knew all that guilt and sense of duty had to come from somewhere.

Listen, I know all about it. All those years at the Christ's Message Baptist Church didn't just let me go unscathed, either.

Alex's mood has been particularly bad on this trip. Shivering as she smoked outside the Italian restaurant where we had our class dinner last night, I asked her about the black coat she was wearing. "What happened to the red Dior one?" I had said. Alex looked like she'd seen the messiah when she found that coat. Either she'd gone back to find out they'd sold the last one, or her credit card trouble had never been sorted out.

"I decided that coat was fug," Alex snapped. "The color looked like—it *aged* me. It looked like something my mother would wear." She'd stubbed out her cigarette with her brown riding boots—the same ones she'd been wearing all week, which was unlike Alex to wear anything over and over. Then she flounced back into the restaurant, careful not to look at George, who was cozy at a corner table with the twins and Drew, listening and laughing as Drew was drumming out the beet of a French techno-pop song that all the girls on the program are obsessed with.

Now, in the cathedral gift shop, Alex lifts up a purple rosary, the beads crafted from real roses like they used to do in the olden days, to show me. "We should get this for Livvy," she says with a snicker. "Since she's such a good little Catholic girl all the time."

I look at the price tag. It costs forty-five euros.

"Ha!" I say. "Way too expensive for a gag gift."

Alex smiles without looking at me. "Hmm," she says. "I guess you're right. Let's go find that nun-in-training before she runs away to a cloister in the hills."

We find Olivia at an altar in an alcove to the right of the nave, lighting a candle and fervently praying with her eyes closed.

"Look, Liv," Alex pulls Olivia from her prayers. "We got you a present!" Alex reaches into her pocket and hands Olivia the purple rosary.

Olivia smiles and turns the heavy beads over in her hands.

"Oh, Alex!" she says, touched. "It's gorgeous. It looks just like the one my grandmother gave me before she died last summer. I'd been wishing lately that I had it with me in Paris. How sweet of you."

"Well, it seems like you've been talking to God more than your best friends the past few days," Alex jokes sweetly and gives Olivia a hug. "Mme Cuchon is calling us, too. I hate to cut off your conversation with the divine, but the bus is leaving, sister."

The girls start to hurry over to join the rest of the group leaving through the heavy wooden cathedral doors. I pull Alex back. "What the hell, Alex?" I ask sternly. "Now you're stealing religious paraphernalia?"

Of course she is. It dawns on me that rich girls like Alex *love* to shoplift. She's just a thrill-seeker with no other thrills available at the moment.

"Oh, grow up," she growls at me, tossing my hand back at me. "What, are you jealous I didn't get anything for *you*?"

I let her walk ahead of me, unwilling to kiss and make up right now.

Mme Cuchon takes us next to the Museum of the Resistance, which in its exhibits tells the story of the French Resistance to the Nazi occupation during World War II. Later, everyone is quiet as we walk out of the museum toward the McDonald's where we are having lunch. Some of the girls, including Olivia, are still wiping tears from their eyes as we line up to order from the counter.

"It's your turn," Alex hassles Olivia, who can't figure out what to get.

"Ummm," she tries to decide. "I'm not really that hungry."

"Liv!" Alex sighs in exasperation. "Get on with it! You're holding up the line."

Olivia looks behind her, embarrassed. "Oh, sorry," she says. *"Je voudrais un jus d'orange, s'il vous plaît."*

"Jesus, that's all you're having?" Alex says. "Is your ballet school making you anorexic on top of all your other neuroses?"

"Alex!" I scold. "Give it a rest! What's your deal?"

Alex doesn't answer me. She mumbles her order to the cashier, who can't understand her. Unlike usual, Alex doesn't ask me to help her. She just points at one of the pictures for a Value Meal on the menu placard. "I hate McDonald's," she mumbles. "Whose brilliant decision was it to come here?"

I order a chicken sandwich, careful to specify to keep the mayonnaise on the side. The French love affair with mayonnaise is one of those things I'll never understand.

"Zack, over here!" Jay gestures for me to join him, Sammy, and another guy named Cory at a table after I've collected my tray from the cashier. As I plop down next to Jay, I feel my body relax. I was really not looking forward to sitting through a sullen meal with Alex this afternoon.

"Zack," Alex calls sharply from across the room, where she's picking at her fries. "We're sitting over here!"

I shake my head at her, a fake smile plastered over my face. *Just leave me alone, Alex. For a few measly hours. Just this once.*

Alex's eyes widen at the indignity of being ignored. Olivia looks on, ever fearful of Alex's temper, as Alex hustles over to our table.

"Zack, are you deaf? We're sitting over *there*," Alex says, pointing at Olivia who won't meet our gaze. Olivia looks humiliated, her face still puffy from the emotional museum visit.

"I thought I'd sit with these guys today, Alex," I say evenly. Jay looks at us, puzzled. This *really* shouldn't be a big deal. With Alex, however, *everything* is a big deal.

"Oh, I see," Alex laughs harshly and pulls me roughly out of my seat by the arm. "Excuse me for a second, guys," she says to Jay and the others.

"Oh I get it," she hisses at me when we're a stone's throw from them. "The boys wanted to play with you for once."

"Alex! Keep your voice down!" I turn back to look at the guys to see if they heard her. I'd *die* if they did. Literally die.

Jay looks at us from the table, puzzled. "Your food's getting cold, man!" he calls to me. "You better come eat it before I do. French portions are way too small. I could eat three Value Meals."

"Isn't that the truth," George agrees from the table where he sits with Patty, Tina, and Drew, just like at dinner last night. Alex looks at Jay, and then at George, chowing his burger and ignoring her.

Olivia gets up to throw away her orange juice cup. "You guys, what's going on? Why aren't you eating your food? Mme Cuchon's hot to trot. You should hurry up."

"Oh, we're just having some boy trouble," Alex says, her voice still low but not as low as I want it to be. I look at Jay. There's no way he missed what she just said.

"Boys like Jay don't know how to play with boys like you, Zack," Alex whispers bitingly, her lips inches from my ear. "Jay wouldn't even know what to *do* with a boy like you. You're not his type, darling. You never were."

17. ALEX

Big Mouth

George sat with Patty at the class dinner we went to right after we got to Lyon, but afterward, Patty went to bed early while George stayed up playing cards in the lounge with Drew and some of the other guys. I sat expectantly in the corner, smoking while Olivia braided my wet hair so that it would be all kinked for today when I woke up, but George didn't look at me, not once.

When we get back from spending way too long at the Basilica Notre Dame de Fourviere (seriously—why do we have to go to the Notre Dame here when we already spent a whole day at the Notre Dame in Paris? That one was better, anyway), I stomp up to the second-floor dormitories at the state-run youth hostel where we are all staying for the weekend. Changing into my super short track shorts and form-fitting zip-up hoodie, I watch the other girls who've been assigned to my dorm room, among them the hideous Patty.

I've forgiven George for the night at PJ's party, the night he ditched me and left with Patty, and I understand if he now feels he can't shun Patty in public. A girl like Patty would go straight home to Texas crying if George publicly rejected her so soon after she came onto him. I know George, and he's just being nice to her to keep her from having a breakdown and ruining her transcript by leaving the program early. He's keeping *me* waiting, which isn't fair, but this weekend is a big opportunity for us—a chance for us to clear the air, and remove Patty—and all other girls—from the equation, once and for all.

Mme Cuchon lets us have free time all evening, giving us a choice to go see Voltaire performed onstage at the University with her, for which goody-two-shoes Olivia jumps at the chance, or hang out under the auspicious gaze of Mlle Vailland at the hostel.

Seriously, Patty can't even hold a candle to me. She's wearing *pearl* earrings. Not glamorous, vintage pearls, but pearls like you'd wear to a sorority sister swear-in or some other heinous Texan tradition. And New Balance running shoes. Talk about aging yourself. Youth is about being young and fabulous, not dressing like a bridge and tunnel secretary.

A big group of them are stretched out on their beds, giving each other the *Cosmo* quiz of the month.

"You should join us, Alex," Sara-Louise invites me over. I lean over so that she can help me pin back my bangs with the bobby pins I hold out to her.

"Yeah, Alex," Mary snorts. "I'd love to know which sexual position suits *you* best." She points at the diagrams printed next to the magazine quiz.

"Very funny, Mary," I say dryly. "I would, but I can't stay. I've got some things to take care of downstairs."

It's true, I do think it sounds fun to listen to punk-rock Mary try and convince Southern belle Sara-Louise of the greatness of Iron Maiden, or watch while Sara-Louise tries to smooth down Mary's spiky hair with her gigantic can of hairspray. But I have no time for silly games right now.

Patty's eyes narrow.

"See you guys," I call cheerily as I bounce out of the room.

Before I go back downstairs, I wander the dark hallway of the youth hostel for a while. It being almost winter, with few backpackers and young school groups traveling around France at this time of year, the dorms are barely half full.

I hear George laughing from downstairs. The boys are sneaking shots of Jager—I saw the handle they brought with them. Soon George will be drunk and horny, and I think I've found an empty room—apparently left open accidentally by the cleaning staff—to take him when the time is right.

I just have to keep him from drinking too much, I think as I secure the lock on the door with one of my bobby pins so that I can get back in later. *All I need is to have a repeat of the night at Sara-Louise's.*

I did return the Alexander McQueen dress to PJ, just like Olivia made me promise I would, even though I *really* wanted to keep it. However, admiring myself in it the next day, when I got it back from the cleaners, I had to acknowledge it was too big for me.

PJ led me into the Marquets' master bedroom so she could return the dress to its rightful place among the other black-tie crinolines and satin sheaths. I whistled.

"Woah," I said appreciatively. "This is one smoking wardrobe. It's better than my mom's!" I surveyed the shelves, crammed full of luxurious fabrics and gorgeous colors.

"Really?" PJ asked.

"No," I scoffed. "Of course not. Please. My mom works for *Luxe*. Going into her closet is like going to Bergdorf Goodman, but with more vintage."

I unfolded a dark green silk-cashmere blend sweater from Tehen and held it up to me. It looked like it would fit perfectly.

"Alex, please!" PJ stopped me. "Enough!"

"Oh, stop it," I brushed her off. "It was just one dress, one time."

The antique princess phone next to the Marquets' bed rang.

"Oh, God, that's probably them," PJ groaned. "I'll be right back. Stay quiet, I don't want them to know anyone's here." She rushed for the ringing phone. "And *don't* take anything!"

"I won't," I smirked. "How many times do I have to tell you?" I just want to try on the Yves St. Laurent sandals I spot on the shoe rack.

Reaching for them, one the sandal's straps got stuck on a shopping bag shoved behind the rack. "Well, well, well," I said to myself as I poked around inside the bag, full of silky La Perla lingerie. "How scandalous!"

Mme Marquet seems to have a penchant for—or perhaps it was M. Marquet with the penchant for—negligees in every color, each with a matching thong. PJ's host mom is a crazy fox! She must have been stocking up for the season. I figured she'd never know if I took a couple. There had to be two dozen sets in there, all with the tags still on! And God knows *I* couldn't afford to buy sexy new lingerie. Not anymore, anyway.

So I slipped two negligees—there were *dozens* in that shopping bag— into my spacious tote bag, along with the corresponding underwear.

"Alex?" PJ said, coming back into the walk-in closet. "Are you alright? You're so quiet I thought maybe you'd passed out from couture exhaustion."

"I'm fine," I answered her, swinging my tote bag over my shoulder. "I better go. Thanks for understanding about the dress."

On my way home, I chewed on my cuticles, ruining yet another manicure, worrying about how mad PJ would be if she ever found out. Then I remembered about the Ming vase and grimly comforted myself that once I reminded her of that, she'd keep all my secrets.

Tonight, after everyone falls asleep, I rise from my bunk bed as quietly as I possibly can. In the darkness, I slip out of my thermal top and shorts. Removing my white cotton briefs, I stand shivering in the cold for a delicious moment before pulling the white silk negligee over my head. The thong fits perfectly, too.

Having swiped Zack's hostel keycard from his wallet when we were on the tour bus this morning, I sneak silently into the boys' dorm, tiptoeing across the cold linoleum floor from bed to bed to find out which one is George.

Thank God he's on a bottom bunk. In the moonlight, I look down at him. He looks so child-like bundled up in his sleeping bag like that.

Alex, my mom told me once, *there's nothing better than the beginning of a relationship—all the promise, the expectation, the goodwill, the lack of resentment and hurt feelings. If you're lucky*, she also said, *that's all you'll remember when it's over.* I argue with her a bit in my head, my mom who everyone always says looks just like Juliette Binoche. *If you're lucky*, I want to say back to her, *if you're smart, it won't ever be over.*

Pulling my hair out of the pins I used to put it back, I shake it out so it looks full and wild. I then very slowly unzip George's sleeping bag, opening it just enough so that I can slip inside but not enough so he'll feel a chill and wake up too suddenly.

Pressing my body against his, I reach down, hoping to wake that part of him up before the rest of him. He moans a tiny bit, stirring awake.

Fear and surprise register in his eyes, but I clap my hand over his mouth before he can blow my cover. I put a strict finger to my lips. He rubs his body against mine as he becomes more and more conscious of what's happening.

"Am I dreaming?" he whispers. "This is like the best dream I have ever had."

Less than half an inch from his ear, I whisper softly, "I know a place where we can go."

George smiles slyly and nods with raised eyebrows. I knew this was a good idea, I just knew it!

I pull him carefully out of bed, leading him toward the door. "Wait thirty seconds," I instruct him. "Then follow me. Fifth door on your left. The door's open." I slip out into the pitch-black hallway and begin to tiptoe toward the empty room I found as I poked around the hostel earlier.

Suddenly, the corridor explodes with fluorescent light. *Please don't be there.*

Oh, God. I almost wish I was a Catholic like Olivia so I would know which saint I needed to pray to right now. The saint of half-naked girls sneaking into an empty dorm with the hottest guy at the Lycée? Surely God will forgive me for *that.*

God might, but my chaperones won't, not if they see George and put together what I'm up to. I turn around, feeling like sand is slipping between my fingers. Just a moment before, George was following me, everything was going so perfectly . . .

George isn't behind me. He followed my instructions to wait. Good boy.

"Alex!" Mme Cuchon bellows from one doorway, her red hair set free from its usual chignon and sticking out in clumps around her head.

Mlle Vailland, peeking around the door to the other girls' dorm, looks just as pissed as Mme Cuchon. "*Qu'est-ce que tu fais?*" she asks, pulling a sweater over her head.

The racket in the hallway draws out the boys from their dorm as I try to charge back into my room. I'm not quick enough for them. The boys congregate at the door hooting and hollering as appreciatively for me as they did yesterday when Jay miraculously jumped onto the moving train.

I catch Zack's eye. He should look delighted, after how I treated him today, but he just looks like he wants to go back to bed.

"You want some fries with that shake?" Drew jeers after me. I clap my hands over my naked ass and try to hide the bare cheeks as I run past Mme Cuchon into my own dorm.

"I just had to go to the ladies' room," I tell Mme Cuchon. "I don't know what all the big fuss is about."

"Just go to sleep, Alex," Mme Cuchon sighs wearily. "And next time, don't forget to bring your bathrobe when you need to get up in the middle of the night on a class trip."

At breakfast I'm greeted by catcalls and wolf whistles, as well as scowls from Patty and her ugly twin sister. (*Get it? They're identical twins, so they're both ugly. I'm hilarious.*)

I look around at everyone in the hostel's dining hall, wondering if I should take a bow or run for cover. I decide to hold my head up high.

George looked *so* elated to see me last night. Undeterred, I spot him eating cornflakes with Drew in the back of the cafeteria. Hooking my thumbs in my belt loops, I sashay over to them.

George and Drew have been up early, and are discussing the football stats they were reading on ESPN.com this morning. God, can you think of *anything* less compelling to discuss?

"George," I butt in. "Are you so excited for Le Corbusier?"

"The what?" George and Drew look at me blankly.

"*Sainte-Marie de la Tourette*," I remind them, emphasizing my comfort with speaking in French by pronouncing every word perfectly. "The monastery we're going to this morning?" In truth, I'm not much looking forward to the excursion, but I want George to know that I take French culture very seriously—after all, it is in my blood.

"Oh, yeah, the silent monastery," George remembers. "Think you can handle it?" Supposedly the monastery we're visiting today on the outskirts of Lyon demands a vow of silence for the monks who live there.

"No way," Drew answers for me, drumming his fingers lightly on the table and rocking back and forth in his chair. "I'll bet you ten euros she can't shut up for even ten minutes inside the monastery."

Bristling, I glare at Drew. "I'll take that bet," I say hotly, deeply incensed by Drew's characterization of me. I'm *outgoing*, not to mention incredibly *interesting*. *Of course* I have a lot to say.

Drew quits with the drumming and shakes my hand, sealing the deal. "You've got to keep quiet from the moment you get off the bus, and then all through the tour until we get back on. There's no way you're gonna make it, motor mouth."

"We'll just see about that," I say. I never could resist a challenge.

"Father Marie-Alain Couterier asked Le Corbusier to design the cloistered *Couvent Sainte-Marie de la Tourette* in 1956," Mlle Vailland drones over the bus PA system as we drive up the forested hill to Eveux-sur-Abresle, the site of La Tourette not far from Lyon. "Le Corbusier designed many notable buildings around the world, including the United Nations in New York. The monastery is a fine example of late Modernist architecture. Regard it carefully, *mes étudiants*. It's a masterpiece."

As we drive up I see a drab concrete building that looks more like an old Williamsburg factory building than a sacred cultural institution. Totally indifferent to the monastery itself, I like the idea of George and Drew sticking by me for the whole tour in order to make sure I'm keeping my end of the bet. With any luck, George and I can sneak away for a few minutes. . . .

I don't like, however, how Drew keeps drumming on the back of my seat on the bus. I can't tell him to quit. I can't say anything at all.

Like I imagined, Drew follows me closely, with an amused George egging him on from the sidelines. Trying to get me to respond, Drew lobs silly questions my way all morning.

"But you wouldn't know anything about this, would you, Alex? I mean, you've had so little contact with French culture before coming to Paris," Drew teases me after a longwinded speech about the role of the

Catholic Church in French life from Mlle Vailland. "Didn't you say you wished you were less ignorant of French customs?"

Drew knows perfectly well that I am a connoisseur of French customs, and that of anyone on this program I've had the most contact with the French. Well, excluding this kid Cory from Denver who has actual French parents— both parents—who live with him at home in the States. Regardless, I am the resident French culture expert at the Programme Americain.

I resist Drew's goading, even when he offensively calls the convent "Saint Marie of the Tourette's syndrome." What a moron.

The monastery might be wordless for the monks who live there, but of all the visitors here today, I seem to be the only layperson who's taken a vow of silence.

One challenge that presents itself rather quickly is how to effectively pull George into seclusion without being able to come out and tell him to follow me.

Finally, Mme Cuchon tells us to wander the grounds for a while and to keep out of trouble. She looks right at me when she says that.

Slipping my hand into George's, I pull him towards a bank of trees near the chapel. Behind the little cement block of a church, I silently unzip my jacket and undo the top few buttons of my slim fitting vintage plaid cowboy shirt. Cocking my head to one side, I invite him to come closer with my best come-hither stare. Inside, I'm trembling.

"Oh, Alex," George laughs. "You're a real original."

He groans a tiny bit as I slip his hand into my demi-cup nude bra. Just as he's about to kiss me, Drew comes around the chapel, doubling over with laughter at finding us *in flagrante delicto* in what essentially amounts to a churchyard.

"Alex strikes again!" Drew shouts gleefully. "She never quits! She's the hardest working girl at the Lycée de Monceau."

I snap the top buttons of my shirt closed as I stomp angrily past him. "You're an asshole, Drew," I spit my words at him. Why do these things always seem to happen right when I'm about to make real progress with George? Why do people keep ruining the only thing that will really make me happy here in Paris?

"Ha!" Drew calls at my back. "You owe me ten euros. I knew you'd never make it all morning without talking."

"You hate me." It's not a question. Zack hasn't spoken to me in twenty-four hours. He really, truly must hate my guts. He crosses his arms and stares straight ahead at the empty tracks as we wait for our TGV train back to Paris at the Lyon train station.

"Seriously?" I ask. "You're really giving me the silent treatment? After all that we've been through."

Zack turns his back to me.

"Fine," I say. "I'll apologize to the back of your head then. I'm really, really, really sorry that I was such a bitch at the McDonald's yesterday. I hate me, too."

No response.

"Come on, Zack! Let's move on. I hate being in a fight with you," I plead. Zack taps his foot with annoyance. I can tell he's about to crack, at least say *something*, with the way he's fidgeting.

I'm right.

"You don't get it, do you, Alex? You humiliated me, you talked down to me—" he looks around to make sure no one can hear him.

"Why do you think you can talk to me that way? And you did that in front of the guy I like. What if I did that to you?"

"Drew does that to me all day long," I point out.

Zack's nostrils flare in rage.

"Okay, okay!" I say. "That was the wrong thing to say."

"Alex," Zack whispers. "Jay could have heard you talking about him and me. He might know now that I'm gay. Everyone might know. Can you even comprehend how scary that might be for me? Some of these kids might hate me, just for that. Some of these kids might want to beat me up. And I don't even know everyone yet. The only one I really know is you, and I don't know if I want to know you anymore."

My eyes swell with tears. "Don't say that," I beg. "Please don't say that. We're so fabulous, you and me. There's no one else like you here for me. I can't bear it if you won't forgive me."

But why should he? I hadn't meant to, but I'd done the one thing I'd promised Zack that I wouldn't do, all the way back the night we went out at Odeon. I hadn't kept his secret safe.

I throw my arms around him and his backpack. "I'm so sorry, Zack. Please, please forgive me. I'll do anything."

"You treat me like a lapdog, Alex," Zack says, shaking me off. "Just leave me alone."

"But Zack." My voice rises in alarm. "Jay didn't even hear me! I know he didn't! No one did." The TGV train, over an hour late, shudders into the station.

"It doesn't matter," Zack says, walking over to the train. "What matters is that he could have, and if he had, there'd be nothing that you could do about it."

Before we board the train, George taps on my shoulder.

"Yes?" I say, arching one eyebrow at him. I've had about as much humiliation as I can take with him today. I just want to get on the train, put something soothing on my iPod, and fall asleep.

George hands me a pack of Gauloises and a free matchbook from the shop where he bought them. "For all the cigs I've bummed off you so far this term," George explains when I look at him questioningly. "I wouldn't want you to think I don't pull my weight in this little arrangement of ours." He gives me a friendly kiss on my forehead. "What do you know? Looks like we're finally boarding. Catch you later, Al."

We climb aboard the train, all of us much more mellow than we were when we boarded the train in Paris on Friday. George takes a seat across from Patty and Tina, who are wearing matching new grandpa cardigans with elbow patches

The thing is, I *need* these cigarettes. Smoking is just one of the many expenses quickly draining my teeny bank account at the moment. Not only did George get me a present, he got me something I truly needed.

Olivia plops down next to me, lagging behind the group since she's been checking her email in the Internet kiosk at the Lyon station.

"Alex!" she announces breathlessly, throwing her arms around me in a jovial hug. "Something amazing just happened! I checked my email— the day I danced on my ankle? When I wasn't supposed to? There was a scout from the Paris Underground Ballet Theatre there, you know, that Left Bank company you told me your mom went and saw during spring fashion week last year?"

I can hardly follow what she's telling me. "Yeah? What happened?"

"The scout from the dance troupe—the one who came to my class the day I danced on my ankle when I wasn't supposed to—she emailed me! They want me for the troupe! They want to *pay* me to dance! And I never even knew I was trying out because I was late, and I'm *never* late! The scout wanted to know why I left in such a rush after the audition!"

"Oh, Olivia!" I congratulate her. "That's amazing!" I'm genuinely thrilled for her.

"Isn't it?" she giggles, then hesitates. "I actually got two emails just now. One from the scout, and one from my mom."

"What did your mom say?" I ask, terrified. Not a letterbomb.

"Well, it's good news and bad news," Olivia says. "She's—my whole family—is coming for Christmas."

"They are?" I ask. "I thought you were going home to California."

"I did, too," Olivia says. She stares off into space. "I really wanted to. It feels like forever since I got to talk to Vince, really talk to him. I was really looking forward to talking to him in person finally."

I consider this for a moment, then tweak her ponytail. "Livvy. Don't think about Vince right now. You just got hired by a major dance company! That's incredible! My mom is going to be so excited for you." If my mom ever returns my calls, that is.

"It is incredible, isn't it?" Olivia, says, the smile returning to her face. "Let's find Zack and tell him the good news!"

"You go," I say, not wanting to own up that Zack and I are still on the outs. She'll worry about it too much; she'll let it take away from her moment in the sun. "I'll make sure no one takes our seats."

I tap the pack of Gauloises against the heel of my hand. *These mean something,* I think, jittery with hope. *They have to mean something.*

18. PJ

Second Chances

"I am so very sorry to have had to alert you to this situation," Mme Cuchon apologized when she called M. and Mme Marquet into her office last week. It was the Monday morning after the party. "I am afraid that the freedom you have allowed her has backfired a bit. She is perhaps used to more parental guidance than she has had here in France."

Oh, lady, if you only knew the kind of parental guidance I'm used to.

Mme Cuchon continued, "I'm thinking that a fair consequence of Penelope's behavior would be to suspend her from the weekend field trip to Lyon that we'll be taking next weekend."

"No!" I said loudly, feeling suddenly close to tears. "I wanted to go so badly." And I did. I wanted to see the *traboules* that Mary had told me about—slender, narrow covered passageways that were used by tradesmen since the Middle Ages, and then used by the French Resistance during

216

the Second World War. The *traboules* are one of those things that you have to go to Lyon to see; you can't just pick up a book and feel like you've experienced the history.

"Girls who look like Penelope always attract trouble, *n'est-ce pas?*" Mme Marquet remarked to Mme Cuchon, who looked uncomfortably away.

"We will watch Penelope more closely from now on," M. Marquet said magnanimously, looking relieved that the meeting was almost over. He gazed at me for a second, and I was shocked to see true fondness, rather than revulsion, in his expression. The Marquets hadn't even noticed the broken vase, or the dress Alex borrowed for her balcony scene.

No, of course not—it had been Mme Cuchon, with her uncanny ability to sniff out a rat, who intercepted a note passed between the Texan twins about, among other inane things, "how cute George and Drew were to walk us home after the rager at PJ's."

"Penelope," Mme Marquet said, smiling hesitantly at me as I walked into the apartment after PE class that afternoon. "We would like you to come with us to our château next weekend now that you are no longer going to Lyon. We do not wish to leave you home alone again."

I smiled back uncertainly. "Really?" I asked incredulously. "You're not mad that I lied to you? And had a party at your house? *Vous n'allez pas vous mettre on colère?*"

M. Marquet shook his head. "*Non*," he said. "You're not in trouble for lying. What matters to us is that we don't have discord here in our house. And sometimes that means just keeping our feelings to ourselves rather than drawing out any drama."

I see. I'd certainly never heard of this parenting philosophy. But not wanting any problems with the Marquets—ever—I nodded vigorously. "Thank you. I won't let you down."

"Let's just forget this whole disturbance ever happened," Mme Marquet said.

Indeed. It must just be the French way of letting things go. And if anyone is jumping at the chance to let go of unpleasant events in their past, it's most definitely me.

As I got ready for bed that night, I tried to reason with myself the way the Marquets had reasoned with me. Letting things go . . . avoiding drama . . . that's what I'd done when I left Vermont for Paris, right?

Wrong. It might be one thing to forgive myself for having a house party in an apartment where I'm a yearlong guest. But to abandon your real family the way I did?

I think of the misty fields behind the château, how beautiful the French countryside is. All I know is that I'm so relieved to have a second chance.

After breakfast the following Saturday, M. Marquet offers to finally take me for a horseback ride. He helps me saddle up a dark brown horse, buckling all the tack into place and snapping a belt on the velvet-covered riding helmet under my chin.

"What's the horse's name?" I ask, petting its soft, furry nose with the back of my fingers.

"*Vanille*," replies M. Marquet, laughing jovially. I can't help laughing too. The horse's fur is so dark that it is almost black.

M. Marquet gallops ahead. I barely know what I'm doing, but Vanille stays astride M. Marquet's horse. I just hold rigidly to my reins.

"*Regarde!*" M. Marquet shouts, gesturing broadly at the landscape. It's stunning, like a scene from a fairytale. We're riding along a bluff, below which stretches the town of Périgueux and a snakelike river and ravine topped by small, slender bridges called *ponts* in French. The skies are gray today, with a tiny bit of drizzle in the air, but not threatening real rain or snow.

"*C'est magnifique!*" I shout to him. He smiles at me. It seems that he really has forgiven me after all.

When we get back to the house, Mme Marquet greets us at the door to the mud room. "I didn't realize you were going for a ride with Penelope," she says crossly to M. Marquet. "We have the hunt this afternoon with the Lafontants. Did you forget?"

"Adele," M. Marquet goes over to his wife and puts his arms around her. "You know I love to ride. I won't be too tired for the hunt this afternoon!"

One thing rich Europeans seem to do a lot is go fox hunting with their rich friends, and then have a giant dinner afterward with a bunch of different kinds of meat. Alex had told us about the custom, which grossed out Olivia, who's a vegetarian. Then Zack had told us how his dad makes him hunt every spring with his uncles and male cousins, and they all have to pray before they kill anything.

"*Tu me rends folle,*" Mme Marquet says in a low voice. "We have so much to do to get ready for the Lafontants. I won't be able to go with you now."

"Isn't that what Marie is for?" M. Marquet asks. Mme Marquet glares at him, then looks at me as if she hadn't realized I've been here this whole time.

"Penelope," she says, "the gathering tonight is for adults only."

M. Marquet looks embarrassed. "Adele, you don't want Penelope to join us?"

"No! This dinner is far too important," she says.

"It's okay," I reassure M. Marquet. "I'd be happy to help you get ready," I tell Mme Marquet sweetly. "What do you need?"

"Well," Mme Marquet says generously, "as long as you don't mind." She leads me into the kitchen. "Just help Marie with whatever she needs." She gestures around at the table full of fruit, vegetables, and potatoes. Hanging above the sink is a hock of beef that needs to be cleaned and butchered.

I, of course, want the Marquets to think of me as helpful, and useful, and never, ever as a burden to them. Hell, if they asked me to clean their château from top to bottom, I'd do it with a smile after letting their vase get broken.

"*Merci, cherie,*" M. Marquet says, touching my cheek with his wrinkled hand. "Adele, let's go dress for the hunt. Did Marie wash my new jodhpurs?" He guides her out of the kitchen. Neither of them looks exactly comfortable in here.

Marie puts me to work chopping chunks of beef for *boeuf bourguignon*—a hearty, delicious beef and vegetable stew served with peeled, boiled potatoes topped with butter and parsley. It's hard work, and messy. Soon my T-shirt is covered with splatters of meat juice. The cubes I've cut are rough and hardly the same size.

"Is this okay?" I ask Marie. She nods.

"Some caregivers you've got," she mutters quietly in French. "At least I'm getting paid for this work. They've got you working in here like servile labor."

I pretend not to hear her, even though the same thought occurred to me as I was tearing cow's flesh from the bone.

We cook all afternoon in the hot kitchen, washing and peeling vegetables, baking bread and praline cake. By the time Marie excuses me I look like I'm about to be battered and fried myself.

I take a bath in the old tub down the hall from my room, soaking in the steaming water for over an hour. After I'm good and clean, with all the vegetable matter dislodged from my fingernails and soaked out of my hair, I wrap myself in a big towel, lie on my canopied bed, and try and read Annabel's old copy of *Madame Bovary* I've been carrying around with me since she left. Unlike my sister, I've never been much of a bookworm. I can't sit still for long enough.

Downstairs, I hear a car drive up and Marie let in the Lafontants.

Even though I'm not invited to the dinner, I take care to look less rumpled than usual before I head down to my own dinner, left in the oven by Marie, who'll serve dinner buffet style, then go back to the little caretaker's cottage she shares with her husband across the pasture from the main house. I'll eat in the kitchen.

I run a comb through my long hair, shaking it out so that it makes a shiny yellow fan over my shoulders. I brought one of my nicer sweaters with me, a simple black cardigan that I button over my tucked-in white collared shirt in an attempt to look more polished. I wear my cleanest jeans with the least holes in them.

The Lafontants and the Marquets are drinking wine in the dining room, which seems odd to me. I wonder if Mme Marquet was too embarrassed to entertain them in her sitting room, since it's not as nicely kept up as other parts of the house. I wonder when the last time the

Marquets had anyone over socially. I pass by the door to the dining room as quickly as possible to keep myself out of the way.

The trees outside rustle in the windy autumn night, their branches tapping the kitchen windows. Marie is a fantastic cook. Each bite of the *boeuf bourguignon* is absolutely lovely, though it's a shame to eat something so cozy all by myself.

I think about my horseback ride today, how lucky I am that the Marquets were so forgiving about the party. One of the things I've missed about my life in Vermont is being in the outdoors and roaming around the woods by our house. The château is almost like being there, except even more stunningly beautiful.

I wonder how Dave's doing. In Vermont, there's probably already frost covering the grass every morning when he wakes up. I bet he's lonely, wondering where Annabel is, not having my parents' house to go hang out at. When he realized finally that I don't know where she is, and I realized things weren't changing for my parents—they are still facing time, and I've still got to get the Marquets to invite me for winter break so I won't have to go home to Vermont—our conversations dropped off. My desperation to talk to him turned into dread. I figure if there's more bad news, he'll email me. Though I'm not sure I could stand any more bad news.

I wash the dishes I used in the sink, drying them with an old dishrag and setting them back into the cupboards. I hear bells of laughter from the dining room, M. Lafontant and M. Marquet gloating over their success during the hunt today.

"Would you men like some more wine?" I hear Mme Marquet ask them. "I'll have to go down to the cellar to get it. Marie did not bring out enough for our dinner."

"I'll come with you," Mme Lafontant tells her. I hear them scoot their chairs back, and their shoes clack the floor as they come toward the kitchen, behind which are the stairs to the Marquets' wine collection. I duck into the shadowy china closet, hiding among the dishes used by Marquets over hundreds of years, each imprinted with their initials. A curtain hangs between the kitchen and me, and as Mme Marquet and Mme Lafontant pass through, I can hear them talking softly.

"So what happened to *l'americaine*?" Mme Lafontant asks Mme Marquet. "I thought she was in the Dordogne with you this weekend."

"Ah, Penelope," Mme Marquet responds. "She's upstairs. I told her to make herself scarce tonight. The men would be falling over themselves trying to impress her if she ate with us."

Mme Lafontant laughs. "How do you stand it? Such a young, pretty girl in such close proximity to your husband. Doesn't it make him wild?"

My mouth hangs open. M. Marquet is an old man! That's revolting!

"It's miserable," Mme Marquet confesses. "But he knows he can't touch. Besides, it makes him appear quite the benevolent patriarch to his voting public. Taking in American brats so they can learn the beauty of French culture. It promotes his image as a harbinger of cross-cultural interactions! The citizens of the Dordogne are so zealous for tourist dollars, they will do anything to kiss American ass."

"You really think it's worth it?" Mme Lafontant says as they go down the stairs to the cellar.

"If it would help my husband get more votes, I'd let Carla Bruni come and live here," Mme Marquet jokes. "In fact, it probably would help!"

I creep out from behind the curtain and stand at the top of the stairs to keep listening. I never understood before why on earth the Marquets had signed up with the Lycée to take on an American student. Now I see it's to make M. Marquet's image more family friendly!

"How is she behaved?" Mme Lafontant asks.

"Oh, you know," Mme Marquet says. "We let her do what she wants."

I hear them coming back up the stairs and scramble out of the kitchen and back to my room.

I guess this means staying for winter break shouldn't be that hard to accomplish.

DECEMBER

19. ZACK

Allez! Allez!

'm sitting in a hard wooden desk behind Jay in history class at school. We're reviewing for the Final Comp, now that the test is only two weeks away. He's so close to me I could reach out and stroke the back of his lovely brown neck.

And I *never* would!

Not unless . . . not unless I *knew* he hadn't been freaked out by what Alex blurted in the McDonald's in Lyon. And to know *that* for sure, I'd have to actually come out and ask him.

I *never* would.

I wonder if Jay is worried that his scholarship won't be renewed. I know I personally would just be hung up to dry if he didn't get his 90 percent.

Watching him now, hunched over his French history textbook, taking notes on Mlle Vailland's epic lecture on Louis XIV and the *Ancien*

Régime, I can almost understand why Alex would think it was better to have my crush out in the open. Not knowing what Jay thinks of me is torture.

When Alex stormed off to go smoke after her scene at the McDonald's in Lyon, I went back to the table to eat the rest of my cold sandwich and soggy fries. When I sat down, Jay sympathetically clapped me on the back and asked if everything was ok. Was he trying to tell me he understood? Had he, oh God, heard what Alex said, and was he trying to tell me that it was ok?

Since we got back from the trip, I've agonized over that moment, that hard, friendly thump of Jay's hand against the back of my cardigan, the genuine caring in his voice. If I could only figure out what he meant. If only I knew if I had a chance with him or not.

It's too risky. Not knowing is better than knowing the awful truth, if Jay turns out to be straight, or worse yet, gay but doesn't like me back. Then I won't have anyone but myself—the geeky, awkward kid from Memphis—to blame.

U r not geeky! Pierson gchats me later this evening. U r a rock star. U r MEGACOOL!

Hehe. Hannes always says that. MEGACOOL. LOL.

Tell JAY that, not me, I type back.

Why don't U tell Jay that? Pierson counters. Why don't u tell him u like him? Give him a list of all your great qualities. Tell him there's no better offer in town. Just see what he says . . .

Easy for you to say, I sulk. Now that you're in raptures with Hannes, you forget how hard it is to make a move. Any move.

Maybe HE's the one who's shy. Maybe U have to make the first move, because if u don't he never will. I roll my eyes at Pierson's grinning avatar. But I know he's right.

Even though I'm a basket case about what happened in Lyon, I can't hold a grudge against Alex. She won't let me.

"Alex, I told you I needed some space from you," I endeavor to blow her off during PE one afternoon. Mme Cuchon had gotten wind of the fact that we'd not been to one PE class this term and basically blackmailed us with failing the Final Comp if we didn't at least go take the end-of-the-year fitness evaluation.

Mary and Sara-Louise are recording our scores as we do basic exercises like push-ups and pull-ups and crunches, keeping time with a stopwatch. I can't really get away from Alex, since she's lying right next to me on the wrestling mat, grunting as she does her crunches.

"Haven't you had enough time away from me? Don't you miss me?" Alex asks. "I miss you."

"It hasn't even been a week since I told you that," I remind her.

The stopwatch beeps. "Time!" Sara-Louise calls. The way she says it, it sounds more like *Tam.*

Alex wriggles over to me. "Cut it out, Zack," she demands. She sits up on her elbow and looks at me gravely. "This is getting ridiculous."

I roll over and start doing some push-ups. "I don't have to talk to you."

"But Zack! It's almost my birthday. My seventeenth," she whines. "I wanted you to get dressed up with me and sing Stevie Nicks to me all night. *Just like the white-winged dove, ooh, ooh, ooooh,*" she sings campily. She knows it's one of my favorite songs. "You know, 'cause I'm at the edge of seventeen?"

"Oh, you're on the edge, alright," I retort. "And I'm fixin' to push you over it."

"Good lord!" Sara-Louise cries in frustration. "I've had enough of this, you two. I don't know what Alex did to you, Zack, but I'm sure it was par for the course. Stop acting like such a little bitch and get over yourself!"

Sara-Louise is standing over me, her hands on her hips. Besides PJ, she's the tallest girl in the class, and she's about twenty pounds heavier. From this angle, she's a little scary. "Y'all are gonna do what my brother and I do whenever we need to work somethin' out—leg wrestle!"

"Awesome!" Mary approves. "Good one. Go!"

"Yes!" Alex says. "Let's do it. I will leg wrestle you for your forgiveness."

Once again, I'm struck by the irony of the situation. I'm surrounded by three girls who want to wrestle, and I'd rather run naked down the Champs Elysée wearing nothing but Alex's red Christian Louboutins.

"Ugh," I say. "Fine. When I kick your ass will you leave me alone?"

We lie down side by side, toe to head. "One, two, three!" we count along with Mary and Sara-Louise, kicking our legs toward each other. On the third count, we interlock our legs and try to flip the other one over.

Well, Goddamn. Alex is strong. She has me doing a somersault in three seconds flat.

"Best of three!" I protest. But she does it again the second time, too.

"You're beat, bestie," she says, jumping up and embracing me. "We're friends again! Aren't you so happy?"

I hug her back. "I think, actually, that I might very well be."

Alex wanted to have her birthday dinner at one of the trendiest, hardest to get into spots in Paris—*L'Atelier* on the *Rive Gauche*. As we all know by now, what Alex wants, Alex gets, so here we are, about to be feasting on chilled octopus and squash foam and feeling not the slightest bit satiated by the ridiculously small portions. Or at least that's what I expect, from the descriptions of the other restaurants Alex tells me about in New York.

Alex gets everything she wants—except having George at her seventeenth birthday party. Apparently, when Alex extended the invite to George earlier this week, George said, "We'll see." When she texted him this afternoon to see for sure if he would be there, he texted back a taut Can't make it. Have a great one! I thought Alex would have broken down into tears from his dismissal, but she managed to keep her head up.

"You look stunning," I tell her at the restaurant. Besides George, the only other friend of hers that can't be here is PJ, and I think Alex was a little relieved by her absence, to tell the truth. As much as Alex recognizes that she has no reason to dislike PJ, really, I don't think she can wrap her head around the idea of being friends with someone that disarmingly gorgeous.

Crowded around our table are me, Olivia, Sara-Louise, and Mary. I'd been too afraid to ask Alex to invite Jay—too afraid he'd say no, and also too afraid he'd say yes.

Alex told all the girls (and me!) to wear all black on her birthday, so that no one at the restaurant would know that we're in high school. Alex has on a high-necked lace number with little black suede booties, and her hair is piled on top of her head like a *fin de siècle* Gibson Girl, with loose tendrils falling romantically around her beautiful face.

"Thank you," Alex says into my ear. "I hope you have a *great* time tonight. I owe you, after what I did in Lyon."

"Thanks, Alex," I say, sincerely.

The waiter fills our glasses with an expensive, delectable Merlot. "Tell him we all want the prix fixe," Alex says to me. The waiter, used to rich girls with bad French, understands her. I don't have to translate for her like usual.

"To the birthday girl!" I raise my glass and clink with everyone else's.

"And to Olivia running off with the Paris Underground Ballet Theatre!" Alex chimes in. Her eyes are wet with feeling. "To leg wrestling!"

"To new friends," Sara-Louise says warmly, squeezing Mary's hand.

"To new challenges," Olivia adds with a big smile. Her ankle is finally fully healed, and she's wearing new patent leather high-heeled pumps with her black pleated miniskirt and tights for the occasion. Her hair is pulled back in a French twist. This is the most grown-up I have ever seen her look.

"To new places," Mary says, gesturing around us at our adopted foreign city. Alex has given her the skull necklace she got at Colette, seemingly out of pure generosity, or because Mary always seems to have an extra cigarette, and lately, Alex doesn't seem to have any.

"To realizing our goals," I say for lack of a better toast. I'm thinking of the Final Comp coming up, and also Jay.

"I'll say," Alex agrees heartily. "Starting . . . *now*." As if to illustrate her point, she winks suggestively at the team of waiters serving our dinner.

"My friend thinks you're cute," she tells one of them. "You should give us your number." When the waiter returns, he slips a folded piece of paper with his name and digits on it into Alex's hand.

"Did he realize you meant your *male* friend?" I snort.

"Of course he did," Alex says, but then she's suddenly not so sure.

We all tuck happily into yet another hopelessly modish dish, this time a tiny bowl of soup with chicken ravioli in it and crème fraiche poured into each bowl individually at the table. It might be the most wonderful soup I have ever had. Then there's a miniature filet mignon resting on a bed of arugula and peppers, dripping with a tangy sauce with notes of orange and garlic, two things I never thought I'd find on the same plate. I chuckle to myself, contemplating the bill. Good thing CAB is so bighearted with that black Amex!

The next waiter who comes over to clear the dishes and the remnants of our bread basket is a hot South Asian guy with brilliant white teeth and a tendency to rest his left hand saucily on his hip in such a way that his sexual orientation doesn't keep us guessing.

"This is Zack," Alex says suddenly, interrupting the other girls' conversation. The waiter and I lock eyes until I blush.

"I'm Rajiv," the waiter says with a slow, sexy grin. "If you want, you all should stick around after we close the bar."

The five of us exchange grins. Rajiv brings over the crowning glory of the birthday dinner—a light lemon layer cake filled with raspberry and vanilla crème and lemon-thyme sorbet. I strike one of the matches from the matchbook sitting in the ashtray on the table and hold it up so Alex can blow it out.

"Make a wish!" Sara-Louise prompts her.

"I wish you'd all stay and get wasted with these waiters and me tonight!" she says.

Sara-Louise, Mary and Olivia beg off, but I'm down. We all kiss and hug and wish Alex a happy birthday again.

"I'm so glad y'all made up," Sara-Louise tells me. "Get home safe!" I usher the girls into a cab and head back inside. L'Atelier is about to close. It's nearly midnight.

The waiters sing French pop songs with the radio as they break down all the tables. Drinking wine at the bar, Alex claps her hands.

"Shots!" she cries. "*Prenons des verres!*"

Rajiv comes over with a bottle of Grand Marnier and some small Turkish apricots. "Try this," he shows us, filling shot glasses with the liqueur and then drowning the fruit in it. "Now eat," he instructs, and we bite into the sweet, alcohol-infused apricots with relish.

The waiters pour us all kinds of inventive drinks, turning the music up and dancing around our high stools. Alex kisses them all on their cheeks as they twirl around her. Rajiv pulls me to my feet, swaying his hips back and forth in a seductive move I can't imitate. I fall back onto my stool, the restaurant spinning a bit.

Rajiv's boss, the head waiter, comes over with our bill. Alex and I stare at it. She owes L'Atelier two thousand euros! The wine alone was half the cost.

I need some air.

I find my way from the bar through the dark, empty restaurant to the door. Pushing hard on the ornate door handle, it won't budge. What the hell?

I try again. The lock holds firm.

I've really got to get out of here. The drinks, the rich food . . . it's all starting to make me feel dizzy rather than drunk.

I rush back to Alex, red-faced from being dipped low by Rajiv in an impromptu ballroom dance number. "Alex, dollface," I sidle up to her. "Pay the bill so they'll unlock the front door. I'm down for the count. Let's go home."

Alex bites her lip. "That's the thing. I . . . I forgot my credit card."

"What?" I whisper. "You don't have it with you? How are we going to pay? We're stuck here! The doors are locked."

I really, really don't want to wait here as ransom while Alex goes home and gets the card. How could she have forgotten the Amex?

I look over at Rajiv. Now that I've lost my buzz, I can see that his face is more wrinkled that I'd noticed before. He's old, probably close to thirty. His smile when he sees me looking at him is slick and oily.

"Or . . ." I look through the kitchen to the stockroom, its shelves bulging with bags of potatoes and garlic and packages of salt and mineral water. Alex reads my mind.

"Go!" she shouts, loud as a shotgun announcing the beginning of a race. Running headlong through the stockroom and throwing our full weight hard against the heavy back door, we fall into an alley with piles of trash bigger than we are on either side of us.

"Go!" Alex shouts again, and off we do go, not stopping until we get to the St. Germain-des-Pres.

"What have we done?" I ask her, gasping for air. In the cool night air, the restaurant seems far away. I clap a hand over my mouth, thinking of Rajiv and his wiggling hips; the sweet, slightly burning sensation of the soaked apricot as I put it to my lips, the staggering amount of the bill we didn't pay. What on earth had I been thinking, busting out of the storeroom like that?

Alex stops a passing man on the street. "Can I bum a smoke?" she asks, using all her American-in-Paris charm. The man gives her a cigarette and lights it for her.

"Well, Zack, I think that's what they call a classic dine and dash," Alex answers nonchalantly.

"Alex."

She smiles expectantly. "What, darling?"

"Your mom cut you off, didn't she?"

She laughs. "What the hell are you talking about?"

"Admit it, Alex."

Alex's face falls. "No, stupid. I forgot the Amex at home. I actually forgot my whole wallet. I didn't have my ATM card, either. That was so dumb of me. I hate myself!" Her laugh is forced.

"What about the coat? How come you never got one? Why are you always wearing that brown sweatshirt to school?"

"Because I like it," she tells me, not meeting my gaze. "It's boho-chic. It's high-low."

"And the cigarettes?" I ask. "How come you're always bumming them from people now? Like Mary? And that guy just now? And you don't smoke as much as you used to."

She takes a long drag. "I thought you told me to cut down on my smoking. I'm just following your advice."

"Alex! Why can't you just tell me the truth?"

Alex throws her cigarette into the gutter and starts laughing hysterically. I laugh, too, though I'm not sure why.

"You know what, Zack? You're right!" she holds her stomach. "She did! My crazy mother actually cut off my credit card. That and she hasn't put any money in my bank account for a month! That's my secret, darling. You got me. Congratulations!"

"And you took us to dinner anyway?" I ask incredulously. "How did you intend to pay?"

She shrugs and bursts into more laughter.

"Oh, my God." I can't help it. It's too bizarre for me to be mad. Shaking with laughter, I pull her into a cab, which I pay for myself.

20. OLIVIA

Excess Baggage

I bid the stuffy Opera school goodbye and attend my first rehearsal at the Paris Underground Ballet Theatre this afternoon. Located in the basement of a dingy building near the Place d'Italie, the dancers I meet there are lounging around in the craziest outfits I've ever seen anyone try to dance ballet in. One of the men is wearing a tutu! And unlike the prima ballerinas I danced with at the Opera, not a single girl is wearing a long-sleeved black leotard. Most of them aren't even wearing leotards at all—just their dance bras and tights.

The choreographer in charge of today's rehearsal is wearing silver eyeliner and has a Mohawk. When he demonstrates the lift he wants at the end of the sequence, he grabs me and lifts me high into the air, his hands firmly gripping my crotch. Even though it's completely nonsexual, I turn beat red all the way to the neckline of my new black Lycra dance dress.

"*Bien fait*," the choreographer says when he puts me down. "Great form. Just remember to keep that back leg in a firm arabesque. Really great arms."

His praise floats me all the way home.

Thomas has been hanging around the apartment again lately while studying for his semester finals, but I've been at school when he's been home. I burst into the front door, hoping he hasn't left yet, anxious to tell him about my great news.

When I find Thomas isn't there—he's gone back to his dorm for the night—I realize that I was rushing home to tell him how great my new job is. I didn't go straight to the payphone to call Vince or my parents. I wanted to tell Thomas.

In fact, I haven't even told my parents or Vince about the Paris Underground Ballet Theatre at all. But there's only so much longer that I can put it off.

Saturday morning, I wake up way before my alarm goes off, a funny feeling deep in my stomach. I lie in bed and wonder how I will ever be able to stand my family here in Paris for two whole weeks. After we take the final comp this Friday, the semester will be over, and all of us, including Brian, will celebrate Christmas the following week here in Paris. Mme Rouille, who is taking Thomas to the Alps for the holiday, even told me we could open presents over at her apartment, under the Christmas tree a hired decorator came over and set up for her while I was in Lyon.

I love my family. I've missed them. So why am I dreading seeing them?

I think of the Mohawk guy, Henri, of how I quit my classes at the Opera school without even telling my mom. That's why. Because this is the first time I've ever gone against her wishes in my whole life.

As the sun starts to appear outside my little room's window, I get up and get ready to go meet their flight at Charles de Gaulle. I dress purposefully, for some reason wanting to prove to them, especially my mom, that I am more stylish than just Pumas and jeans. I take out the black wool trousers I got at Zara, wide-legged with a flat front, sailor type side button closure, and with those I slip on a cream angora-wool blend sweater I found at Le Bon Marché. I blow dry my hair and iron it carefully, wondering if my mom will notice how far my roots have grown in and how bad my split ends are.

Early in the term, Alex and Zack had taken me to the famous Galeries Lafayette, and showed me the nylon Longchamp bags with the brown leather handles. I had chosen one in a Kelly green, which Alex approved of. It cost so much money, but with it dangling from my shoulder, I feel so *French*.

By myself last week, I hunted through the shoe department in the Galeries before finally settling on a pair of simple black boots with a narrow, curved toe. With the coat, gloves, and chenille scarf I had bought at H&M, I feel like I look like a whole different person than when my family saw me last. It's stupid to get too caught up in clothes, especially since I spend half my life in sweaty leotards and leggings, but in this outfit I feel more like a Parisian teen, or better yet, a student at the Sorbonne. And today that's important for some reason.

I latch together the Tiffany's "O" pendant my mom gave me for Christmas last year. I look nice.

I am one of the only people on the metro this morning, slowly creeping across Paris toward the Gare du Nord. I pay the extra fare for the RER to CDG. I am starting to get jumpy. A guy in a business suit and a rolling suitcase across the aisle from me is staring at me. I look down and see it's because I am literally wringing my hands.

I see my mom first.

Long hair with highlights, done by the same colorist as the one I used to go to in San Diego, wearing an unzipped pink hoodie sweatshirt over a green spaghetti strap tank top with Seven jeans and Ugg boots—basically, she's dressed like a teenager. Typical Mom.

Dad sleepily trails her through the crowded airport, clutching Brian's hand as if the French people around him might kidnap him at any moment. Dad is wearing jeans and a sport coat—looking less like an overgrown *TRL* fan than Mom does—but is also wearing slip on sneakers with no socks, like he thought it would be seventy degrees out when he got off the plane instead of forty.

Brian has his little backpack and a pillow, and stares at the floor. As soon as I see his freckled face and red mop of hair, my gut wrenches. He must be so freaked out, by the plane, and the busy terminal, and all the emotion of me, Mom, and Dad, and yet he's keeping it together so well. I know better than to tackle him—that would set him over the edge—but I have to hold myself back from embracing him. How could I have made him come here? How does he know to be so brave? With Brian, I know that I will never know.

My mom shrieks when she sees me and grabs me in a close hug. I hug her back just as hard, letting the crowds of people weave around us. I've missed her—all of them—so much.

"Let me get a good look at you, beautiful," she says after a bit and pushes me within arm's length. Her face falls as she peers at my dark roots and chomps her gum.

"Oh, Livvy, your hair," she clucks at me. "We'll fix it while I'm here."

My dad hugs me happily, then gently leads Brian to me so that I can hug him without setting him off—he *really* doesn't like to be touched, especially without warning.

I am trying to tell them everything at once—how we'll get to the hotel, how frigid it is outside, when I see someone next to my dad.

"Livvy—we brought you a surprise!" my mom squeals. My heart catches. It *can't* be.

Next to my dad, laughing at how long it took me to notice him, is *Vince.*

I immediately burst into sobs, so debilitating that I can't form words, just base noises.

"Look how happy she is!" my mom exclaims to my dad. She leans over to Brian. "Look, sweetie, look at Livvy. She's *happy.*"

"Vince?" I say, choking a little on his name.

Vince, in baggy hip-hop style jeans and a yellow Bruins sweatshirt, is standing right in front of me. His chin is covered in sexy morning-after stubble after the long flight, and he's wearing his glasses. I bet that the dry air in the plane was irritating his contacts. His familiar cologne—Polo Ralph Lauren—fills the space between us. I'd brought one of his dirty T-shirts with me to Paris, but that smell faded from the cotton fabric sometime around Halloween.

I don't really believe he's here. I must be hallucinating. Vince is at

UCLA. I just talked to him last night. He wasn't about to get on an airplane . . . he was going to shoot hoops with his buddies. And yet, it is him, right here in front of me, smiling that same golden boy smile.

"Hey, babe," Vince says, his eyes reddening a bit too. "Good to see you." His voice is quiet.

I bury my face in his chest, clinging to his sweatshirt. I never knew how deeply I missed him until this moment. But there's something else there—guilt for kissing Thomas, for sure, and something more unrecognizable. Something that makes me feel like I am swimming and can't quite get to the surface soon enough for air.

"Thank God you're here," I say into his jacket. "I don't think I would have survived even one more day without seeing you."

You don't even know all the things I could have done to us if you hadn't come.

I can't wait to show my family and Vince *my* Paris. My dad booked a room at the Hilton Hotel right near the Arc de Triomphe, and after my mom gets her fill of the Champs Elysées, I want to show them *Cambronne*, the area south of the Eiffel Tower near where Alex and Zack live. Pretty far away from the touristy stuff, I think they'll appreciate how picturesque the streets of Paris are without sidewalk vendors trying to sell us cheesy framed photos and asking if they might do caricatures of us for the low price of just ten euros. Under the Cambronne elevated metro station is an open-air fruit market that sells the most mouth-watering apples in the world, and across the street is a *chocolaterie* that Alex, Zack, and I *adore*. I also think they'll get a kick out of seeing the Statue of Liberty's French sister statue in the fifteenth arrondissement. I know I did. It looks so out of place, even though everyone knows that the statue in New York was originally a gift from France.

"But, baby, I don't want to see the Statue of Liberty. I've already seen that when we went to New York to look at dance schools out there. I want to see the Eiffel Tower," my mom tells me when I bring up the idea.

Well, I've *already seen the Eiffel Tower,* I think, but hold my tongue. *And I never got to see the other Statue of Liberty. I was practicing for auditions the whole time,* I remember bitterly. Our trip to New York in eighth grade had been a disaster—my mom decided she couldn't handle me living so far away so young, after a brutal week of trying out for New York school.

It's not like the Eiffel Tower is anything special, just a bunch of twisted metal that Parisians used to say was ugly when it was built for the World's Fair a million years ago.

To my mom, though, it *is* special. She takes about a hundred photos of us in front of the thing—Vince and Livvy at the Eiffel Tower, Mom and Dad at the Eiffel Tower, Livvy and Brian at the Eiffel Tower, and on and on. I feel guilty being so resentful of doing the things she wants to do. My mom is obviously having an amazing time so far, and to be fair, this is the first vacation she's had since that New York trip.

After Brian's shrieking at the top of the Eiffel Tower gets us all kicked out for good, I strike a deal with my parents. Vince and I will hang out with Brian doing things that are more to his liking, such as long walks and eating sandwiches on the quiet banks of the Seine while bundled up in our jackets, and my parents can go explore Paris on their own.

Brian can't handle the crowd scenes of places like the Louvre or Les Halles a week before Christmas, and to tell you the truth, neither can I.

"Are you sure you don't mind?" I check with Vince.

"I just want to be with you," he whispers, wrapping me up in his arms.

My parents are now gratefully and energetically touring Paris by themselves, showing us a slideshow of everywhere they go on their digital camera when they return to the hotel at night. I urge them to wander Paris, let themselves discover the wonders of the city slowly, patiently, but their pictures prove that they are pouncing on Paris with a voracious appetite. My mom brings to her trip to Paris the same rabid organization that she brings to Brian's specialized education, to my dancing and the UCLA scholarship. Her Lonely Planet Paris guidebook is carefully flagged and highlighted to all the places she can't miss—the Musée d'Orsay, Notre Dame, the Moulin Rouge (though not, of course, to see the risqué revue—just to take a photo of the windmill on the top), and everywhere else all the tourists go.

The French Lycée operates much like Thomas's classes at the Sorbonne when it comes to the Final Comp. Rather than have class this week, they give us all week off to study on our own. I have to say I haven't been studying as hard as I could be, even before my family and Vince got here. Something about the offer from the Paris Underground Ballet Theatre made me not as nervous about the test. I spend the free time this week hanging out with Vince and Brian each day, and meeting up with my parents at night for dinner. I tell my mom I have dance class every day at three, but really I take the #7 metro down to the Place d'Italie and dance my heart out learning Henri's intense new routines.

Vince is too polite and too good a friend of Brian's to say so, but I can tell he wishes we could be alone. It would be more romantic, but at the same time, I like that Brian is there. Sometimes I wish Brian and I could be alone, wish that we could be rid of Vince. Brian's a good listener and certainly understands more than people give him credit for. There's so much that I want to tell him.

"What do you want to do today?" Vince asks me on Wednesday morning when I get to the hotel. My parents have already left for the day.

"I don't care," I answer. "It's not like we're doing anything. Just the same thing every day." It comes out more bitterly than I meant it to, but I'm too weary to spend another quiet day alone with Brian and Vince, wandering around the wealthier arrondissements and stopping for coffees and sandwiches and bathroom breaks.

"Livvy," Vince says, careful to speak in a low voice so Brian wouldn't hear, "you were the one that suggested that we hang out with Brian. You yourself said you preferred it."

"I know," I grumble.

Hanging out with Brian isn't the problem. The problem is Vince. All day, I feel like we run through the things we have to say to each other really quickly, usually before lunch time. Then every moment is agonizing after that, trying to have a good time. If we could go to a museum, it might provide us with some conversational fodder.

We leave the hotel after pulling Brian away from French cartoons in the mid-morning. As we have all the other mornings, we find a pastry shop and get breakfast. This one is full of locals, lingering over buttery croissants and coffee and reading the papers. The blustery winter day keeps people inside for much longer than perhaps they would normally spend. We're lucky to get a table.

"Livvy!" Vince exclaims after we place our order. "You drink coffee now?"

I'd ordered a café crème without even realizing it. I miss the Café Dumont, where I haven't been in forever. I'm longing for Alex's bouncy cattiness and Zack's acidic banter. I miss PJ's wry smile and easy companionship, the way she refrains from inquisitiveness and yet focuses her unflinching attention to whomever she's with.

"Oh, yeah," I say, not sure why I ordered it. "I wanted to try it. Alex, Zack, and PJ are always getting them. I want to try one, I guess."

"You're not going to like it," Vince tells me. "Trust me."

"How do you know?" I say, suddenly defensive. "Just because you don't like coffee, I won't either?"

"Whoa, Liv, calm down," Vince says.

We sit in silence. The waitress brings over our food and drinks. Vince is right. The foam on top of the café crème tastes good, but the coffee underneath it is gross. I pour a bunch of sugar in and take a thick gulp so Vince won't be able to tell he was right.

"You should invite some of your new friends to hang out with us," Vince pressures me. "It would be fun to meet them."

"Oh," I defer. "They're all really busy studying for the Final Comp." Though I know Alex and Zack would be over the moon to get a good look at Vince after hearing about him for so long, Brian's condition would surely weird them out, no matter how hard they tried. I don't want to risk the discomfort of us all hanging out together.

At the mention of my friends at the Lycée, I feel distracted wondering whether Alex has worked her way back into George's good graces and worrying about her if she has not. I wonder about poor Zack, and what's been getting him down lately.

"Hey," Vince says after a while. "It's cool if you want to drink coffee.

Everyone else in the world does it. I just noticed it was something different about you."

Brian chews his Danish. I know he can tell things are tense between us. I feel really, really bad all of a sudden.

"Hey, Bri," I say to him. "How's your breakfast?"

He takes a while to answer. "Good."

"That's good. You want to walk down by the river today, watch the boats?"

"Yeah."

"Sounds great," I say. I look at Vince.

"I'm sorry, babe," I say, taking his hand. "I'm just stressed about the Final Comp."

"No worries," Vince says. "We're gonna have a great day. How's your café crème?"

"Disgusting," I laugh.

"Thought so," he says. "I know you too well."

By the time Friday finally comes, I'm actually looking forward to the test and going to school. Everyone's a little hyper from lack of sleep and too much caffiene. We're all wondering if the rumors are true, that you'll really be sent home if you don't pass the test. There's a nervous energy in the air as we wait by our lockers for the bell to ring and Mme Cuchon to let us into the classroom.

"Good luck," I tell Alex, giving her a hug. "You'll be great."

"Oh, I know," Alex says. "I've been speaking French—"

"Since you were a baby?" Zack finishes the familiar sentence for her. "Don't blow this, Alex."

"*You* don't blow this," Alex sneers. "I have to go pee. See you guys in there."

"Seriously, Livvy, she didn't study at all," Zack confides, keeping his head down. "What if she fails?"

"She won't fail," I assure him. "You're sweet to worry, but Alex always keeps her head above water." I'm feeling surprisingly confident. Last night after rehearsal, Henri told me I was in the running for a lead in a spring dance performance. The formal auditions were going to be held after the New Year, but he told me he had been thinking of me.

"It's got to be weird to have your parents here," PJ remarks as we file into the classroom, "not to mention Vince." PJ avoids looking at me, but I feel accused by her mention of him.

"It's not weird, it's great," I answer her. "Everyone I hold dearest in the world is in Paris right now—why would that be weird?"

As Mme Cuchon passes out the scantrons and the blue books for the test, I think for the first time how I know nothing about PJ's own relationship to her family. I don't even know if she has any brothers or sisters. How odd. Even Alex, in all her bravado, has told us of the troubles she has with her mom, and of course her father, who she jokingly refers to as "The Invisible Man." But PJ might as well be an orphan for all that we know about her life at home in Vermont.

Wearing my pants from Zara again, this time with a grey turtleneck sweater, I meet my parents for a celebratory dinner at their hotel. The Final Comp flew by, and I think I'm finally ready to tell them that I've joined the Underground, as I've learned is the way everyone refers to the troupe.

I burn with embarrassment at all the other Americans in the dimly lit restaurant, ordering hamburgers and fries with extra ketchup and demanding to have more ice in their water glasses. Even though I've definitely been known to order extra ketchup sometimes, too.

"Oh, Livvy," my mom says, her cheeks flushed red with happiness. "You must love it here so much."

"I do!" I tell her brightly. "I really, really do." This is a perfect time to tell them, a perfect time to segue into my news that I'm staying indefinitely, as long as the dance troupe will have me. Not just till June, but through the summer, and until I'm too old or too injured to dance anymore. That's how much I love Paris, I will tell them. That's how much I long to stay.

"It really has been so lovely to be here with you," my mom gushes. I want to roll my eyes, since we've barely seen each other since she arrived, but I also know how much this all means to her. She so rarely gets to do the things she wants to do. *Especially since I left for Paris,* I think with a cold flash of guilt.

Just do it, I think, unable to even look at Vince. My mom is one thing, she'll be disappointed, yes, but also proud of me and my dancing. She'll relish telling her friends and the other parents at Brian's school about her talented daughter the ballerina in Paris. Vince, on the other hand, will look even more the fool, waiting years for his girlfriend to never arrive at UCLA.

Just before I can say anything, my mom starts to cry. My dad looks at her, then back at me with a horrible grimace. "We want you to be happy—" he starts.

"Oh, Livvy, my baby," my mom says, pulling me into her arms.

"What's going on?" I say loudly, looking at Brian with alarm. Is someone sick? Is something wrong with Brian? With mom? With me, and I don't even know it yet?

My mom's voice cracks, "We want you to come home."

I look around at all of them, and then back at my mom. "What?"

My mom covers her face with her hands. "Livvy, it's been just awful without you. Brian's been steadily declining since you left—his teachers think he's been horribly depressed without you."

I think of Brian happily slurping sticky lemon sugar from his crêpe as he, Vince, and I strolled around the Jardin de Tuileries. "He seems okay to me," I protest. Right now, he's humming and staring at his plate.

"That's because he's with you," Vince says, speaking up for the first time.

"Stop talking about Brian like he's not right here!" I snap at Vince. "How would you know, anyway? You've been in L.A.!"

"It's true," my mom says sadly, wiping at her smeared makeup with the white cloth napkin. "We're not doing good at home, baby, not without you."

It's then that I feel it, all the energy flowing out of my body like a balloon deflating. It's sort of like when I step down off the points of my shoes and walk off the dance floor on my flat feet. *The show's over*, my shoes clunk awkwardly as my body winds down from the routine.

Now it's Paris, the dance troupe, my new friends—the show's over, time to go home.

It was a show, I realize regretfully. *This was never my real life. I never belonged here, as much I always wanted to.*

"Okay," I say finally, refusing to look at any of them except Brian. "I'll come home at the end of the term."

Why did I even bother coming to Paris at all? Why would they let me fall in love with something, I think with a hard lump in the back of my throat, *if they were just going to take it away?*

"I better go tell my friends," I say, putting my napkin on the table. "They're all going to be really disappointed." I actually just want to go back to Mme Rouille's apartment and be alone for a while. But I want my mom to know that there are other people in my life besides the ones sitting at this table.

"Livvy, wait!" my mom cries.

"Just let her go," my dad advises. "Just let her go for one night."

21. PJ

Too Many Belles at the Ball

*A*fter the Final Comp, my feet drag all the way to the train station. The train feels like it is hurtling at breakneck speed toward Bordeaux, then Périgueux. I drink several cups of bad coffee from the café car on both trains, feeling like I need to sharpen my senses, stay on track, do all the right things when I arrive.

When M. Marquet picks me up, I try and give him my most appreciative smile. "Thank you so much for picking me up. And for having me back to the château. I love coming here so much."

"We'll go for a ride tomorrow," he offers. "Right after breakfast. Vanille has missed you!"

What was once mysterious and charming about this big old house is now just plain spooky. All night, I toss and turn, jumping awake at the strange creaks in the floorboards above my head, hearing voices though everyone should be asleep.

Mme Marquet knocks softly on my door Saturday evening, just as the dusk is settling out the windows. I jump a mile at the noise, then dread letting her in. I know I need to talk to her about the break. Mme Cuchon reminded us just before the test that all of us staying in Paris for the break need to make sure and have our host parents call her to formally take responsibility for us for the extra time before Spring term.

"Penelope," Mme Marquet says, swooshing into the guest room with her arms full of brightly colored satin, silk, and taffeta. "Would you like to come with us to the hunting ball this evening? The ball hosts, you remember *les Lafontants*, have a daughter your age, and they'd like you to keep her company if you don't mind." She spreads a metallic gold empire-waisted strapless sheath over my bed. "Maybe this Lanvin gown will fit you. I wore it on New Year's last year. M. Marquet just adored that color on me."

At Mme Marquet's urging, I slip out of my T-shirt and into the dress, kicking off my corduroys modestly once the dress is on. I look at myself in the mirror. The bust fits perfectly, giving way to a slim fit through the waist and along my hips. The shimmery gold fabric complements the skin of my bare shoulders. I so rarely wear anything this form-fitting that I barely recognize myself. I lift my long hair and twist it up with my hand, wondering if I should ask Mme Marquet if she will do my hair.

"*Mon dieu*," Mme Marquet says when she sees me in the Lanvin. "You'll be a scandal in that dress. You can wear this old Oscar de la Renta."

I turn away from her as I slip out of the gold dress and into a light blue taffeta ball gown that fits much less nicely. It's about four inches too short, and princess seams were designed for a body much more voluptuous than my own. Even I can see that the gown is out of fashion, despite the sumptuous fabric and delicate stitching. It looks like a costume from Disneyland; something from a TV montage about Princess Diana's gowns.

"*Très belle!*" Mme Marquet says, though I know the dress fits badly. "That one is much more appropriate."

"You really think it looks okay?" I say doubtfully.

"*Oui!*" she confirms. She sounds so sure that I decide the dress really isn't that bad. It was obviously very expensive, and the fabric feels amazing against my skin. After all, Mme Marquet knows much better than I do what to wear to a function like this one.

"*Ma princesse,*" she then says as she leaves to go get herself ready, and her approval feels so good I want to hug myself.

"Mme Marquet?" I ask her. This would be the perfect time to ask her to call Mme Cuchon. But she's already gone.

It turns out the Lafontants' daughter, Aimee, is not, in fact, my age. She's fourteen, and has a gaggle of friends to entertain her. Everywhere I turn, there are older people, married couples in long-sleeved black-tie attire, and then younger kids in party clothes, buffed patent leather Mary Janes and taffeta dresses for the little girls chasing the little boys around in their shorts and knee highs. There aren't any people my age here at all.

Mme Marquet takes an unprecedented interest in my well-being as soon as we arrive at the Lafontants' mansion, which is even grander than the château. She introduces me to all of her friends with pride.

"*Ooh la la!*" the women fuss over me. "*Très, très belle!*"

Glamorous people, amazing food, chandeliers, an honest-to-God ballroom right here in the Lafontant mansion. I can't help beaming as I absorb it all.

"Are you having fun?" I turn to find M. Marquet at my elbow, handing me a glass of champagne. I nod happily.

"Oh, yes! It's all just so out of this world. I'm having an amazing time." I take a timid sip of champagne. I'm usually not a huge fan of booze, but this tastes like heaven—bitter and sweet at the same time, and fizzing its way down my throat so easily that within a few minutes my flute is empty.

"Have another," M. Marquet says, lifting two more flutes off the tray of a passing waiter. "And don't forget to take a look around. It's magnificent."

A woman in a black two-piece beaded gown beckons to M. Marquet. "Have fun, *cherie!*" I can tell by the lightness in his voice that M. Marquet is drunk, but in a good way. "And, *cherie*, I have to tell you. I just *adore* that color on you."

I giggle. A walk does sound nice. Pretty soon I'm going to be drunk, too—I need to pace myself.

I've only been drunk once, at a party Dave and Annabel had to celebrate their engagement. Before Annabel decided she couldn't trust Dave, either. It didn't have to be that way, but Annabel didn't know the whole story when she disappeared.

The Lafontants, I'm discovering as I walk around their little palace, are one of the oldest and most established families of the French aristocracy. Their medieval crest is hanging everywhere, proudly showcasing the lineage of the family from before the modern age. Ducking into a candlelit corridor lined with old woven tapestries on one side and huge iron-framed windows on the other, I feel like I'm in an old fairy tale, especially with my big, puffy blue dress and my hair tied up off my neck, however inexpertly I had done it. I look at myself in the reflection of the window. It doesn't matter that the dress isn't a perfect fit or that strands of my hair are falling out of my messy updo. I look like I'm in a fairytale. I almost feel assured that I am going to have a happy ending here in France

Guests—and there must be more than a thousand of them here—are wandering about the château like it's their own home, so I feel comfortable doing the same. Imagining that there must be an old library somewhere, I start to poke into the little rooms lining the corridor. Some look like offices, with stately desks and a thick layer of dust over all the papers, while others are storage rooms full of antiques. I even see a suit of armor in one of them. I long for Annabel, or even Olivia or Sara-Louise or Mary—someone else to explore this magical place with me. At the moment, I'd even take Alex—how envious she will be when I tell her the company I kept this weekend!

Farther down the hallway, I see a door cracked open, the light from a fire making shadows on the floor. I hear voices, making me curious. What is it about rich French people that compels me to go traipsing through their houses as if hunting for treasure?

I push the door open.

Mme Lafontant is spread out over a large banquet table on her stomach, her black satin skirt hunched up around her waist and her pale hips and thighs looking shockingly white against her black garter belt and silk stockings. And with her, I'm absolutely shocked to find, is M. Marquet. The bodice of Mme Lafontant's dress is pulled down, and M. Marquet's spotted hands are squeezed harshly around her breasts. M. Marquet lets out a loud, awful moan that I'd just as soon forget I ever heard.

I try to back out as quietly as I came in, but in my haste I smack face first into the doorframe. "Fuck!" I say aloud, trying not to cry in pain as I rush back down the hallway toward the ballroom. The train of this stupid blue dress is so long I keep tripping over it, slowing me down.

"Penelope!" M. Marquet calls after me, catching up with me easily. He's tucking his tuxedo shirt back into his black pants. He still has the scent of Mme Lafontant's perfume on him, plus another rich smell that makes me gag. He feels too close, too heavy.

"What are you doing?" I spit out at him. "Isn't Mme Lafontant a close friend of Mme Marquet?"

"Ah," M. Marquet says. "You Americans are such sensitive babies. Don't be upset, Penelope. Nothing is the matter here. In France, marriage is much more open than in your country. Affairs are accepted; it's commonplace . . ."

I lift the heavy hem of my dress and walk briskly away from him. The whiskey on his breath makes me nauseated, and remembering how affectionate Mme Marquet had been to me earlier, how she called me *ma princesse*, my loyalty is to her. When I come back into the ballroom, I can't look at her. I might throw up at the memory of what I just saw, or cry. I put my hand to my forehead, willing the mental image to go away.

"Penelope!" Mme Marquet rushes to my side. "Are you ill?"

What if I was? Would you call me an ambulance? Or would you sneak me out the back door and call someone who wouldn't embarrass you?

I breathe in for three counts, out for six, just like my mom said. "I'm . . . I'm . . . not okay, actually." I take another long breath. "M. Marquet is—I just saw him—Mme Lafontant—on the table—"

"My husband was fucking Mme Lafontant on a table?" Mme Marquet asks archly. "Says who?"

Me! I want to say, but something about her tone tells me this is one of those situations she'd rather not discuss in real terms.

"That's an ugly rumor, started by jealous, silly girls," Mme Marquet says with finality. "Silly girls who don't belong with the good society of this ballroom. Go find our driver. It's time for you to go home. Just look at you."

"But, Mme Marquet . . ." This has all gone horribly wrong. I look down and see with horror there is dark blood seeping through the front of my dress. I must have cut my knee when I banged into the doorway. "Oh, God," I choke out.

"And Penelope?" Mme Marquet goes on, clasping my forearm forcefully. "Don't think I don't know about your trouble back in the United States. Don't think I don't know how badly you are relying on our generosity. I know all about the lies you've told, the things you've neglected to tell us, to tell Mme Cuchon."

I gape at her, panic taking over me. "You want me to pose as your daughter so that M. Marquet can look like a family man to French voters. What about the lies *you* tell? The things you've neglected to tell me?"

"Shut up! Just shut up you stupid, ignorant *vache*," Mme Marquet says. "You slut. You tramp." She's drunk, and slurring her speech. Mme Marquet staggers as she pushes me out the front door, past the caterers and the servants and the butlers and the long line of valets and chauffeurs waiting for their passengers to come out. "I told you! It's time for you to go home!"

"How can you be so cruel?" I ask, truly flabbergasted.

Our driver spots Mme Marquet and pulls up the car. "Go! Just go," says Mme Marquet. "You think I'm cruel? You think I'm cruel? You don't know anything about cruelty, you whore. Just go."

I'm trying to go, but she won't let go of the back of my dress. I fling her off me, and the strap she was holding breaks, ripping the back of the dress so it's hanging off my back. The driver looks away as he opens the door for me. He's the only witness, and he'd lose his job if he tried to stand up for me.

As we drive away, I see Mme Marquet fall to her knees on the gravel driveway, clutching a tuft of light blue fabric in her hand.

22. ALEX

The Right Girl for Him

 don't know how Olivia puts up with her parents staying at the Hilton. It's so tacky and . . . *American*. It's not her fault, but sometimes Olivia is hopelessly gauche.

"Well, where is Madame Caroline staying?" Zack counters as we move up the stairs of the Ternes metro station on Monday afternoon. We're headed to the Lycée, but just for a few hours. Mme Cuchon wanted to have a last meeting with us before the holiday break, most likely to lecture us on staying out of trouble while we are out of her direct supervision.

Zack knows how excited I am for my mom to finally come visit. I can't wait to show her off! And she's been so distant since the credit card incident and bailing on fashion week, barely emailing or texting me at all. She must have been really pissed! I'm ready for her to forgive, forget, and reinstate my line of credit.

"My mom is staying at the de Crillon, like always," I tell him breezily. "You'll have to join us for dinner there one night."

"You're kidding," Zack whistles. "At the Place de la Concorde? You guys don't mess around, do you?"

"Nope," I say, lighting a quick cigarette as we walk to the Lycée. My mom was definitely not messing around when she canceled my Amex, that's for sure.

Miraculously, we have time not only for me to smoke before school but to check our mailboxes in the office as well. It will be the last time we can check them before the break.

"Empty as always," Zack groans, then goes to find Olivia. I bite my lip, noticing how careful he is to avoid Jay and the guys sitting on the couch in the computer lab, waiting for the twins and a bunch of other home-obsessed girls to finish checking their email and Facebook accounts. *I really screwed that up for him,* I think with a sharp pang of remorse.

"Zack!" I gasp. "Look!" Zack, out of earshot, doesn't respond. There's a package in my mail slot. Having a package in your mailbox is the most wonderful thing any Programme Americain student can hope for at the beginning of each school day. A student who gets a package is the center of attention throughout the whole of the day, everyone wanting to know what American goodies they have and whether they will be willing to share them. Katie from Ohio is always getting gingersnaps from her mom, which are gone by the end of our first class. George's mom sent him the *Bourne* trilogy, immediately sending all the other kids to their email asking for all their favorite movies on DVD. Mary orders books in English from Amazon.fr, and can usually be seen furtively reading a British version of *Life is Elsewhere* or *One Hundred Years of Solitude* for the rest of the day after she gets her package.

Personally, I've yet to have a package, and I want to make the most of it. I pull Jay up off the couch. "Jay!" I whoop. "Help me open the box I just got from my mom in New York!"

A bunch of kids surround us as Jay pulls out his Swiss Army knife and struggles to cut cleanly through the heavy layer of packing tape. They all must be dying to know what I would be getting from my mom. I mean, my mom is *practically* a celebrity. CAB works for *Luxe*! And I'm the only New Yorker on this program. *My* package is going to be good.

"I hope it's chocolate from Jacques Torres," Sara-Louise says excitedly. "My daddy got me some of that on his last trip to New York, and I could eat those chocolate-covered macadamia nuts with the powdered sugar for the rest of my life. . . ."

"Is it from Barneys?" another girl, Elena from Chicago, who watches too much *Gossip Girl*, asks breathlessly.

Jay has successfully opened the package. "Thanks!" I say breathlessly. I reach into the box to find . . . a stuffed animal. I grab it and show it to everyone.

"My mom knows I just love baby seals," I gush, though until this moment I've never once professed to have any affinity for baby seals. "Look! There's a card."

This is it, I think. My mom's put a check into the card, which will have a message on it that all is forgiven and understood, that my expenses in Paris are much more than in New York, and not only is she sending me this check so I'll have some cash to last me till her visit, but the Amex has been reinstated as well.

I open the card, careful not to rip the check. French banks can be very finicky about sloppiness. I don't want them to hassle me when I cash it.

But there is no check. The card is simple, my mom's regular monogrammed stationery she's had my whole life. CAB.

My dearest Alex,

You will be so pleased with me. I've found a way for you to pay off your astronomical debts. My dearest friend Margerite—you remember, from Lyon all those years ago?—has a friend from school who lives in the fifteenth like you. Madame Sanxay—her number's below—call her right away. Give the seal to her lovelies!

Yours,

CAB

With blurry vision and barely able to comprehend what I've just read, I smile at everyone around me. "My mom's not the gingersnap type," I tell them, and cradle my seal in my arms as I walk off to find Zack. When I find him, I don't say anything. I just show him the note and burst into sobs.

Zack hustles me into the hall.

"Hey, hey," Zack comforts me. "What's the deal? I don't get it. What is she talking about?"

"Look at what she wrote!" I point at *Yours, CAB.* "She doesn't even call herself Mom! She doesn't even write that she loves me, or misses me!"

Olivia joins us in the hall. "What's going on? Alex, why are you crying?"

I wipe at my eyes. "No reason."

"You don't have to tell me," she says. "But I have to tell you guys something."

When Olivia tells us she's going home with her parents the day after Christmas, she can't hold back her own tears. "I never told you guys how hard it was for my family for me to be here. They need me at home. Vince needs me, too."

"I need you!" I wail. "Please don't go."

"You'll be okay," Olivia sniffles. "You guys will take care of each other."

Zack takes both of us into his arms, burying his face in my hair. I think he's crying, too.

I call Mme Sanxay from the privacy of my bedroom at my homestay. Some morose-sounding child answers the phone.

"*Je cherche Mme Sanxay,*" I tell him in my kindest voice.

"*Quoi?*"

"Get your mother," I command him in English. The kid drops the phone and shrieks for Mme Sanxay to get the phone. I shudder.

"*Bonjour*, Alex!" Mme Sanxay greets me. She starts explaining the after-school job to me in rapid French. I can't understand a word she is saying.

"Sorry," I interrupting, forgetting how the French despise bad manners. "How's your English?"

Mme Sanxay pauses. "Your mother told me you speak French."

"I *do*," I say. "Just not right now. Long day. So what's up?"

"Can you come by Thursday? I know it's Christmas Eve, but I'd love to introduce you to the children before we fly off to Mallorca."

"What children?"

"My children! The ones you'll be taking care of," she laughs, confused. "Didn't your mom tell you?"

"No," I say. Now I'm confused.

"Everyday from three to six," she goes on. "You'll meet us here after school. I'm just so eager to have a few hours to myself."

I can't believe it. I numbly hang up with Mme Sanxay, telling her I will see her tomorrow.

Never, ever, in my whole life, has my mom done anything so cruel.

I dial her number on my cell phone, even though I know the call will cost a fortune from my BlackBerry. Another thing for my mom to get mad about.

"MOM?!?" I shriek into her voicemail. "What is going on? You can't do this to me! You can't just get me a job without asking me! I don't even like kids. How am I supposed to survive?"

The voicemail cuts me off. I stare at my cell phone in my hand.

A cold sense of injustice descends onto me.

I call her again. This time she picks up.

"Yes, Alex?" my mom answers.

"I hate you. I really do. You are a *terrible* parent," I say quietly, and hang up.

A few hours later, I write my mom on my BlackBerry.

Mom — don't bother coming to France for Christmas this week. I was really excited to introduce you to my new boyfriend, George, but now I don't want to subject him to the cruelty of having to be in the same room as you. I'll have a better Christmas if you just stay in New York.

If she wants spitefulness, spitefulness is what she is going to get.

All I have left in this ruthless world is George. And I will have him. Make no mistake about that.

• • •

My mom, before she worked for *Luxe,* was a young fashion publicist working the Paris shows right out of college. Her best friend in Paris was a model named Margerite who now lives in Lyon. Margerite's brother, until about three months ago, was married to Mme Sanxay and is still, of course, the father of the Sanxay children. I won't be meeting M. Sanxay today, however, because he's in the south of France with the woman he left Mme Sanxay for.

Say hi to my dad, I think. My dad has a house on the beach in St. Tropez. The Riviera must be where all the worthless cheating husbands congregate.

Mme Sanxay leads me into her living room, the carpet lush and elegant but the floor strewn heavily with gaudy plastic toys. Two shrieking children, the boy a little smaller than the girl, wrestle each other in front of a blaring television set. Off to the side is a playpen with a little baby in it, wailing helplessly. I cower in the doorway, not wanting to get any closer.

"*Les enfants!*" Mme Sanxay barks at them sharply. "*Silence!*"

All three children stop for a moment to register her presence, then go back to their loudmouthed misery. I shiver in horror.

Mme Sanxay picks up the baby. "*Je te présente Charles,*" she tells me, holding out the little squirming child for me to hold. I shake my head quickly. "*Non, merci,*" I say, as politely as possible. He smells like Johnson & Johnson bath powder, a scent that has always made me want to barf. I gag.

"Let's go into the kitchen, shall we?" Mme Sanxay leads me to a messy table covered in old junk mail and French newspapers. Like my own homestay and in fact, the apartments of my friends in New York,

Mme Sanxay lives in a reasonably sized flat that probably costs a fortune with rent and maintenance. Right now, it's looking particularly unmaintained.

"Pardon the mess. It's just so hard to keep everything together. That's why I was so thrilled when your mother called me last week to offer your services. My nanny lost her work permit and was sent back to Venezuela. Alexandra, you're a godsend." She smiles at me for a long time, too long. I look away.

"I know you are busy, dear," she continues, shifting the baby from one hip to another. Charles screws up his little face, mashing his lips together. To my horror, Mme Sanxay responds by unbuttoning the first few buttons of her shirt and unhooking one of the large cups of her maternity bra underneath, exposing a large, veiny breast that the baby hooks onto immediately, sucking vigorously.

"Charles is eating some solid food now, but he still loves his mother's milk best," Mme Sanxay tells me, looking down at the little beast fondly. I clench my jaw to keep from gagging.

"I wanted to put together some information for you, emergency phone numbers, maybe a list of what the kids like to do and eat, but I ran out of time. When you come back, I promise to be more organized! Alexandra, dear," she goes on, reaching for the pocketbook on the chair next to me. The purse has some liquid dripping from it. She doesn't even notice. "I'm so grateful to you. Here's the money you'll need for incidentals—diapers, metro fare—while you are caring for *les enfants* next month, if you want to put it in your checking account, and I'd also like to give you a deposit to show you how glad I am to have you working for me in the coming months. I couldn't find *anyone* in Paris willing to

donate the kind of time I need for the amount I'm able to afford to pay."
Mme Sanxay pulls a large wad of cash out and folds it into my palm.
For the first time since I stepped into this filthy, miserable apartment, I
smile.

"Go and play, *cherie*," she says to me. "We'll see you soon."

I skip down the stairs to the street, unable to flee fast enough. She'll
see me *never*. That place was a den of pure wretchedness. How does the
old song go?

Oh, right. *Take the money and run.*

I take the money (there is quite a lot of it, actually) and run right to
Le Meurice, the little boutique hotel on the Rue de Rivoli I've always
begged my mom to let us stay in when we visit Paris. My mom always
says that Le Meurice is not for little girls and their mothers. It's for *lovers*.
Which is what brings me here tonight, on Christmas Eve.

A few well-distributed fifty-euro bills gets me immediate entrance
into Le Meurice's luxurious spa, even though the receptionist tells me
they've been booked for months. Stripped naked on the waxing table,
Clotilde, my expert aesthetician, peels and plucks until my whole body
is silky smooth. When she is done, I head for the steam room, then the
exfoliation treatment room. By the time I'm back in the junior suite on
the top floor that I've paid for in cash, my skin is as rosy and soft as the
silk duvet on top of the four-poster king size bed.

Just as the in-room nail technician, Patrice, gets to work on my
pedicure, George responds to the text I sent earlier. *Would love to stop by*,
it reads. *There's something I really want to tell you.*

I can't help but wiggle my toes excitedly, even though it messes up the nail polish and Patrice has to start over, wasting valuable primping time. Tonight is going to be *perfect*. I hoot with laughter, recalling all that George and I have been through since we got to Paris in September. I can't believe it's been over two months since we first kissed at Sara-Louise's party.

Sure, we've had our ups and downs. I frown at the hazy memory of screaming down at him from PJ's balcony and comfort myself by thinking of the look of total pleasure George gave me when I slipped into his sleeping bag in Lyon.

Patrice lets in the room service guys, who set up a bottle of Dom Pérignon, two crystal champagne flutes, and a big bowl of juicy red strawberries. My own hands are too fragile from my fresh manicure to tip them, so Patrice dispenses some cash from my camel tote for them, and ducks out of the suite.

This morning I wrote my cousin Emily and proudly filled her in on my progress. I never thought I'd be able to report that I'd so completely moved on from Jeremy, but in fact, it's true. Old heartbreaks don't even register when I consider my future with George. Who cares if my mom never sees it for her own eyes? Who cares if the first couple months of our romance have been shrouded in secret? That's the kind of guy George is—surprisingly shy when it comes to love.

He won't be shy when he sees me tonight, though, I giggle to myself as I step into the La Perla set I swiped from PJ's host mom's closet. The creamy silk chemise just skims over my backside, barely hinting at the thin matching underwear. In front, the neckline dips low to set off my cleavage. I could dance at the sight of myself.

Just a few minutes later, a light knock at the door announces his arrival, and suddenly I feel like an actor on opening night. I know all my lines but still don't know how I'll be received. With a deep breath, I slowly and discreetly open the door.

"Oh, Alex," George says, his face breaking into an appreciative smile. "You shouldn't have."

"No?" I say coyly. "Should I put on a robe then?" I stay put, knowing full well that is the last thing he wants.

"Is this all for me?" George asks, taking in the champagne, the strawberries, the candles I had Patrice light while my nails dried.

I push him gently toward the bed. "Yup," I tell him. "And this time, there's no chance of us getting interrupted."

He kisses my chest first, his lips soft against my skin. Pulling the strap of my negligee off my shoulder, he moves his mouth up and down my arm and over my neck and the top of my back. He moans softly as he pulls down the other strap, my boobs falling out of the chemise and into his mouth.

I can't help it—I want him so badly I could almost weep. As he takes off his shirt, then his chinos, I'm overcome with how intense everything is with George tonight. He's gorgeous, of course, and I've always been crazy about him. But there's something more tonight, something I've never felt before. I feel vulnerable and bold at the same time, simultaneously scared and confident. Every time he touches me, my desire for him heightens. Soon I'm fully naked, totally exposed on the bed next to him in his plaid boxers. I can see how much he wants me, and I know he knows how much I want him back.

"Wait," I say, suddenly needing to hear him say it, to tell me what I already know is true. "Before you . . . before we . . ."

"What?" George says, still devouring my neck.

"Let's have some champagne," I say, leaning over to pop the cork. I giggle a little as I pour, George kissing a trail down my sternum toward my belly. "Here," I laugh, handing him a glass. "Try it."

George takes a sip. "Amazing," he says. "You're amazing."

I smile like a fool. "That's what I want to talk about," I say as I try and gently lift his head back up to my face. "I want to talk about how we feel about each other."

"I feel pretty great about you right now," George says. "I think I'm going to feel even better in a minute . . ."

I swallow hard. "Before we do it, I need to know that this is real. That all the drama between us is over."

George stops his nuzzling and stares at me.

"Alex," he says, taking a long drink of champagne. "I did come here tonight wanting to talk to you seriously."

"You did?" I squeak happily. This is too good to be true.

"I mean, I've always gotten a lot of attention from girls," George says, looking out the window for a moment. "I've always been a flirt. It's such a part of who I am. This program is no different. I like hooking up with hot girls as much as the next guy." George moves away from me slightly, and the separation between our bodies lets cool air blast my skin uncomfortably.

"Right," I say, not quite following.

"I mean, with you it's always been about hooking up," he says. "I have to admit I've been wanting to sleep with you since the moment I saw you." I giggle, flattered. "But now I have to say I want something else. And I think I've found it. I never thought I could fall for one girl and want to settle down with her, but I have."

My eyes widen. This couldn't be going better if I had written the script myself. He loves me. I knew it!

"You want something deeper than just hooking up?" I say knowingly.

"Yeah," George says. "It's just starting to get old, no matter what bells and whistles a girl like you can put on it. It's just sex between you and me. It's never anything *real*."

Wait a second . . .

"That's why I came here tonight, Alex," George says, sitting up. "I wanted to tell you that I think I'm in love with Patty, and that's why this thing between you and me has to stop."

"What?!" I cry. "Are you joking?"

George shakes his head.

"What are you talking about, George? Ten seconds ago you couldn't wait to fuck me, and now you're telling me that you love Patty? Patty, who's a born-again? Who's a *virgin*?"

George laughs in spite of himself. "I know—I can't explain it! When I'm around her, it makes me realize . . . it makes me realize that there's more to life than just sex, and hot girls. Though," he says ruefully, "I have to say, her looks might have something to do with how I feel about her. She *is* pretty hot."

I think of Patty with her cheerleader ponytail of dyed blonde hair, tied tight for school with a red ribbon. I think of her garish houndstooth pea coat and her cheap polyester tube top. I look at George, suddenly unsure if I am even on the same planet as he is, if this is still really my life, or if I've walked into some alternate reality where Texan sluts beat out women like me—worldly, sophisticated, charming women like me—in the hearts of guys like George.

"So why then," I choke out in a rage, "did you start taking off my clothes? Why were you about to go all the way with me? Because she won't let you? Because with me you thought it was a sure thing?"

George stops and thinks for a moment. "I guess I thought I could put this thing between you and me to rest. I came here to tell you all that and go, but when I saw you in that sexy nightgown, and you smelled so good, I guess I thought we could have one last hot night together and then go our separate ways."

"Our separate ways?" I repeat in a hollow voice, no longer able to conjure the rage I want to punish him with. My hands start to shake, spilling champagne down my arm and onto the silk duvet. "How am I supposed to go my separate way from you? We're here in Paris together until June!" And besides. I don't *want* to.

George takes the glass and puts it on the nightstand. "Let me get you a robe," he says and turns away from my naked body. That gesture, the way he suddenly can't bear to look at what he was so lovingly touching just a little while ago, breaks my heart more than any of his hurtful words did. I disgust him. Just the very fact that I'm here, and not Patty, makes him want to run away.

George hands me the robe without meeting my eyes, then silently slips back into his clothes.

"I'm sorry, Alex," he says quietly as he leaves. "I fucked up. I just want something better than this." The door's latch catches in the doorframe with a defining *click* behind him. I look blankly at the mahogany grandfather clock in the corner of the suite. It's only eight o'clock. I was expecting us to be here until a least two, maybe all night if we wanted to risk getting in deep shit with our host parents. I was thinking it would absolutely be worth it, just to see the sunrise together, to order room service before school.

In the suite's expansive bathroom, I light a cigarette and sit on the edge of the whirlpool bath. A few swigs of champagne, straight from the bottle, only serve to make me feel worse.

Just look at you now, I imagine my mom saying if she were here. Of course, she isn't here, and that's the whole point, isn't it?

No one is here. I'm too unlovable for *anyone* to be here with me.

I've wasted over a thousand euros on this room and the spa treatments I had earlier to get ready for George, all the money I had left in my account and all the money Madame Sanxay gave me yesterday. I don't have any way to pay her back unless my mom sends me a check tomorrow—and that would be a *real* Christmas miracle. Even the clothes I'm wearing—if you can call them clothes—aren't mine. I stole the lingerie that's been tossed on the ground, for God's sake, and the robe belongs to the hotel.

I open the window in the bathroom, letting out my cigarette smoke and letting in a biting gust of wind. In the moonlight, I see that snowflakes are starting to fall. It's the first real snow of the winter, just in time for Christmas.

George is out there somewhere, texting Patty in Texas.

Even farther away, Jeremy's out there, strumming a guitar, writing songs about love and pain. But none of them are about me.

23. OLIVIA

Bittersweet

"We thought you guys might want to be alone," my mom tells Vince and me on Christmas Eve. "Why don't we chill out with Brian and you guys can go to dinner and a movie? We'll give you some money. Have a great time!"

"Thanks, Mom!" I say enthusiastically, but I'd have been happier just watching TV with Brian all night. It's true, Vince and I haven't been alone at all since he's been here, but for some reason, the buffer Brian creates between us is more comforting that stifling.

"God, finally!" Vince moans with satisfaction as he hugs me from behind on the platform of the Opéra metro station. "I've just wanted to hold you and not let go since I got here."

Parisians are infamous for their high tolerance for public displays of affection, but I'm self-conscious all the same. "Vince!" I squeal, shirking from his touch. "Don't be a perv."

Vince doesn't let go. "The Frogs can think I'm a perv all they like. I've been going crazy for *weeks*." He presses against me eagerly. Normally

I'd blush, flattered, proud of my ability to turn him on without even trying. "You're so beautiful," he breathes into my ear.

Mercifully, the #7 train pulls up then. We're headed to Odéon, one of the many places Thomas had told me is fun to hang out in Paris. Alex and Zack go sometimes, sit in the Rive Gauche bars that will serve them, and watch all the interesting Rive Gauche people walk by, but I've yet to do more down here than just visit the St. Germain-des-Pres.

Vince and I bumble our way through our connection at Châtelet station. Vince laughs when we can't find our way to the train going to Odéon, but I'm more annoyed than amused. Vince looks like an idiot, in his UCLA baseball cap and his bright white Air Jordans. Is this really the same guy I used to swoon over from the stands of our school gym, watching him run down the court, dribbling and passing and making all the cheerleaders go crazy? What changed since then?

I try to ease up on Vince through dinner. He's still the same guy I've been in love with all along—goofy, easygoing in most respects, fiercely competitive in others. He lets me tell him about Paris, things I couldn't tell him with my parents and Brian around. He listens carefully (he's always been a good listener, I have to give him that), laughs at all the right times, and tells me more than once how beautiful I look, even if my roots need a touch up and I've lost my California tan.

"You're really gonna miss all this, huh, Liv?" Vince asks me, taking my hand in his rough one, callused from playing basketball.

"Yup," I say sadly, thinking of the dance troupe, of Alex and Zack, of Mme Rouille's poodles, Mme Rouille herself. Thomas—Thomas I can't even think about. It's too much.

I wave down the waiter for our check. "What do you say we skip the movie and head to bed?" I ask, exhausted by the prospect of all that I am leaving here in Paris.

"Sure," Vince says enthusiastically.

"I meant our *respective* beds," I say. "I could really just use a good night's sleep."

"Sure, babe," Vince says with a compassionate smile, unsuccessfully trying to mask his disappointment.

After I drop him at the Hilton, I walk up the Avenue de Wagram by myself. The frigid air feels good.

That was one of the things I was most scared of before I came to Paris. It sounds dumb, but it's true: I agonized about what the weather would be like here, if it would make me miserable. In San Diego, it rains sometimes, and there are definitely days when I have to wear a sweatshirt to school. But I have never really owned a coat before now. I had to take Alex with me to find my pea coat because I wasn't really sure what I was supposed to get. Now that it's winter, and all the forecasts are predicting snow for Christmas, I'm finding that I really like it. It's invigorating, gets you going.

I wonder if Vince is like that. If my fear of losing Vince is like my fear of cold weather. Once it happens, will it even feel like that big of a deal?

"Olivia!" Thomas greets me, the little poodles yelping at his feet in the doorway. He's barefoot, with his shirt untucked and his curly hair a little frizzy and disheveled. He pushes his glasses up his nose in that adorable way he does. "I've been wishing to see you. *Ça va?*"

"I'm fine," I say measuredly, though my heart is pounding. The last time I saw Thomas, my tongue was down his throat and I never wanted it to stop. "What are you doing home?"

"I just finished my term paper and handed it in early, so that I wouldn't have to do it on holiday," he explains. "*Maman* is at a party. I was about to head out for a celebratory drink. Want to join me?"

"Don't you have to be up early tomorrow for your train?" I ask.

"Olivia," Thomas grins. "It's just one drink. And it's Christmas Eve."

"Okay," I agree, not even taking my coat off. "Let's do it."

"So, what's happening in your life since I last saw you?" Thomas says as he opens the door for me at the local neighborhood pub, *La Belle Chambre*. We snag a cozy table near the back.

Thomas is so friendly. I can't believe that after I led him on like I did, he's still taking me out for a drink.

"Well," I say, not knowing where to begin. "Remember that day you came to the Opera school and I was dancing when I wasn't supposed to be?"

"Yeah?" Thomas says, pushing his hair back from his forehead. "I'll never be able to forget it."

"There was a talent scout there from the Paris Underground Ballet Theatre. I was late, so I didn't know our class was actually an audition of sorts. They emailed me a few weeks later and asked me to join," I tell him in a rush, realizing how proud I still am of that accomplishment. "I've been a member of the troupe for two weeks now. I love it!"

"Olivia, *c'est formidable!*" Thomas exclaims. He throws and arm around me and vigorously pounds the table with the other hand. "*Félicitations!*"

He looks truly impressed.

"Thank you," I say modestly, not yet wanting to break the news that I can't take their offer. I just want to bask in his admiration for a few more minutes.

Thomas orders himself a whiskey, but I just want sparkling water. I didn't want to drink tonight. I just wanted to be with someone who'd be happy about the Underground. Clinking our glasses together for the first round, I toss my head back and let the fizzy water rush into my stomach as if I'm taking a shot. Thomas drains his whiskey and laughs.

"Another?" he teases, laughing.

"Very funny," I say. "We've got a big day tomorrow, my family and me." I don't mention that Vince is in town, too. "And you know I'm not the most seasoned drinker."

Thomas laughs. "This is true." The waiter brings Thomas another drink, which he drains just as quickly and wipes his mouth with the back of his hand. Is he nervous, too?

I sort of half-laugh, half-sigh. "Yeah." I'm remembering how it felt, goofing off with him at PJ's house. Even before the kissing, it was one of the most entertaining nights of my life. With the kissing . . .

"Seriously, Olivia, your news is amazing," Thomas says, his tone changing. "That's a true accomplishment. Your family must be so proud."

"Hmm," I defer noncommittally.

"I've never seen anyone dance like that," Thomas says. "I've never seen anyone *be* like that at all. I couldn't help but stare at you. You were—you *are*—stunning."

Thomas doesn't break his gaze. "Olivia . . ." he says quietly.

"You've had a lot to drink," I say. "We should get back to the apartment. It's late."

Thomas slaps twenty euros onto the bar as we leave. In the elevator back up to the apartment, I tell him thanks. Thomas nods. "Anytime."

I have a lump in my throat that keeps me from saying anything else. There's so much between us, and yet what can I say? *I'm afraid to say your name because it makes me feel so vulnerable that you even exist. I can't be with you; I can't even stay in your city. My family is my whole life.*

Yeah, right.

As he reaches for the front door, Thomas drunkenly trips and falls forward, banging against the door comically. In spite of myself, I burst out laughing. Thomas looks at me, his face red, and then explodes into embarrassed laughter himself.

"You idiot," I say, unlocking the door myself. "You drunkard!"

Thomas laughs. "*Oh, mademoiselle*, I am so very sorry. Please forgive me for all the whiskeys I drank to celebrate your newfound fame! We aren't all as disciplined as you are," he kids me.

I unwind my scarf from around my neck and smack him with it.

"Shut up," I say, grinning. He grabs the end of the scarf and pulls it, tug of war style, to him. I fall forward, right to his face.

"Olivia," he says, doing that thing to my name that makes me melt, and the next thing I know, we're kissing, even more passionately than when we were on the balcony at PJ's party, and we're fumbling at each others clothes as we stumble toward the little bedroom that's sort of mine, sort of his.

"You are . . . so beautiful . . ." Thomas tells me as he slips me out of my dress and tights. All those times Vince had said those same words earlier tonight, they'd never sounded like this.

I can't respond. I just slowly unbutton his shirt, exposing his smooth chest. It feels like a dream when we fall back onto the bed—his bed, my bed.

Even when it's over, we can't stop touching each other. I'm still so entranced by everything about him. I laugh out loud. "Wow," I say, for lack of a better word. Lying next to him, I feel like a whole different person, like when I get up and turn on the light, I'm going to see that I now look different. There's no way that this could have happened and I will go back to being me.

"*Tu m'étonnes,*" Thomas says. "I've never felt this way before." He still has his arms around me. I never thought I'd be in this moment with him, and not Vince, but it feels perfect. I did really fall out of love with Vince this fall. How did that happen without me even realizing it?

I stop laughing. "I have to tell you something," I finally tell him. "I'm leaving. I'm going back to California at the end of this term." I gesture at the open suitcases all over my floor, half packed already. "I'm not coming back to Paris. I'm not taking the position with the dance troupe."

"*Quoi?*" Thomas asks. "Why not?"

"My family needs me," I say. "I just have to go back."

"Do you *want* to go back to California?"

I shake my head, admitting to myself for the first time that I really, really don't want to.

"But you're going anyway?"

"Yes," I say, though I feel like I can barely speak.

"You're a very brave girl, Olivia, walking away from an opportunity like that," Thomas says, cradling me in his arms.

"Brave? I don't think so." I didn't know it was possible to feel so happy, and so confused, and so vulnerable all at once.

"You're brave to walk away from your ego like that," Thomas says with a tender kiss on my forehead. "Would it be okay if I asked you something?"

"What?"

"Is it me?" Thomas says. "Are you running from me? Because of how we feel about each other?"

I look at him and think about that for a long time. Finally, I wrap myself in my pink bathrobe and get up to get a glass of water. I fill up a mug without turning on the light and take a long gulp of tap water. In the dark, I let my tears finally fall where Thomas can't see them. Because then he would know that he's right.

24. PJ

You Never Can Tell

*T*he annual Christmas Eve gala benefit for L'Orchestre de Paris is not to be missed by any member of Paris society. Mme Marquet spends all day on Christmas Eve preparing for the event, while M. Marquet spends all day at his club playing squash.

Her face slathered in a thick sea foam green mask, Mme Marquet pops into the kitchen in the mid afternoon for a cup of tea. Topping it off with a bit of brandy, she doesn't see me come in and sit down until she's turned to walk back into her bedroom.

"*Mon Dieu!*" she exclaims, pressing one of her thin, bony hands against her bare décolletage in shock. She's wearing silk pajamas with a silk coverlet, obviously de rigueur attire for a day of pampering like this one. "Penelope! You frightened me."

"Sorry," I apologize hastily. "How's it going?"

Mme Marquet ignores my question and heads for the master suite with her tea.

"Madame?" I say, following her. "Can I come in?"

"What is it, Penelope?" she says.

Impetuously, I sit down on her bed, watching her reflection in her vanity mirror. She begins to remove the green cream with a soft white washcloth and a small dish of toner, careful not to get any of the residue onto her clothes.

"I just wanted to say that I'm sorry I made you mad last weekend," I tell her quickly without making eye contact. "I didn't mean to upset you."

Mme Marquet lets out a barbed peal of unhappy laughter. "Ha! You don't upset me, child. You could never upset me."

Confused, I stare at the back of her blonde head. "But you were so angry at me," I say. "I thought I offended you . . ."

"Penelope, *arrête!*" Mme Marquet says. "Don't kiss up to me. I've already called Mme Cuchon and arranged for you to stay with us over the break. After all, it would be such a shame to send you back now—people would wonder why. No, no," she says, smiling strangely. "We'll leave for the Dordogne tomorrow morning and have Christmas with the Lafontants."

"*Les Lafontants!*" I exclaim. "But what about . . ."

"We've already been through this," Mme Marquet says with impatience. "*Tout le monde a ses secrets.* Even you, Penelope. Everyone. Why can't you let a sleeping dog lie?"

"I just wanted to tell you the truth," I say, unable to rid my mind of the grotesque image of M. Marquet heaving above Mme Marquet's friend on the table. "I thought you should know. You don't have to just stand by and watch things like that happen. . . ."

Mme Marquet flips around and bores her bright blue eyes right into mine. "You want to start telling the truth?"

Mme Marquet walks toward her closet and flings open the heavy doors leading to the racks of her expensive clothes. "Tell the truth about this, PJ! Tell the truth about the things you've been stealing from me, the Alexander McQueen dress you 'borrowed.' Tell me the truth about the *underwear*, of all ghastly things, that you stole from me!"

I jump up defensively. "Underwear! What are you talking about?" I think of leaving Alex alone in the closet and groan inwardly. I should have known.

"Save it for Mme Cuchon," Mme Marquet says coldly, her face contorting with anger and meanness. I realize that Mme Marquet is not *jolie-laide* like I at first thought. She is just plain ugly. "If you really want everyone to start telling the truth, Penelope, you are going to end up right back in her office. And from there you'll go straight back to the United States! And I know you don't have a home to go to."

"No!" I cry, as much at her threat as for the heavy silver paddle hairbrush she picks up off the vanity table and throws across the room, just barely missing a framed antique photograph of some long dead Marquet relative. With an unsatisfied shriek, she picks up her tea and flings the china cup at me, splashing the hot brown liquid all over my white thermal T-shirt. I scream as it scalds my stomach.

"What the hell is going on in here?" M. Marquet, his gray hair still damp from his shower at the club, bursts into the room in his navy warm-ups. "What are you doing to my wife?" he demands of me.

"*Rien!*" I defend myself. "I've done absolutely *nothing* to either of you! All I wanted was for you to like me!" I run from their bedroom.

I lock myself in my room all night. Even after I hear the Marquets leave for the benefit I don't come out. Late into the night, I speculate darkly on the nature of secrets. My parents had a secret, and it tore my family apart. Annabel was good at keeping secrets, good at hiding her fear. Even Olivia, who I thought was so sweet and pure, had a secret. I guess no one is as innocent as I ever thought they were.

The Marquets have found out my secret somehow. I suppose it must not have been hard—if you knew to look. I tried so hard to keep it from them, for fear they'd send me back home. And yet, that isn't even the problem now. The problem is far worse. They'd planned to hold my secret over my head, control my every move.

There's a scaly red mark on my stomach where the tea burned me. I finger the ridged skin, wondering how to make it right with them. My living situation with the Marquets has never been ideal, but now it's a nightmare.

A knock on my door at close to 4 A.M. jars me from the light slumber I've fallen into. I'm still wearing the stained T-shirt and my jeans. I get up, pull my Grandpa sweater around me and go to the door, finding M. Marquet leaning against the door frame in his tuxedo.

"May I?" he asks, gesturing to come in.

"*Oui*," I say reluctantly.

M. Marquet motions for me to sit next to him on my bed, which I do. With a heavy sigh, he loosens his bowtie and undoes his collar. "Ah," he breathes. "That's better."

"Penelope, *cherie*," he says affectionately. "Things have not been easy for you in France, have they?"

I sigh. "Nope," I admit. "They haven't."

"And why have we gotten off to such a terrible start?" he asks plaintively. "Have Mme Marquet and I not provided a good home for you here? Have you been unhappy with our apartment? With our château?"

I shake my head. "Oh, no, the apartment—the château—it's all great," I say truthfully. "I'm lucky to be here."

"So what then?" he says softly. "You were upset by what you saw? It frightened you?" He brushes my long hair out of my eyes. It feels too intimate to be fatherly, but I don't want to be rude. And the French have different ways of showing affection.

M. Marquet is speaking so softly I can barely hear him. His face hovers near mine. I can feel the breathy whisper of his voice on my cheek and the light tickling of his graying hair on my forehead. He reaches out his finger and lightly traces the inside of my elbow.

"My wife is a bitch," he says, just as quietly. "Adele drinks too much. She doesn't know what she's saying half the time. She knows about Mme Lafontant; you did not have to tell her. And she knows how I feel about you. . . ."

"*Quoi?*" I say, not sure I understood him. The scent of him is suffocating, the close talking and breathing overwhelming my senses. The way he's touching me gives me sickening chills.

"Oh, Penelope," he exhales roughly. "Oh, *mon dieu . . .*"

M. Marquet leans toward me and licks my earlobe, ever so slightly. My body convulses in repulsion.

"What the hell are you doing?" I say, pushing him away. "That was disgusting! You are supposed to be my host father!"

With his right hand, he grips my waist firmly before I can jump off the bed and slips his left hand between my legs and tries to plant his mouth onto mine.

"Penelope . . ." he moans. "Don't fight it. Just let it happen the way it's supposed to."

Taking advantage of his clumsy drunkenness, I shove him forcefully off of me, dart around him so that I am standing several feet away from him, near the door to my bedroom.

"Get out!" I hiss. "You're a filthy old man! You're sick!"

Thrown off balance, he falls toward the empty bed next to him but recovers quickly.

Jumping up, M. Marquet grabs me before I can scream. His hands on my collarbone, he hisses into my ear. "You just don't get it, do you? This is how it's done in France. You American. You Puritan."

He lets me go, tossing me hard against the wall. I feel the wind get knocked out of me.

"You tell anyone about this, you'll be on the next plane back to America," he mutters in my face. I push him away, and he stumbles out my door and into the bathroom. I shove my feet into my Converse, on the floor by my bed, and grab my coat, heavy with the weight of my wallet in the pocket, off the back of my desk chair. Before I dash to the front door, I grab *Madame Bovary* off my desk.

I gasp when I reach the empty Place de Ternes. It's so cold, so calm. I pull my coat more snugly around me, cursing the swift cold spell that everyone had been hoping for, wishing for a white Christmas.

I look southwest, toward the lit up Arc de Triomphe, the traffic around the circle light and spare. The Champs Elysées in the distance is strangely empty as well. Even the restaurants and bars are now closed. The Parc Monceau is to the east, the tall gates locked for the night. Where can I go? It's Christmas. Most of my program has flown back to the U.S. for the break, like Sara-Louise and Mary did, or went on vacation with their host families. The ones who remain in Paris are fast asleep.

I tried to do this on my own and I failed. The burn on my skin, the gash on my knee, the memory of the ripped bodice of my blue dress as I was escorted from the Lafontants' ball. M. Marquet's slimy tongue on my ear, his brutal hands striking me when he did not get what he wanted.

I can't stay here in Paris.

I need Annabel; I need her protection; I need her smarts and I need her bravery.

I pull *Madame Bovary* out of my pocket, fearful and unsure. There is a picture postcard inside it, one that Jay bought for me in the Louvre gift shop. It's a self-portrait of Jean Auguste Dominique Ingres. I flip it over and scrawl a note on the back of it.

I can't—I *won't*—look back as I run down the Boulevard de Clichy. In the early hours of Christmas morning, I'm the only one on the street, odd for Paris at any hour of the day. The city is unusually serene. Mine are the only footprints in the freshly fallen snow.

25. ZACK

Good Friends Are Hard to Find

I forget to close my curtains when I fall asleep on Christmas Eve. Bright sunlight seeps into my room early the next morning, and out my window I can see a thick blanket of white snow covers my street from the Square St. Lambert at one end to the Rue de Lecourbe at the other.

Mireille and Paul are somber children, bookish and nerdy. They aren't the types to greet Christmas at the break of day. Last night, after we all set our shoes out by the fireplace so that *Père Noël* could fill them with gifts and candy, Romy and Jacques took my host brother and sister and me to *la Messe de Minuit*. We did not get back from the midnight service until two, when the fat snowflakes were already coming down. Romy's parents and extended family joined us at the apartment for *La Reveillon*, a huge Christmas Eve feast that lasted until the very first light was creeping over the horizon. The whole family will most likely sleep in until the early afternoon.

Unable to fall back to sleep, I get up and go to the window. I look out at the snow for a long time. I think about Christmas, about my own family and how far away they are. My mom will have been up all night wrapping gifts. My little brother, Freddie, and my little sister, Heather, will stampede the Christmas tree by 5 A.M., but my dad won't let them open any presents until he and Mom tell the Christmas story start to finish from the Bible and they've all prayed about it. One of the kids will try and open their gifts too fast or out of turn, and my dad will yell at them to slow down and remember that greed is a sin. By the time it's over and time for church, my mom will be so tense she'll be dropping things—the pancake batter, the pitcher of orange juice—and my dad will just want to forget the whole holiday and watch the game. My aunts and uncles and cousins will come over to the house for brunch and ask how I'm doing over in Paris and my parents will say just fine. But really they won't know *what* to say because what kind of kid goes all the way to Paris to live far away from his family when he's just sixteen years old? What kind of kid doesn't come back for the holidays and, in truth, wishes he never had to come back at all?

Then I consider an even worse scenario: that the whole family is having the most wonderful, spiritual holiday ever, and it's all because I wasn't there to ruin it for everyone with my long hair, my "fruity" clothes (as my dad never ceases to say), and my bad attitude about the Baptist Church, the Bible and all the other accoutrements of Christmas in Germantown? Maybe they finally have what they want—the perfect Christian family.

The radiator clanks inefficiently in the corner of my room, the way it does every morning now that it's winter. It feels like the toll of a bell, a reminder that life is passing me by. I came to Paris to find myself and to find love. And all I've found, by the looks of it, is loneliness.

Pierson hasn't emailed in over three weeks, too busy with his boyfriend to keep in touch. Sometimes, on a quiet morning like this one, I could wile away hours chatting with him in Amsterdam, comparing notes on our European experiences. Not anymore.

The letter from the Lycée came yesterday morning. I found out that I got a B on the Final Comp. I chalk up the answers I missed to frittering away so much time with Alex, strolling the Jardin de Tuileries, going out drinking just because we can, seeing French movies without subtitles and ending up missing most of them while I explain the dialogue I was able to catch to Alex in the dark.

I hope Jay got an A on the test. I hope he gets to keep his scholarship for the rest of the year.

Flopping onto my stomach, I flip through the contacts list on my cell phone, thinking maybe I'll call Olivia, wish her a Merry Christmas. Before I come to her name, though, I stop at Jay's and look wistfully at his number, wishing I had the balls to call him up.

"Hey, Jay," I'd say casually. *"Did you hear that weird thing Alex said in the Lyon McDonald's? She's right, I'm gay. What's more, I have the hots for you like I've never wanted anyone before. Want to come over?"*

Ha.

While I'm staring at the screen, my phone starts to vibrate with an incoming call. Confused, I see Jay's name flash at me and I start to try and hang up, thinking I've accidentally called him. But no! He's calling *me*.

"Hey, Jay," I say casually, or as casually as I can manage under the circumstances. "What's going on?"

"Zack!" he says. "Oh, man, I'm glad you answered. Listen, I need to talk to you. Can you be at the Parc Monceau in a half hour?"

"At the Parc Monceau?" I ask, perplexed. Neither Jay nor I live up there, in the seventeenth.

"I'll explain when you get there," Jay says hurriedly. "Meet me at the Colonnade."

I dress quickly and carefully, selecting a light blue slim-fitting button down with some loose True Religion jeans and a wide army-print belt. A newsboy cap and my long wool coat will keep me warm, but at the last minute I grab a cashmere scarf Alex bought for me at the Galeries Lafayette. I had thought it was a little too gay to wear to school, but today, I can't help admiring how nice it looks tied around my neck.

The Colonnade de Naumachie is a half-ring of crumbling stone ruins around a small, murky pond in the northeastern corner of the Parc Monceau. The water's surface is thick with fallen leaves. Jay, obviously quite distressed, is pacing around the path that runs alongside the ruins when I arrive.

"Hey, man," I say easily.

"Zack!" He shakes my hand in greeting, the way straight guys always do. "This is going to sound weird, but there's something I have to tell you."

I hold my breath, waiting for the words I've always wanted to hear. *"I'm gay, too, and I love you, Zack."*

"Look!" Jay hands me a postcard with a portrait of a young man from the nineteenth century. "It's Ingres! It was slipped under my door this morning."

I flip over the postcard.

Jay,

I'll never forget you.

One day, maybe we'll meet again and I can explain.

I'll write when I'm ready to be found,

Love,

PJ

Jay can't keep still. "Do you see that?" he asks me. "Did you read what she wrote?"

I don't understand.

"PJ's running away from something," he says. "She must have had to leave all of a sudden and couldn't tell anyone why. I called her house; no one answered."

"Jay, slow down," I say, still totally mystified. "Is PJ in some sort of trouble?"

"That's what I am trying to tell you!" Jay practically shouts. "All I know is that when I woke up this morning, I went out to get the paper and found this postcard underneath it. She must have come by my house while we were sleeping. That *means* something, man. It's got to mean something. I don't know what yet, but I swear I am going to find out."

I read over what PJ wrote again.

"So, wait a minute," I say. "Why did you call me?"

"I need your help, man!" Jay tells me again. "You're the one kid in this program who's got a good head on his shoulders. You've always been solid to me, man. None of the other guys are going to take me seriously. Everyone will think I'm just hot for PJ and blinded by how much I love her and not thinking straight. But this is serious. I've got to find her. I'll never forgive myself if I don't."

"But, Jay," I say. "I'm not 'solid.' You and I aren't *friends*. I mean, we are, *sort* of. But, the reason I've, I mean . . . I *like* you. Because I'm gay. Couldn't you tell? On the Lyon trip, or since then?"

For the first time since I got to the Lycee, Jay stops moving around. "What are you talking about?" he says, not meanly, but plainly puzzled.

"Remember how I went and sat with you guys at the McDonald's in Lyon?" I tell him quickly, each syllable of explanation more heart-wrenching to get through than the last. "And Alex was pissed. Couldn't you tell that she was jealous, when she came over and pulled me away and chewed me out in front of everyone?"

"Alex was chewing you out?" Jay says. He thinks about it. "Oh!" he realizes, coloring red as he puts things together. "I guess I didn't get it. I figured she just didn't want you to sit with Sammy and Cory and me because we're not cool enough for your crowd."

We both fall silent.

Jay's innocence, his fundamental goodness, his naïveté about matters of sexual orientation, about the bitchy things Alex would do to embarrass me and put me in my place, is heartening and heartbreaking at the same time. If it is even possible, I've fallen for him more than ever, and just at the moment he's telling me . . . he's in love with PJ?

"So you like PJ?"

"Oh, man," Jay says in agreement. He shakes his head, but not to say no—to show there are no words for how much he likes her.

"And does PJ like you?"

"Well," Jay says, gesturing at the postcard in my hand. "She trusts me. She wrote to me. That's all I know right now."

"Tomorrow morning," Jay continues, "I'm going to withdraw the rest of my scholarship money. I just got the disbursement for next term. I'm going to use it to find PJ."

"Jay, no! She didn't even say where she was going! How are you going to find her? She probably just went back to Vermont."

"I don't think she did. Did she ever once tell you anything about her family? About missing anything from home?"

"No," I admit. "But where else would she go if not home?"

"She wouldn't leave France." Jay kicks at the snow, already dirty and melting. "There's something keeping her here, I just know it."

"You've got to help me, Zack," he says. "Whatever the reason for your friendship, I know you're a good guy. I don't care if you're gay; stuff like that doesn't bother me. It shouldn't keep anyone from being friends. Please help me find her."

I can see Jay is going to do this with me or without me, and as nasty as it is to be this near to him and know that my worst fears are true—that Jay is straight and will never see me the way I see him—I can't resist how much he needs me right now. My heart feels like it's being squeezed, like my lungs might actually capsize, at the notion that Jay doesn't like me at all; had never even thought of me in that way. But the one thing that keeps me from throwing myself into the muddy, freezing pond next to us is that he also didn't shun me, either. Being gay was no big deal to him. I never thought I could come out to a guy—a guy who was good at sports, running for trains, and playing video games—and that guy would not even blink twice. I can only hope that everyone else I ever come out to is just as cool about it.

"This is ridiculous," I say finally. "Maybe Olivia knows what's going on. She lives down the street, let's go ask her. Before you do anything crazy with your scholarship money."

"Will she mind if we barge in this early on Christmas morning?"

"No," I say, totally certain. "Livvy will want to help."

"Awesome. Let's go!"

Just then, I get a text from Pierson.

Merry Christmas! It says. Wish you were here!

Hustling toward Olivia's homestay, I can't help but relish the feeling of Jay and me together, whatever the reason might be.

You never know, I text back as we wait for a green light at the crosswalk at the Parc's gates. In the new year, I might very well be.

26. OLIVIA

Joyeaux Noël

Zack shrieks bloody murder when he opens my bedroom door first thing on Christmas morning. Thomas and I are still asleep in bed together, our bodies still intertwined from the night before.

"Zack!" I gasp, pulling the sheets up to my neck as I sit up and try to locate my clothes and my senses. Thomas, equally shocked, just stares at Zack.

Zack covers his eyes and goes back out to the hall. "Oh, my God," he says through the door. "I am so sorry. Elise let me in. I had no idea . . ."

I pull on Thomas's shirt and some black dance leggings. The shirt comes down to my knees. I toss Thomas his boxers and pants and let Zack back in when we're both decent. "Shhhh," I say. "Don't wake up Mme Rouille!"

"So y'all are . . . a couple?" Zack says, still unable to look at us. He looks like a scared little boy. I glance over at Thomas and then back at Zack.

"I've got to go," Thomas says as he darts out of the room. "I shouldn't be in here."

"It's complicated," I answer Zack. "What are you doing here? It's only eight o'clock in the morning. And it's Christmas!"

All of a sudden, I'm terrified. "It's Alex," I guess. "Alex is in trouble. I knew something was the matter when I called her yesterday. Where is she?" I start pulling on my Ugg boots and combing out my bedhead with my fingers.

"No, it's not Alex," Zack tells me. "It's PJ. And Jay. Jay's actually . . . Jay's in your living room."

"What?" I freeze. "Oh, God. You guys have to get out of here. Mme Rouille and Thomas have a train to catch. . . . My family will be here any second. Does Alex know anything about this?"

Zack shrugs. "I don't think so. Why would she?"

You never know with Alex. I start walking Zack out to the front door.

"Jay, I'm really sorry but you have to go."

"But Livvy, aren't you going to help us?" Zack asks.

I take a breath. "I am. Just give me . . ." I look at the grandfather clock in the foyer. "Give me a half hour. I'll meet you at Alex's!"

Just as the boys leave, the buzzer rings. Oh, no! My parents! But it's not them; it's the taxi for Mme Rouille and Thomas.

"Olivia!" Mme Rouille greets me. "*Où est ta famille?*"

"On their way!" I answer cheerfully. "Any minute!" I can't help being jumpy. I am, after all, still wearing her son's shirt.

She doesn't notice. "Elise will be here for anything you need today and tomorrow. I'm so sorry that you are leaving me so soon. We were just getting to know each other. You're welcome here anytime. I'm so sorry I didn't get to meet *ta famille*."

"Another time," I say in a rush, trying to push her out the door. "Thanks for everything!"

Thomas gives me a *bise* on either cheek, each one lasting a bit longer than the custom requires. "Well?" he says. "There's still so much of France I'd like to show you. Will you ever come back?"

"I'll keep in touch," I say hurriedly. God, how could I not? Memories of us, our bodies touching, flood me, nearly knocking me over. "Happy holidays!" I wave freakishly out the window until I can see that their taxi has driven off, Thomas looking up at me from the back window. I'm not worried about him, not after last night.

I run back to my room to prepare for my parents' arrival. I put on my "O" necklace, knowing my mom will appreciate the gesture. She's not going to like what I have to tell them.

The buzzer rings again, just as I've slipped into my jeans. I answer the door, their four smiling faces lined up in the doorway.

"I can't go back home with you," I blurt out, not even saying hello. "I don't want to." I stand back to let them into the apartment. My dad and Brian are wearing red sweaters that they bought here (none of their other clothes were quite warm enough), and my mom's blonde hair is in pigtails.

"Livvy, what do you mean?" my dad says, reaching out to me for a hug. I hadn't noticed that I'd started crying, but when I wipe at my face, it is wet with tears.

"I've been offered a place in the Paris Underground Ballet Theatre. I've been dancing with them for almost a month," I tell them, my voice sounding different now that I'm not trying to please them with everything I say. "It's a really prestigious company. More experimental, funkier. I love it."

"What?" my parents gasp. Vince's face is stricken.

"I'm accepting the offer. It's my dream come true."

"But, Livvy," my mom protests, "what about UCLA?"

"What about me?" says Vince.

"Maybe one day, I'll go to UCLA," I say. "But I've made up my mind—I'm staying in Paris for now. I want to dance here."

Some small part of me had been expecting that they would be able to talk me out of my decision, that when they got here, my family and Vince would convince me to come home to California tomorrow with them after all. Some part of me had actually been hoping for it. After all, it isn't going to be easy here. If the guilt doesn't kill me, the rigorous rehearsal schedule of the Underground might.

"Livvy, when did this happen?" my mom asks me. "How could you audition for a job without even discussing it with us? How could you do this to me?"

My dad intercedes. "Leslie, she's not doing anything to us. She's just going after her dream."

"But I thought your dream was to go to UCLA," my mom says. The bags full of brightly wrapped Christmas gifts are still in her hands.

"It *was* my dream," I say. "But my dream changed. I'm a different person than when I left San Diego in September. When I came over here, I was scared, excited, and was having fun, but all I cared about was UCLA. When I sprained my ankle—"

"You sprained your ankle?" my parents ask in unison. Oops, forgot that I hadn't told them that so they wouldn't worry.

"Yes, but it's all better now." I continue. "When I sprained my ankle, I thought my chances at UCLA were over. I even danced on my ankle before I was supposed to because I was so eager to stay in shape."

"Oh, Livvy," my mom clucks in shame. "You know better than that."

"When I danced on it, I made it even worse," I admit. "But the day I went to class, a talent scout from the Underground was there. I didn't even know I was trying out. But my dancing was so good that day because I'd been aching to dance for so many weeks that I felt like all the emotion was pouring out of me. I have to dance just to dance, not as a means to another end. As much as I'd love to be a doctor one day, I don't know if that's really what I want to be going for right now."

My dad and mom look at each other for awhile, and then back at me.

"And what if we had said no?" my mom asks me. "You're still a kid, you know. You still have to run important life decisions by us."

"Then I would have had to defy you," I tell them. "But I would never want to do that. So I can stay? You're not mad?"

"Of course not," my dad says. "This is amazing news. I'm thrilled for you!"

"Oh, Livvy, I've been going crazy without you," my mom admits, hugging me. "And I do want you to go to college—that's why we supported your decision to come to Paris." Here she looks up at my dad, then back at me.

My dad has tears in his eyes. "You're the best daughter we ever could have asked for," he says, his voice breaking. "When you love someone, you have to let them go when the time comes. You deserve this, Livvy. You've worked so hard."

"I'll miss you so much, Livvy!" my mom says through her tears.

I hug them both, not wanting to let them go. Behind us, Vince clears his throat.

I throw myself into his arms next and sob into his chest. "I'm so sorry, Vince," I say, meaning it.

He doesn't say anything, just holds me for a long time.

"So you can cancel my ticket?" I ask finally.

"Of course," my mom says, smoothing my hair. "Just let us know when our superstar ballerina wants to come home for a visit. We never did get your hair fixed, did we? Maybe you can do that when you come home."

"I was thinking I might go back to my natural color," I tell my mom. "I don't know if I want to be a blonde anymore."

She's taken aback. "Livvy, I've had about enough for one morning. Let's just take one thing at a time."

My dad rolls his eyes at her. "Who's ready to open some presents?"

I lead them into the living room and help them set their gifts under the tree.

"Elise made coffee and tea for you guys," I say. "It's all in the kitchen. I'll have her bring it out before she leaves for the holiday."

I hesitate, hating to disappoint them again, but remembering PJ. If she needs me, I have to be there.

"I have to run out for awhile," I tell them, making a break for the door. "Don't open presents until I get back!"

• • •

Zack and Jay meet me outside Alex's apartment building. When I get there, I realize that in all the drama of the past few weeks I haven't seen my friends in quite awhile. I realize how happy I am to be here, despite whatever the creepy circumstances are. I need my new friends right now, to reassure me, to make me feel like Paris is home.

"What's going on, you guys?" I ask Zack and Jay as we climb the stairs to Alex's homestay.

"PJ ran away," Zack says, before Jay can answer. "She left Paris, and we don't know where she went, or why she ran."

Alex looks thin and gaunt when she answers the door and shows us into her bedroom. She curls up on her windowsill, practically drowning in her bulky sweat. I can imagine her sitting here before we buzzed up, her ears plugged into her fancy Bose headphones that are hanging around her neck now, smoking and ashing out the window. Marithe has strict rules about smoking inside the apartment—Alex is well aware that this is way against the rules. But the stink of the room tells me that she's been smoking in here all morning.

I grab her iPod to see what she's been listening to.

"Edith Piaf? Jeez, Alex, what happened?"

Her headphones, combined with the oversized hooded sweatshirt she's got on, make her look sort of tough. She's got a haggard look on her face, like she's seen it all in her short life so far. It's unlike Alex to be so dejected.

"Merry Christmas to you, too," Alex smirks at us. "Nothing happened. I'm just feeling sick lately."

"It's freezing in here," Jay comments, and I realize that whatever is wrong with Alex, it's not very sensitive of us to bring Jay into it—she barely knows him

"Jay, I'm really sorry," I say hurriedly. "Can you give us a minute alone with Alex?"

"Sure," Jay says gamely, though I know he's impatient to get down to business.

Zack plops down next to Alex, closing the open window behind her. "Are you going to tell us what's going on?"

Alex shrugs. "Not much, as you can see."

I look around her room. The scene is grisly. There's a fetid, rotting-food smell emanating from under the bed. Clothes are strewn everywhere, empty cartons and cigarette packages that were tossed near the waste basket but did not quite make it inside.

"Alex, are you ok?" I ask, suddenly aware that we've found Alex in the midst of a deep depression. Her face is thin and her eyes cloudy with undisclosed troubles.

"I'm fine," she snaps. "What brings you here to disturb my tragic malaise, anyway?"

"You can tell us, Alex," I coax her.

"Is it about George?" Zack asks, gently pushing her face towards his. "Did something happen?

"Ha!" Alex snarls. "He wishes."

"Is it because your mom didn't come to Paris for a visit?" I ask.

"No! I told her not to come. I hate her."

Zack and I exchange a look, thinking that maybe we should come back later, when Alex is feeling better. Poking out from the piles of magazines on Alex's nightstand is an envelope whose return address is clearly that of the Programme Americain. That must be her Final Comp grade. Is Alex depressed over how she did on the test? Or is it something worse?

Jay knocks on the door. "Can I come back yet?" he asks.

"Yes," Alex calls to him. "It's fine."

Jay comes back in, and we tell him to show Alex the postcard he got from PJ so early this morning.

"We think she ran away; that she's in some sort of trouble."

Alex snorts. "Right. The only trouble with PJ is that she's a giant *dork*," she says meanly. "After all this time, haven't you guys learned at least that much?"

"Alex!" I scold. "We're all really worried about her. And she is *not* a dork."

"Alex," Jay interjects. "You know France better than any of us. If we have any chance of tracking PJ down, of helping her with whatever happened to her, you are it. You out of *everyone* on the program can make this happen."

"Why do you say that?" Alex asks, perking up just slightly.

"That's just the kind of girl you are," Jay says. "I barely know you and I can see that whatever Alex wants, Alex gets. Am I wrong?"

Alex sighs heavily and puts her head in her hands.

"You are wrong," she corrects him. "But that doesn't matter. You need me, so I'll help you. I hate to say it, but as you can see, I obviously have nothing better to do. Isn't that funny? All these plans, and none of them worked out how I thought they would."

Jay hugs Alex, then Zack, then me. "Alright!" he exclaims. "I knew you'd come through!"

"Let's do this," Alex says determinedly. "She couldn't have gotten to Paris without me. I can definitely get her back here."

"What?" we ask, confused.

"I'll explain another time," Alex brushes us off. "Let's just work on finding crazy old PJ, wherever that girl might be. At least this gives me something to do since I stupidly told my mom not to come to Paris. What was I thinking? Christmas is going to be so *boring* without her."

"God," Zack says, his eyes resting on mine. "If you'd told me four months ago, I'd be spending Christmas Day sitting in a stinky bedroom plotting how to bring a Vermont hippie back to Paris, I'd have told you to eat me."

"That's how Paris works," Jay says. "You never know how things are going to turn out."

"Yeah," Alex says. "Haven't you learned that, Zack?"

"I'll tell you what I've learned," Zack says. "I've learned that a pretty girl who smells as bad as you do right now is a girl in distress. Why don't you take a shower? It's Christmas, darling. Do it for us."

Alex glares at Zack. "I do not smell anything but fabulous."

"Girl, you smell like a pack of cigarettes threw up on you." Jay's face is solemn, but his eyes sparkle.

"You guys," I say. "What are you doing for Christmas morning?"

"My family's still sleeping," Zack says.

"Mine, too," Alex says.

"Mine didn't go to bed till it was light out," Jay agrees.

"Weird tradition, huh?" I say. "Staying up all night on Christmas. You guys want to come over and meet my parents? And Brian? And Vince? We could open presents, be together the way Americans are on

Christmas. Before the sun goes down again." Paris is so much farther north than San Diego. Right now, on the shortest days of the year, the dusk settles before four P.M. "And we could figure out how to find PJ."

"Would we ever!" Zack shrieks. "We finally get to see Prince Charming!" he remembers this morning, and his eyes widen. "Oh, yes, Livvy. I *definitely* want to come over. I've been dying to meet Vince!"

"Is there gonna be food?" Jay asks.

"Yes," I laugh. "Elise made breakfast before she left to spend the day with her own family. There's plenty. Do you want to join us?"

"Definitely. I'm starved."

We all look at Alex. "Your real family is going to be there? And your boyfriend?" she asks me.

"Yup," I say. "Except I don't think Vince is my boyfriend anymore."

Alex's interest is piqued. "And what's your mom like?"

"She's great," I say honestly, remembering how proud she was when I finally told her my news. "She'll love you. Vince will, too."

"Then I'm in," Alex says. "I could use a little love today."

"I think we all could," I say, giving her a hug and pushing her toward the shower. "We'll wait in the kitchen."

I can't help it. I grin at Zack. If he can keep my secret about Thomas for a few more days, at least until my family and Vince go home, I can keep the secret that I am just catching on about. Zack is head over heels for Jay.

I shake my head. Will Paris always be so crazy? Will it always feel like a big, extraordinary ballet, with a million emotions pulling at each moment?

I stop smiling. We've got to find PJ. She could use a little love, too, however cheesy that sounds,

Just as soon as my parents get on that plane, I promise myself, *we'll make sure she knows how much support she has here. She can't have gone far. Right?*

27. PJ

The Escape

Olivia would run directly to Mme Cuchon if I ended up on her doorstop in the middle of the night. Zack would spill the beans to *someone*, if not Mme Cuchon, by the time the sun rose this morning, and Alex . . . we all know Alex. Would she really have welcomed me with open arms?

I considered Sara-Louise and Anouk, or maybe Mary. Not for the first time, I wish I'd made friends with one of the French students at the Lycée. One of them might have been able to keep my secret. The Americans will all have to come clean about how much they know of my whereabouts at some point; for all their sakes I decide not to let them know anything.

The last thing I ever wanted was *another* scandal. If I told anyone what M. Marquet did, how he acted when I was alone with him in my bedroom, he might follow through on his threat to get me sent home to Vermont. It might even make the papers. A newly elected magistrate, with an ambitious wife and lofty political goals . . . *L'Express* would have a field day. Once cast out of France, where would I even go? Home? To be the pity case, the pariah, of our town? The girl with the missing sister and the locked-up parents, forever wallowing in the shame of her family?

Pas de chance.

In the middle of the Gare du Nord is a giant timetable of all the trains running today. It hangs above the tracks, fluttering as the numbers and letters change to update the schedule. The station must be five stories high, and just covered enough to protect the train tracks and the waiting area from snow or rain. It's as freezing in here as it is outside. There are pigeons flying around, and about a dozen kiosks are scattered all over, selling baguettes and cigarettes and magazines. It's so old-world, like a black and white movie on A&E. First thing Christmas morning, it's virtually empty.

I clutch my passport. FLETCHER, PENELOPE JANE, it reads, my photo smiling out from its inside cover. When I took this photo, I'd never had reason to have a passport before. My dad drove me down to the Kinko's in Burlington in his truck and slapped down a fifty-dollar bill to get a half a dozen sets of photos taken. We needed them for the passport, for the student visa, for the Lycée student ID card. When we came home and showed them all to my mom, she couldn't decide which one was more beautiful.

"My girls are the prettiest girls in town," my dad said proudly. "They look just like their mom." My mom kissed him on the cheek and gave him that googly-eyed look they always used to share.

That was last spring before school had even let out for the summer. Annabel and Dave were probably playing guitar on the porch like always. If I remember really hard, I can hear them harmonizing an old camping song from where we were standing in my mom's cramped kitchen, the baskets of strawberries she grew in our garden waiting to be washed in the sink. I didn't have a care in the world. I was headed off to France in the fall, with parents who loved me and loved each other. My sister and her boyfriend, whom I'd loved since we were all little kids, were getting married on the Fourth of July. When she moved out, I would have my own room.

I was numb, heartbroken, terrified after everything came crashing down. I didn't want to go to Paris anymore, not with this happening.

My dad explained it to me after Annabel fled. "I had one last stash to get rid of, and then we'd be free and clear," he told me. "I didn't want all those meds to go to waste. The people we sell these drugs to need these drugs. Some of them will die without them; and some will live for a long time with a lot of pain. Why should the government, private businesses, get to make such a steep profit off of a basic human right like that?"

"You don't have to explain it to me, Dad," I said, more forgiving than my sister. That was why she ran, because they'd sold the prescription drugs even though they'd told her they'd stop before I found out.

"We never even booked the flight," I told them the morning before I was supposed to arrive in Paris. "You guys need me here. I can't leave you guys."

"Just go to Paris," my dad said, handing me an envelope full of cash. "I'll never forgive you if you don't do it. And whatever you do, just stay out of trouble."

I had never wondered why my dad didn't pay for anything with a check, or why my parents didn't have any credit cards. They'd always had cash on them, giving it to me to pay for school field trips, for books, whatever. They'd had me send my Programme Americain payments by Western Union, in my own name. I'd never thought about how they would pay for the plane ticket. I'd never even been to an airport before I got to JFK in New York.

"You, too," I said, breaking down into sobs.

My mom drove me down to the Greyhound station to catch the bus to New York, watching for cops in the truck's rearview mirror the entire time. I wanted to scream at her, but also just sit with her and hold her hand and tell her it was all going to be fine. That this, too, shall pass.

"My baby girls, grown up and long gone," my mom whispered.

"That's what happens," I wanted to say, *"when you risk our safety, when you risk our freedom."* And by the time I talked to Dave from Paris, the cops had their arrest warrant. I made it out of Vermont in the nick of time. And the whole time, I wondered what would have happened, what misery we all could have avoided, if I'd just never made them stop so I could pee.

Voie 8. My train is boarding.

I have my pick of empty seats this morning. Not a lot of travelers this early on Christmas morning. I take a spot next to the window.

Madame Bovary lies in my lap. Annabel loved this book, and wanted me to read it before I went to Paris.

I flip through the old paperback, the cover bent out of shape and the pages beginning to fray at the edges. What was Annabel's deal about this book, anyway?

Deeper into the story, far past where I've gotten in the book, Annabel made notes in the margins. I stop when I see that she's circled something.

Looking over my shoulder, reassuring myself that no one is watching or can see what she's marked—*Rouen*. I don't know where Rouen is, but I repeat it over and over to myself, knowing it will help me find Annabel.

We push out of the Gare du Nord, rumbling through the train yard, littered with old railcars covered in graffiti. I notice bold red letters painted on the side of one of the cars. It reads:

A LA LIBERTÉ.

The End

THANK YOU TO...

My incredible agent, Molly Friedrich, and her wonderful staff; Lexa Hillyer and Ben Schrank at Razorbill, who are both amazing and brilliant; Jane Smiley, Doug Wagner, Julia Dexter, and Lindsey Pearlman for their insightful early reads, Liz Berliant and Kirk Reed for their patience as I fact-checked to write characters who hail from places I've never been; Phoebe Silag and Brian Lane for being generous experts on all things French, and Alison Rich and Gretchen Koss at Doubleday and Spiegel & Grau, who employed me by day as I worked on the novel at night. Razorbill and Penguin also have a large team behind them that I am equally fortunate to work with. I am so lucky to be a part of this imprint and publisher. I look forward to getting to know you and your readers as this trilogy continues.

Since the hardcover edition of Beautiful Americans was published, I have been blessed by the generosity of so many people who helped me promote the book through events, publicity and super-enthusiastic word-of-mouth. These people include: again, my mom, Jane, and again, my friend Liz Berliant, Jack Canning, Peter Scott, Laith Agha, Chelsea Williams, Jamie Larson, Jeanne Silag, my dad, Bill, Barbara Mittleman, Laura Pieper, Mike Kilen, Leslie Patrick, my grandmother, Frances Nuelle, and her friends at BridgePoint at Los Altos, CA, Conor Callahan, Sarah Nord, Shana Heller, Jan Wagner, Lita Weissman, the Borders Books & Music stores in Providence, RI, Ames, IA, and Hollywood, CA, Book Passage in San Francisco, The Corner Bookstore in New York, Jennifer Smith and the Carmel Valley Library, Elena Loomis and Carmel High School, and, of course, everyone at the amazing Bookshop Santa Cruz in Santa Cruz, CA. I'm also super happy to get to work with Jessica Kaufmann in Publicity at the Penguin Young Readers Group.

Thank you all for sharing so many fun experiences with me my first time out!

Be sure to read **all** of the books in the
Beautiful Americans trilogy!

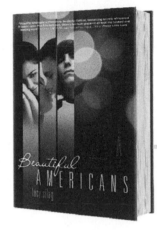

Beautiful
AMERICANS

WANDERLUST

EXPERIENCED